ESCAPE AND FREEDOM

CLAIRE HIGHTON-STEVENSON

ISBN-10:1722225599
ISBN-13:978-1722225599

<u>DEDICATION</u>

In loving memory of David C Furze, My friend.

You escaped your pain and found your freedom.

I miss you!

ACKNOWLEDGEMENTS

As always, Michelle Arnold, I am forever in cake debt!

My Arc team.

Maria Siopis.

Artwork by the amazingly talented Angie Sklavenitis.

As always, My wife.

THE PAST

2003

WEMBLEY,

NORTH LONDON,

ENGLAND

One

Wembley Arena was filled to the rafters with teenagers and parents alike. Every seat in the house had sold out within minutes of being on sale. The sound system rocked the very foundations as the band began to play, kids screaming in expectation. The bassists and guitarists found the beat of the drum and on she walked through the dry ice and bright lights. The crowd erupted again as the lead singer of Solar Flare threw out a "Hello Wembley!"

Song after song after song played out. Nobody sat in their seat; they danced in the aisles instead. It was loud and fun, the band enjoying the show just as much as the audience were.

Lucy Owen was stunning. Her long bleached-blonde hair swept up and to the side, her green eyes shone with anticipation and excitement as she stood there in the centre of the stage and gave her all, the centre of everybody's attention. This was what it was all about: all the hard work and constant rehearsals, nights in the bus, back and forth from one town to the next. It was all for this: this atmosphere, this moment where it all came together, and she was the star.

The music pumped like a heartbeat that thrummed through your very core. Voices rang out, singing and screaming as the concert goers were whipped up into a frenzy of excitement. When a number of them were allowed to come on stage and sing with the band, it was euphoric.

It was the last night of an exhausting European leg of their world tour, and Solar Flare was looking forward to a few weeks off as they headed to America for a series of concerts that would catapult them to superstardom. Their first two albums had gone straight to number one and they were already a hit on both sides of the pond, but this would be the first time they had toured there, and nobody could wait!

When the curtain finally came down and they walked off stage to find their dressing rooms, Lucy Owen was pumped. The guys were all talking about hitting the bar once they got back to their hotel, but she had other ideas on how to spend tonight.

The plan was simple: they were to grab quick showers and get changed, then jump on-board their tour bus and be driven to Heathrow, where they would be staying in a 5-star hotel for the night. In the morning all of them would be flying straight out to the States. Once there, they would get 3 weeks to themselves before the tour prep started and a 63-date tour began. It was going to be the most hectic and tiring time of their lives, but it would also be the most exhilarating and adrenaline-filled time too.

All of them had dreams, and every single one of them took them to America.

British acts didn't do well in the US that often, but when they did, it was the bigtime, and that was what Solar Flare was aiming for. They had worked hard. For 3 long years they had either been on the road touring or in the studio recording, and it had been torturous at times for all of them. They lived together, ate together, slept together too at times when all they could do was grab a few hours on sofas and chairs. They were a family; they had their share of arguments and disagreements, but on the whole, they were having a blast.

Lucy's girlfriend Nicky was going with them and was already waiting for her in the dressing room. Her own mother had described her as tall and gangly, but to Lucy, she was gorgeous. Not just ordinary gorgeous, but the kind that comes along once in a lifetime kind of gorgeous. Her mocha-coloured skin glowed with a light sheen of sweat she had worked up dancing backstage. She was a long drink of something hot, rich, and vibrant that set Lucy's mind racing with all kinds of possibilities. They were a striking couple, their skin tones complementing each other perfectly. They were a yin and yang, dark and light, but they shared the colour green in their eyes, almost exactly the same hue. They had to keep their relationship under the radar as far as the media was concerned, but everyone they knew was aware that they were in love, hopelessly.

"Baby, you were fucking brilliant!" Nicky said, her accent perfectly British unlike Lucy's more common approach to the vernacular. She threw her arms around her neck and kissed her hard. "God, it makes me so horny watching you on stage."

"Yeah? I hadn't noticed." Lucy laughed. "However, we don't have time," she replied, smirking at the pout she knew she had just caused. "Oh, come on now." she said, lifting Nicky's chin and staring into luminous green eyes, "You know that once we get to the hotel I am going to make it up to you?"

"You had better, darling," Nicky said, smiling. "I am horny as fuck right now," she whispered against the shell of her lover's ear, sending delightful shivers of anticipation down Lucy's spine in an instant.

It always amused Lucy whenever Nicky used such crass language. Her father had been born and raised in Jamaica, but had joined the British army at an early age, and that was where he had met her mother, while stationed in the UK. Looking at her and the way she dressed, the people she chose to hang out with, you would never guess that Nicky had been raised and educated in some of the best schools money could buy, until she spoke. When she did speak, it was eloquent, and every word was enunciated correctly, meaning that when she did choose to swear, it was fundamentally more enticing than anything anyone else could have said to Lucy.

A loud banging on the door followed by a deep voice bellowing, "Five minutes and we're leaving!" ended the moment.

"Let's just leg it and go to the airport by ourselves later," Nicky suggested with a wink.

"You know we can't do that, anyway it will be fun on the bus with the guys, a last hurrah," Lucy argued. "They've got cham-pag-ne," she sing-sang as she teased, knowing just how much Nicky loved to drink the bubbly stuff.

"I guess so. Why do I always let you get your own way, huh?" Her palm caressed Lucy's cheek.

"Because I love you?" she smirked, kissing her quickly.

"I love you more," Nicky countered, kissing the corner of her mouth once again.

"I doubt it."

"Oh, it's true, who else would put up with all the teenage boys that want to have their way with you?"

"Well, they don't get to, do they?" Lucy challenged, raising an eyebrow and the sexual tension as they kissed once more. Lucy tugged Nicky's body into her own by her belt loops. Someone banged on the door again, and this time it opened when Scott popped in and jerked his head towards the hallway. "Come on, we're off," he said. "USA here we come!" he continued to shout as he moved on to the next door down the hall.

They smiled at one another before both grabbed their bags and then, holding hands, they ran for the bus, laughing as they stumbled along the corridor.

There was a small group of about 50 fans outside, and they had to run the gauntlet to get through it. People always wanted to touch her, grab at her, talk to her, and on the whole, she accepted that as part of the job, but right now she just wanted to get to the hotel and spend a few hours naked with the woman she adored before hours of travelling and jet lag took its toll.

~E&F~

Greeted by whoops and high fives from the guys as they finally clambered aboard, they were all still bouncing on the

5

adrenaline a show provoked. Scott played bass along with Jenna; Sarah and Ben played the drums; Chris, Rob and Mike played various guitars; and Sasha played keyboards. Lucy played the piano too, but she was the lead singer with the other guys all having their moments on the mic. Jenna, Sarah, and Chris did most of the backing and between them, they had a fantastic sound. A sound that was going to transcend the Atlantic and bring them worldwide success.

Someone opened a bottle of champagne, the loud pop of the cork causing more whoops and cheers. Plastic glasses filled quickly as they all toasted each other, all except Sasha. She was strapped in and taking a nap like she always did after a show. They toasted the end of this part of the tour and for further success in the future, swallowing down the liquid in one. They were cruising, through life and along the motorway. They were young, famous and rich, with the world at their feet one minute and in the next, it all came crashing down, literally.

Two

There had been no time to even think about what was happening. It was a small bump, barely noticeable, and then the bus careered out of its lane, skidding back and forth, tossing them around a little in their seats and down the aisle as the driver tried desperately to get it back under control, but it was too late. The road was wet from an earlier shower and the wheels had locked up, forcing the cumbersome vehicle into a skid. The back of the bus where all the weight was held swung violently into the central reservation and pushed the front of it out of control even more. The driver slammed on the brakes in a last-ditch attempt to gain control, but all that did was cause them to lock up further, and the bus rolled over onto its side. What had once been windows and a wall was now the floor as the bus careered along the ground at speed. Sparks flew as the metal came into contact with the tarmac. Its occupants were thrown around like rag dolls in a dog's mouth. Glass shattered as windows hit and then imploded on impact. Boxes and bags that had been held in overhead compartments were now tossed around hitting anyone in their way. The cacophony of metal scraping was like a painful screech. Finally, the roof buckled as the motorway bridge pillar halted its forward momentum with an almighty crash, stopping it from sliding any further, crushing anything in its path.

The impact was earth-shattering. There was silence for just a moment and then the screams, the terrifying god-awful screaming of people hurt and frightened. Debris was strewn across the road leading a trail of destruction to the mangled and crushed vehicle.

A mere 45 seconds had felt like a lifetime, the power of the event monumental in its destruction. Lives that were full of promise and expectation just evaporated in a heartbeat that stopped dancing to its own rhythm, to any rhythm. Nothing would be the same again, for any of them or anyone connected to them.

~E&F~

Blue and red lights flashed around her. It was almost hypnotic, the way the colours danced around and over one another like a ballet of light that lit up everything for a second, before plunging into darkness once more. Over and over the colours swept across her. One minute there had been silence and then the roar of screams and machinery had deafened her. Her hands covered her ears and she felt warm tears slide down her face. She heard herself call for Nicky, but she couldn't hear a reply through all of the noise.

And there was pain, a lot of pain, and yet, she couldn't pinpoint where from; it was everywhere all at once. She tried to concentrate on each part of herself, to locate the epicentre of the agony. Her leg definitely hurt, her head hurt too, and when she tried to move she found she was pinned down. At some point, she tried to move again, and the pain that shot through her was so intense that it caused her to pass out.

The next time that she came around, she realised that she was still on the bus and a paramedic was attending to her. She had no concept of time; it could have been a minute, it might have been a day, and she didn't know or care. She had no clue as to what had happened other than the obvious. Something was sticking in her arm, she knew that much; a drip maybe? And she was asking where Nicky was, but he just kept talking to her about her injuries. It was frustrating, and she was getting more worked up and annoyed. The paramedic was explaining that they had to move her.

It all went black.

Three

Everything was bright, so very bright. When she tried to open her eyes, that was the only thought she had: too bright. Her head pounded when she rolled it to the left. A window. Blinds open and the sunshine was streaming through so clearly, she could see dust particles hanging in the haze of it. It was confusing. She didn't remember making it to the hotel or going to bed, and she was definitely in a bed. Taking a deep breath, she rolled her head the other way and tried to work out what the machines were for. She tried lifting her head, but that wasn't happening. So, she lay there and wondered if she was just having a bad dream. One that when she woke up would disappear into the subconscious, never to be thought of again.

The ceiling was white, the walls were white, and there was noise, she could definitely hear a lot of noise. Someone was crying, weeping really. Who was it? It sounded familiar. Her mother maybe? It wasn't Nicky though, where was she? She tried to speak, but she wasn't quite sure if she had said it out loud. God, this was tiring.

~E&F~

Lucy Owen was just 23 years old as she stood by the graveside of Nicola Abigale Jackson, supported by two crutches and her parents. She had been 19 years old when they had first met, 20 years old when they had first kissed, and 22 years old when they had last kissed. Her birthday had been just weeks ago, and it had passed by like any other day. She had received cards and flowers from well-wishers and fans, but with all the cards and flowers from the accident, none of them stood out as anything special; there was no happy birthday girlfriend card like there had been the year before. The card had been a happy birthday darling wife one, but Nicky had crossed out the word "wife" and written "girlfriend" instead. She smiled as she remembered that, and then she cried when she remembered there would be no more.

She thought back to when her doctors had explained it was a miracle she was even alive. The police had been equally amazed that she had lived; she had been sitting in the area of the bus that had had the biggest impact and where everyone else had not made it.

She had stared at herself in the mirror. Bruises that had been deep purples, blue and black, now just a sallow yellow and orange. They were everywhere, and it was obvious that at one time she would have been a horrific sight to look at. Stitches marked a zipper down her face. She hadn't dared to even look at the rest of her body; her face was awful enough. One leg had been trapped in a cage-like contraption, screws drilled into her bones, holding it all together.

There wasn't a minute of the day that she wasn't in some form of pain. The physical pain she could numb; drugs could do a lot for a person like her. The emotional anguish was a different story. She pleaded to be sedated. The only time she didn't dream of them was when she was anesthetised. Her only solace from the torture of it all was when she went under the knife to fix one part of her or another. Skin grafts, bone reconstructions. She would pray not to wake up, but each time she would come around, still breathing. In the end, she realised that death was too easy. She wasn't supposed to die, that much was now obvious. She was meant to live. To live forever with the knowledge that she was the reason that Nicky was dead. It was her fault, and the pain of knowing that would be her penance.

~E&F~

She had stood by the gravesides of four others too. Scott, Ben, Sarah, and Mikey. She had missed every funeral. She hadn't even known about them; goodbyes from her had had to wait. Her hospital stay had been two days shy of eight weeks.

She had 168 stitches, 23 of them down the left side of her face. A punctured lung, ruptured spleen, four broken ribs, and a leg broken in two places had meant for the first three weeks she hadn't even been conscious. The families of the deceased had waited long enough to bury their loved ones, and so Lucy had missed them. The press had been to them, well they went to Scott, Ben, Sarah, and Mike's. They printed nice little back stories about each of them and added photos of them and the flowers at the funerals. Nobody went to Nicky's, she was of no interest to the media, not until afterwards when they got wind of the lesbian angle and then they wanted to know everything.

For Lucy, it was the end.

Solar Flare was no more. Nicola Jackson was no more, and that meant that Lucy Owen was no more.

THE PRESENT

2018

KINGS BEACH,

LAKE TAHOE,

CALIFORNIA.

Chapter One

"Girls, don't wander too far, ok?" Nicole Granger shouted down the overgrown path of her new home towards the lake where her three daughters had taken off to explore. Shouts of "Ok mom!" were heard before they were out of sight. She listened for a minute. They were safe, she reminded herself.

The three-bedroom cabin in the woods was in need of a lot of tender loving care, but on the whole, it had a sound and well-built frame. It had all its windows intact, and importantly, the door was sturdy and had bolts that locked. Nicole had managed to agree to a low rent on the place in exchange for doing some repairs; a lot of repairs.

They had been lucky to find this place, off the beaten track and next to the lake; it was the perfect place to keep her girls safe. It was the middle of April, and most of the vacant cabins would normally be rented out by now to holidaymakers; however, this cabin hadn't been rented to tourists, or anyone, in a long, long time.

Her eldest daughter Storm was 8 years old and had the smaller room to herself. A bed, desk, and wardrobe were all it held. Her two younger daughters, 4-year-old twins, Rain and Summer, were to share the larger room, sparsely decorated too. It also held a double bed that they would have to share and a double wardrobe, as well as a large chest of drawers that would dwarf them both. The sun shone through the windows on this side of the cabin, lighting up the room in warm, soft reds and browns. Slightly threadbare rugs covered some of the floors, but it was safe, and that was all that mattered.

All of the rooms had beautiful old-style hardwood flooring and wonderful stone fireplaces. They just needed a rub down and a varnish and they would be like new; things were built to last when this old cabin was constructed. The cabin had electricity and running water at least, as well as all of the usual mod cons one expects in a house nowadays, albeit they were old and probably in need of replacing. All in all though, it was a great place.

Nicole's bedroom was the master, with a small walk-in closet and a tiny en-suite bathroom. The bed was an old-fashioned double: metal frame with beautiful ironwork and covered in hand-stitched blankets that would keep them warm when winter came calling, and all three of her girls would climb into bed with her for cuddles, something they hadn't been allowed to do until now.

She worked quickly to unload the sparse personal belongings they had brought with them from her car, a second-hand SUV she had picked up just a day before. There were only three bags and a box. Minimal clothing for each of them and a few toys for the twins and books for Storm. Everything else they needed she would have to buy when she could afford it.

When she had finished bringing everything in and placing each item in the correct room, she set about making some coffee for herself and some lunch for the girls. She smiled as she listened to them giggling and screaming with excitement at whatever it was they had found to entertain themselves. It was good to hear; there hadn't been a lot of laughter in their short lives lately.

"Hey girls, come on in, it's time for some lunch!" Nicole called. Within seconds six tiny legs scurried in through the door. Three smiling and laughing faces looked up at her as they sat around the small table in the kitchen.

"So, what did you find?" she asked them, caught up in their excitement.

"Mom it's amazing, the lake is like literally just there." Storm pointed out of the door. "There's a wooden path that leads out too, for a boat, can we get a boat?"

"Oh, I don't know honey, maybe one day. And it's called a jetty." She couldn't help the grin that spread across her face. "Mommy needs to find a job first and get you guys settled in school."

"Mommy? Do I have to go to school?" Rain asked imploringly. "Cos I can stay here with you and learn from books."

"I am sure you can baby, but school is more fun, you'll get to make lots of new friends and find out all about where we live now."

"Is Daddy coming to live here too?" Summer asked. Before Nicole could answer, Storm replied gruffly, "No, don't be silly, I already told you that."

Summer's eyes watered and her little lower lip began to tremble. "Will I see Daddy again?"

"I don't know baby," Nicole said, immediately scooting around to where her two youngest sat. She wiped away Summer's tears. "Daddy has a lot of things he needs to do first." She noticed out of the corner of her eye that Storm had rolled her eyes and slowly shook her head. So much resentment. Her beautiful little girl had witnessed far too much and was growing up far too fast.

"Ok, can I have some juice please?" Summer asked as Rain nodded. Grateful that their attention span was limited when it came to their father and that they could be easily placated, she reached for the juice.

"Of course, sweetheart, and then when we've finished lunch I think we should all go to our rooms and unpack our things, okay?" Nicole said, smiling at them all. "We've got a lot of work to do."

Chapter Two

For several years, Lucy Owen had been in some kind of therapy or another. Initially, it had been a lot of physical therapy. Getting her back on her feet and walking again had been a painful and drawn-out experience that she was thankful was over, although she still had pain occasionally – always would have – and she still walked with a limp, but she was lucky she could walk at all, so she rarely complained. Her leg had been virtually crushed when it had been caught under the metal column that separated the windows. They had buckled as the coach concertinaed. Emergency services had had to cut her out from that, and then she had gone through numerous operations to keep her alive and so they could completely rebuild the bone with plates and pins. But she was lucky, or so they kept telling her, that it hadn't just been ripped off.

Then the *other* therapy had started; the record company insisted on it. Talking wasn't something she enjoyed. She simply didn't want to discuss it; what was there to say? "Hey, my friends and the love of my life were killed, and I wasn't!"

God, she was so over talking about it with people who had absolutely no fucking idea what she was talking about when she used words like pain and longing and heartbreak! What could they possibly understand?

She had used to be an outgoing happy-go-lucky girl. When she and Nicky were out with friends, everyone would be entertained by the pair of them, but since the accident and Nicky's death, Lucy found she had no heart for anything anymore. One by one her friends dropped her from their social circles. She was glad; she hated their pity, the sympathetic looks they gave her when they didn't think she was looking. The whispering about her when they thought she was out of earshot. And when her parents decided to move to Spain and enjoy their retirement early, there really was nothing keeping her in England.

The record company was very helpful in the beginning while they were still getting coverage in the press and using it to their own advantage to boost sales of Solar Flare albums, making a fast buck in the process. But they had finally realised that Lucy Owen was never going to get on stage again, so they dropped her during a huge publicity campaign for one of their other major stars. Her contract was torn up by mutual consent, and her career in music was officially over.

Eventually there was nothing left in the UK for her, so she sold up. Packed up her stuff that littered the modest mansion she lived in with Nicky in leafy Wimbledon and put it all in storage. She couldn't deal with it, she wasn't ready to throw Nicky's things away. Her own things she didn't want to take with her; she wanted no memories other than the two photographs she had with her always. One was of Nicky and the other was of Solar Flare, the entire group in their heyday. It had been taken during a shoot for *Monster Hits* magazine and was probably their most popular, their merchandising always used this image on posters.

She wanted to exist somewhere that nobody would recognise her, nobody would ask her about Solar Flare, about the accident, about Nicky. She found a place online and took the next flight out, going to America like they had all planned to do. It seemed fitting.

The cabin on the shores of Lake Tahoe was nothing luxurious. She didn't want that; she had had all of that, and look where that had gotten her. What she wanted, needed, was somewhere she could just disappear. She had been here for nine years now, and all the locals knew of her was that her name was Lucy and she kept herself to herself. Half of them thought she had some form of learning difficulties and that suited her; it kept them away, frightened to speak with her in case she actually replied. Her cabin was pretty remote, with only one other cabin within walking distance to hers; it was empty, and she liked it that way.

Chapter Three

Lucy heard screaming and naturally ran towards it, pushing aside the fear that rushed through her as she was reminded of the cries of her friends and bandmates that awful night on the motorway, ignoring the pain that shot through her leg with the sudden movement.

The screaming quickly turned to laughter as she rounded the bend and saw two young children splashing around in the shallow water's edge. They were very alike, twins most definitely; both had long honey blonde hair that hung loosely down their backs, and they wore the same clothes, denim shorts and little white t-shirts with some kind of giant cat head smiley face thing on it.

Lucy looked around, searching for a reason why they would be here. There was a third child, a little older with long, dark wavy hair and glasses. She sat by herself on a rock watching the younger ones, the protector of the group. It was she that looked up and saw Lucy first. The young girl clearly hadn't expected to see anyone out here, but she smiled shyly as she got up and walked towards the other two, ushering them out of the water.

As they walked away, the older one looked back towards Lucy and waved goodbye. Lucy pulled her cap down lower to cover her face, but she found herself waving back.

Wandering back to her own place, she wondered where the children had come from. Probably a family camping nearby, and they had wandered off, she assumed. She didn't like the idea that people were nearby though; it left her feeling uneasy. She didn't deal with people very well anymore. They saw the scars and couldn't help themselves from prying or worse, pitying. The scars didn't bother her, not anymore. She was more than used to them, and they were a reminder of something, someone she used to be. But other people were always interested, and it was the questions she didn't like, couldn't deal with and didn't want to listen to.

If she had to go into town she always wore her cap. She would acknowledge some of the locals with a nod of hello, but her only real friend was Rita. The older woman ran the local store. Rita had always taken time with Lucy. She seemed to understand there was something deeper there, something Lucy didn't want to talk about. Over the years Rita had managed to garner a few titbits of information from Lucy, like where she was from or how old she was, but she had never asked her about the scar that ran down one side of her face, a pretty face if you looked at her from the right, but the scar marred it on the whole and Lucy hid it, always kept her long golden brown hair hanging loose on that side.

When she had first arrived at the lake, she had only ever shopped at night or first thing in the morning when there was nobody else around. As time had gone on though, she had become a little more confident about going out in daylight. It helped that the locals kept their distance, not that Rita thought that that was a good idea. She wanted Lucy to understand that not everybody would judge her. Most of the local folk were good people who wanted to reach out to her, but they felt they should hold back until Lucy herself made it clear she would welcome their attention.

It was something that Rita would continue to encourage, but after all these years she wasn't so sure anymore that it would ever happen.

Chapter Four

Nicole and the girls entered Rita's store a couple of days after arriving. The *help wanted* sign and the need to replenish the meagre stock of food they had drew her in. Everything had been a blur these past few days, but she hoped now she could finally settle and give the girls some stability.

Storm had been enrolled in the local school and would start the following Monday. She would at least get to finish the spring semester before the holidays arrived. She had missed too much already. The twins needed to start socialising with other kids too. She had been able to get them into a local pre-school program that would have them for 3 hours a day, 3 days a week until September when they could start kindergarten. She just about had the money to pay for it, but it had eaten into her meagre savings, and now she really needed to find a job.

"Hi there, what beautiful girls you have," Rita remarked to Nicole as they all wandered up to the counter. She looked Nicole up and down and made a quick assessment of the newcomer. Something about her screamed well-to-do, the way she held herself, and yet, she could barely keep eye contact. Her eyes darted around the room as though she expected somebody else to be there.

She was dressed simply, in a plain white t-shirt and old ripped jeans with a well-worn pair of sneakers to top it all off. And she wore barely any make-up. She was stunning in an understated way, and yet her face held a haunted look about it too. Rita was intrigued.

"Thank you, yes they are, aren't they?" Nicole suddenly changed from nervous to proud and gushed adoringly at her brood; it was the only time her eyes lit up. "I uh, I saw the ad in the window for help, I hoped maybe...I could apply if it's still available?"

"Oh right, yeah sure I'm still looking, do you have any experience?" Rita asked, aware of three small pairs of eyes watching her expectantly, the older one taking a bigger interest in the conversation than the smaller ones.

"Uh, not really, but I'm a quick learner and—"

Rita cut her off before she could finish speaking. "It's okay, I was just figuring I should ask, I can teach ya whatcha need to know." She smiled. "It isn't big pay, but it's a fair deal, and you get a discount in the store, thirty hours a week and I'm guessing with these three you're going to need to be a little flexible, am I right?" A slight southern twang to her accent was just about discernible still.

Nicole glanced at her girls and back at Rita before nodding. The bell that was attached to the door and rang anytime a customer entered dinged from behind them, and she flinched slightly at the unexpected noise. Rita nodded an acknowledgement to whoever had entered the store and continued on with Nicole.

"I have a room out back the girls can do their homework in or watch TV if you can't find a sitter."

"Really? Because I really need this job," Nicole declared, her need for a job finally outweighing her nervous disposition.

"We help each other out around here. I hear you've moved into the old Maxwell place? Ain't nobody lived there for years, so I can imagine the state of repair it's in, and if you've rented it then I can only imagine the desperate need you find yourself in too?" she said sympathetically. Nicole blushed at the honest appraisal from the woman in front of her. "In fact, Lucy over there is your neighbour, ain't that right Lucy?" she said to the woman who had entered the store moments earlier. Nicole turned to find a tall, skinny woman in jeans, with long, light brown hair hanging loose and her face half hidden beneath a red baseball cap.

Lucy had already seen the family stood together at the counter and realised they were the same children from the lake just a couple of days ago. She hated when Rita tried to get her to engage with people, but she tried so very hard not to be rude.

"Yes," she answered quickly, adjusting her cap as one of the smaller children turned to look at her and was soon followed by the other two and their mother.

"Hi...I, uh...I'm Nicole and this...*these* are my girls." She stammered out their names and waited for Lucy to react. When nothing happened, she quickly held out her hand instead and waited. She looked nervously back at Rita, who just smiled. For a moment Lucy just stood still, staring down at the floor, but slowly she reached out a scarred hand and gently let her fingers touch Nicole's, then hastily thrust her hand back into her pocket. She didn't like the way that had felt, like electricity passed through their fingers and struck her somewhere inside that she didn't quite recognise and yet, it felt so familiar. She hadn't felt anything like that in a very long time, and it unnerved her.

"I like your hat," one of the smaller ones said, cheerfully looking up at her.

Lucy turned her head slightly in her direction, thankful for the distraction. The kid was smiling at her, so she nodded, but remained silent.

"I have one like it, at my old house," the little one continued.

Nicole shushed her. "Rain, don't bother the lady. I'm sure she has lots to do, just like we do." Lucy was about to turn and retreat when another voice piped up.

"I saw you at the lake, didn't I?" Now it was the taller one that had spoken. She was the image of her mother, just in miniature.

Lucy nodded again. "Yes." She began to fidget, feeling a little uncomfortable with the close quarter scrutiny. She didn't like this; it felt like an interrogation, and any minute an inquisitive mind would ask about them: the scars.

"You don't talk much, do you?" the taller one added, tilting her head slightly so she could see under Lucy's cap. Lucy turned her head away and took a step backwards.

"Storm, don't be rude and let the lady be," Nicole chastised, before turning her attention to Lucy. "I'm sorry."

"Sorry," Storm repeated. She looked about as sorrowful as her mother did. "I just, I like talking."

"I'm sorry." Nicole apologised to Lucy once more. "I'll try and keep them out of your way." She realized that maybe Lucy was a little uneasy around the kids.

"Okay," Lucy said quickly before turning to pick up a basket and walking to the other end of the store. Four pairs of eyes watched her limp away. Only Rain was too busy looking at all the candy bars to take any interest in the strange woman.

"Lucy is, well she's a little different, but she wouldn't hurt a fly so don't you be worrying about that," Rita made clear as she spoke in hushed tones. "She just doesn't like people much, or not so much doesn't like, she just finds it difficult, I don't know why, but she ain't stupid so don't be treating her so and you'll be alright with her."

"That's okay, we all have our secrets, right?" Nicole said, her gaze still firmly on the strange woman under the cap. She certainly had enough secrets of her own.

"Sure do, so when can you start?" Rita smiled at her.

"I can start right away." She smiled brightly, and for the first time in a long time, she felt that maybe, just maybe, things were looking up for them.

Chapter Five

Over the following days, Nicole slowly adjusted to life in her new home. It wasn't anything like what she was used to, but she would make do. Right now, it was everything she needed it to be.

Storm started school. With 7 weeks left of the spring semester, Nicole hoped it would make it easier for her to make new friends right away. The twins loved their new school too; it amazed Nicole how little they were fazed by all the change that had gone on. For the first time, she was able to relax a little and let them just enjoy being kids, making noise and running around like kids should be doing. Of course, as long as they didn't bother the lady in the next cabin. She hadn't seen Lucy at all since their first meeting. There was something about Lucy that made Nicole want to know more about her, but the idea of orchestrating a conversation with her just overwhelmed her, and so she had not sought her out.

On a sunny afternoon towards the end of April, however, Storm wandered down to the lake to do some homework. Her sisters were back at the cabin with their mom, singing and dancing and generally making a lot of noise. And so, she wandered the banks of the lake to find somewhere quiet to sit and do her work, or just ponder the things that ran through her young mind. She noticed Lucy up ahead sitting peacefully on a rock. Unsure what she should do, she just stopped in her tracks. Having been told not to bother Lucy, she didn't want to interrupt her and get in any trouble, but at the same time it wasn't her fault if the strange lady was on the path leading to where she wanted to go, and it would be rude to just ignore her, because despite everything, she had been brought up with manners. She had learned the hard way what happened if you weren't polite.

Making her mind up, she decided she would just continue on with her walk, be polite and say hello, but not linger and then that way, she couldn't get into any trouble. As she neared her, she could tell that Lucy was unaware of her presence. She had her cap off and her hair was tied back. The first thing Storm noticed was the long, jagged scar that zigzagged its way down her left cheek.

Deciding that it might be best to make herself known, she said a quiet, "Hello," her footsteps gaining speed as she attempted to walk past without disturbing Lucy.

Lucy froze, realizing that the kid had seen her without her cap on. She had to have seen the scar too. She placed her hand over her heart, which was beating like it would thump right out of her chest, to try and steady herself.

She had met many a kid since the accident, and most couldn't help themselves from pointing out the obvious, or pointing literally, usually rather loudly and always in front of other people who would then turn to stare.

"I'm sorry, I know I'm not supposed to bother you, but I didn't know you would be here and I'm just walking through, so please excuse me."

Lucy studied her some more. The girl was polite and considerate. She felt her heartbeat slow as she breathed evenly, in and out. "It's ok, you can walk through."

"Thanks, I don't want to get in trouble. I was just going to sit over there and do my homework," she said, pointing to a spot not too far away. "I won't bother you if you want to carry on sitting here."

"Okay," answered Lucy. Not counting Rita, this was the most she had spoken to anyone this month. Usually her anxiety would spike and she would begin to sweat, searching for an escape route, but something about the kid calmed her.

For several long minutes, Lucy continued to just sit and hold her face to the sun. The heat always helped to dull any ache that her scars caused. Her leg was often stiff and painful, but it was better now that she lived somewhere hot. Her thoughts were drifting, not really thinking of anything much. When she heard the small voice speaking again, it shocked her that she had almost forgotten she wasn't alone.

"Don't you get bored?" Storm asked from her spot on the shore. She had her books open on her lap and was trying to concentrate, but the women along the shore from her intrigued her too much.

"No." Her answer was quick and snappy. She didn't want to open a channel for conversation, but the kid had other ideas.

"I would, I like talking to people," Storm admitted, looking up into the sky as though all the answers to life existed within her grasp.

"Clearly." Through hooded eyes, Lucy surreptitiously watched the young girl. She could almost see the cogs working inside her mind as she tried to come up with her next question. But there was a battle there too, not wanting to get in trouble. She had her hands tucked underneath her legs in an effort to keep herself quiet. Something about the gentleness of her piqued Lucy's interest. "Why do you like talking so much?"

Storm was a little bit excited at the new turn of events. Lucy hadn't moved, but she was talking to her. "It's how you find out stuff," Storm answered quickly in case Lucy withdrew her question or got up and walked away.

"What kind of stuff?" Lucy inquired. Knowing she was potentially opening a Pandora's box, she stiffened slightly as she waited for the inevitable questions.

"Lots of stuff, like—" She looked around, thinking. "Why do you sit there and not here?"

That simple question threw Lucy a little, but she answered. "I just like it here."

"Yes, but why?" Storm closed her book and placed it down gently on the floor beside her so that she could twist around to face Lucy properly.

"It's my spot," Lucy answered honestly. She could feel more intenseness forming in the young girl, like she was building up to something. "What else do you want to find out?" Lucy had turned slightly in her own spot to face Storm. She folded her good leg to press against the inside of her bad one. The young girl's eyes searched Lucy's face, but she didn't fixate on the scar. "Ask me," Lucy said quietly. It was the first time someone had seen her scar unhidden and not asked her about it. She felt herself relaxing a little.

The young girl bit her lower lip gently and pushed her glasses back up the bridge of her nose, looking away across the lake as she considered how to ask the question she most wanted an answer for.

"How?" she finally said out loud, feeling brave enough to fix her eyes with Lucy's.

"How what?" Lucy pushed. She wasn't trying to make the girl uncomfortable, but she was succeeding in doing so. "Come here." She patted to the spot next to her.

Adults telling her to 'come here' usually meant she was in trouble, and being in trouble meant a punishment. So, she moved slowly, keeping her eyes firmly on the woman.

"Sit," Lucy demanded gently when she finally stood in front of her.

Storm sank gingerly onto her knees and looked up at Lucy, biting on her bottom lip. Her big brown eyes were so full of questions and apprehension. She looked as though she was about to be scolded and was preparing herself for it.

"How what?" Lucy asked again, her voice softer now as she studied the child. Storm relaxed, understanding instantly that she wasn't in trouble and there wouldn't be a punishment.

Storm studied her face once more. Slowly she lifted her finger to Lucy's cheek. Lucy's first reaction was to flinch, and Storm instantly pulled her hand away, but Lucy nodded and jutted her chin out. Storm concentrated, her tongue poked out between her teeth, and as she gently touched the scar tissue she asked, "How did you get this?"

Lucy sat very still, her heart beating wildly, and allowed this young girl to gently explore her. It was a first. It confused her how easily she had allowed it. Only medical personnel had ever touched the scar on her face; she had even stopped her own mother from doing so. She wondered why this girl – no older than 8 or 9, maybe younger – how had she managed to sneak through her defences so easily.

"I was in an accident," she mumbled. Gulping air, she tried to swallow it down. It was the first time she had told another person in over 10 years.

"What kind of an accident?" Storm asked, still innocently investigating the line that drew its way jaggedly from her left eyebrow and down her cheek almost to the corner of her mouth. Lucy placed her hand on the child's fingers and pulled them gently away from her face, taking deep breaths that were becoming faster and harder to control.

"This is why I don't talk, too many questions," Lucy said too quickly as Storm tried to decide whether she should keep talking or not.

"I have a scar too," Storm blurted out, looking at Lucy. "On my arm."

"That's nice, did you fall over roller skating?" Sarcasm dripped from Lucy's voice. She was starting to feel uncomfortable now. She could feel her heart racing, the blood pumping hard, cortisol flooding her system as her fight or flight instincts began to push to the fore.

Silence passed between them. Lucy watched her as she tried to decide something, her little face frowning while her eyes misted a little.

"No...my daddy dragged me away from Mommy and broke my arm." She looked away for a moment before turning back to Lucy. "I had to have an operation and have a plate put in," she divulged sadly as she held up her arm so the scar was visible to the woman. "It's held together with tiny pins."

Lucy froze at the words. *My daddy broke my arm.* She turned back and looked at the girl. "I'm sorry that happened to you." And in that moment, she realised that this little girl had more in common with her than anyone else she had known in the last 10 years. This young kid understood pain and loss as much, if not more than she did. And what about the mother? Was this why she always looked so sad when she thought nobody was looking?

"Me too, it hurt a lot," Storm continued, trying to smile, but the sadness was too evident. "Mommy says we all have scars even if they are not visible, that some people carry them in their heart."

Lucy nodded. "Your mum sounds like a very wise lady.

Chapter Six

For almost a week, Lucy would go down to the shore every day and find Storm sitting in her own spot. They would acknowledge each other, with a wave from Storm and a nod of the head from Lucy, and then Lucy would sit in her spot and the world would continue to move around them. It was as comfortable as Lucy had been with anyone in the last 15 years, and that unnerved her a little.

Storm had made no further attempt to speak to her again, and she found that unsettling too. In fact, she found herself thinking of ways to engage Storm in conversation with her, which was ridiculous. She was a 30-something adult and this was an 8-year-old kid, for Christ's sake. But this kid had scars too, physical and mental, and she felt a connection with her. She was starting to realise she wasn't the only person on the planet dealt a shitty hand.

She didn't bother with her cap when she went to the shore now. What was the point? Storm had seen the scar and hadn't run away screaming; in fact, she had touched it. With gentleness, with care and reverence, and she had asked about it without it sounding like she was just being nosey, and she hadn't then gone on to question incessantly either.

Today she had even tied her hair up in a ponytail. It was darker now, much more like her original colouring, but still sun-kissed. She preferred it that way to the bleached look of her youth. She felt eyes on her and looked up to see Storm looking her way.

"What?" she said to the kid, narrowing her eyes at her.

"Nothing."

"You were staring?"

"No, I was looking." The kid had a sharp mind, quick and witty, and Lucy enjoyed the repartee with her.

"Well, what were you *looking* at?"

"I was looking at your t-shirt, it's my favourite colour and reminded me of something else," Storm replied, getting up and walking towards Lucy. "May I sit?" she asked, pointing to the spot next to her.

Lucy nodded, and Storm sat down in a heap next to her. She crossed her legs and picked up a small pebble in front of her, examined it, and then placed it back exactly where she found it.

"What does it remind you of?" Lucy spoke quietly, still unsure of her own voice.

"My old bedroom," Storm answered. She looked up at her, and just to be clear she added, "In our old house."

"Well, maybe you can paint your new bedroom the same colour," Lucy suggested.

"No!" Storm shouted. She suddenly got up and rushed back to her own spot. Flopping down in the rock, she pulled her knees up and wrapped her arms around them and just stared out across the lake.

"Or not then," Lucy muttered to herself, unsure what exactly had happened. They didn't speak for the rest of the afternoon, and at four p.m. precisely, Lucy stood and went back to her cabin like she always did and watched from the window as Storm stood. She then wandered off back to her own cabin further along the track.

~E&F~

At dinner that night, Nicole placed down three small plates and a bowl for herself. She dished each child a healthy portion of macaroni and cheese with some broccoli on the side. Her own bowl contained the other half of the tinned soup she had had for lunch, with a small slice of bread to go with it. It wasn't much, but it was the best she could do until things settled down and she could afford to splurge a little more. The discount at the store was a godsend, and she made the most of it.

"So, what did you get up to today, Storm?" she asked, taking her seat at the head of the table. She didn't like it much when her eldest took herself off somewhere; anything could happen. It wasn't safe for them to be wandering too far, but she knew that she needed to start giving Storm a little space. Today though, she looked a little down, and that worried Nicole.

"Just sitting," she replied quietly before sliding her fork, loaded with macaroni, into her mouth.

Nicole studied her a little before gently probing some more. "Must be a nice spot you found, you were gone all afternoon, I got a little worried." She broke up the piece of bread and dropped each bit into the soup.

"Sorry Mama, I was just along the shore," she said. Looking down at her plate, she followed it up with, "Just in front of Lucy's cabin."

"Storm, baby, I've told you don't go bothering that lady." Nicole spoke gently, but she needed to be firm with this, they couldn't afford to be upsetting anyone or drawing attention to themselves by creating a problem.

"I'm not, I just sit there and read my books," she replied honestly. "Sometimes we talk though, is that so wrong?" She looked up at her mother with the exact same brown eyes. Mirror image.

"She talks to you?" Nicole put her spoon down, intrigued and a little more concerned. Trust wasn't something that came easily just now. Rita had been clear that Lucy wasn't anyone to worry about, but as a mother, that was her job.

"Well I talked to her first I guess, but she replies and we talk about—" She thought about the best word to describe what they talked about and settled on "Stuff."

"What kind of 'stuff'?" She was not surprised that her 8-year-old child had managed to get a woman who didn't speak to people to talk to her; Storm just had that way about her.

"Well, did you know she has a scar on her face?" Storm confided, drawing her finger down her cheek replicating Lucy's scar. "Like this."

"No, I didn't," Nicole said, shaking her head. "Is that why she doesn't talk?"

"I don't know." She shrugged. "I didn't ask her why she doesn't talk, I just asked her how she got the scar?"

"Hmm, ya know baby sometimes you shouldn't ask people things they might prefer to keep private." She picked up her spoon again and began to eat her food before it got cold.

"I know, but she told me to ask her, so I did."

"I've finished, Mommy, can I go play now?" interrupted Rain, holding up her empty plate as proof, completely uninterested in the conversation her older sister was having.

"Me too!" Summer piped up, her little goofy grin showing off her toothy smile.

"Go on then, don't make a mess though." Nicole smiled as her two youngest hopped off their chairs and ran to their bedroom. They didn't have enough toys to make a mess right now, but that didn't seem to bother them, the innocence of youth so encapsulated in them both.

Turning her attention back to Storm she asked, "So what did she say?"

"She was in an accident, I think she has other scars, but I didn't ask her, you can see them though when she moves and her shirt lifts," she said, showing on her own torso where she saw it, but then she hesitated a moment before adding, "I told her about my scar."

"You did? What did she say?" Nicole was surprised as her daughter rarely opened up to anyone about it, not that she had had much opportunity before now. She hoped that it would be good for Storm to talk about it.

"That she was sorry that it happened to me."

"Did you tell her how?" Nicole coaxed gently.

Storm looked down at the table, embarrassed? No, anxious.

"It's okay if you did, baby. It isn't a secret or something to be ashamed of. You—" She stopped and corrected herself. "*We* did nothing wrong, okay?" She cupped her daughter's cheek reassuringly and smiled.

Storm nodded her head in agreement. "Yes, I told her daddy did it when he grabbed me." Her little face grew red and tears pricked at her eyes. When her lower lip began to tremble, Nicole moved from her chair to kneel beside her and wrapped her arms around her.

"It is all going to be okay, baby. I promise, Daddy can't hurt us now, and he doesn't even know where we are, remember? Plus, we have a new name now too, so don't you be worrying," Nicole assured her child for the hundredth time, still trying to convince herself too that Paul Nixon would not find them

Chapter Seven

Saturday morning found Nicole behind the counter at Rita's store when Lucy came in for her weekly shop. She had taken to the job quite easily, and it was helping her get back into the groove with social interaction. The store wasn't so busy that it was overwhelming, but there was enough footfall of traffic that she had plenty of gentle interaction each shift. But the strange woman in the hat always made her a little nervous. She wasn't afraid of her, that wasn't it at all, but something about Lucy brought an inhibition to Nicole that she wasn't used to.

"Good morning," Nicole mumbled, averting her eyes as Lucy wandered in and grabbed a basket.

"Hi," Lucy muttered back in reply before she dodged quickly down an aisle.

There was nobody else in the store. Nicole followed Lucy up and down the aisles. Picking up tins that had been placed in the wrong spot, she checked dates on the dustier-looking ones and gave them a quick wipe if they were still saleable. Quick glances towards the tall, skinny woman made her skin heat.

"Anything I can help you with?" Nicole asked Lucy quietly. "I...I'm new and need the practice finding things," she said with a smile she hoped would convey honesty and friendliness. She was trying to find her own feet again with making new friends. Maybe she had bitten off more than she could chew with Lucy though. "Nicole," she reminded her.

The bar was packed as Lucy headed up for another drink. She had a buzz on and was enjoying the music and laughter with her friends. She squeezed into a space at the bar and shouted a sorry when she realised she had bumped against a girl and spilt her drink.

"Hey!" Green eyes shone with a sparkle of humour as their owner turned fully to face Lucy. "I would say you owe me a refill, wouldn't you?" she grinned.

Leaning in, Lucy said, "I suppose that's the least I can do." She returned the grin.

"Nicola." She held out a delicate hand, "I prefer Nicky, but if you're going to take me out then you should know my proper name, right?"

"Nicole?" She said the word almost reverently as she glanced up. "Nope, all good thanks." Lucy shook herself, not looking at her. From her profile, Nicole could just make out the scar that Storm had told her about. It was a shame, she thought; Lucy was a beautiful woman. Nicole had always taken care of her looks, not that she was vain, but she liked the way she looked and had spent time on cultivating her style. Of course, none of that mattered now, but still, she couldn't imagine how she would have coped if she had had to live with such a marking on her face. Then she remembered how close she had come to that.

Feeling eyes on her, Lucy continued staring at the tins on the shelf in front of her. She could feel the rush of blood flood her cheeks. She followed the old familiar breathing technique she had learned a long time ago and settled herself.

"I was in an accident," Lucy muttered. She breathed out, surprising herself that she had said it out loud once more; that was twice in the same week and to two different people, albeit from the same family.

"Oh...I'm sorry, I didn't mean to stare, I was just—" She flinched, suddenly aware that she had spoken out of turn. She had gotten better with it, but sometimes she still felt the fear. "Sorry." Looking downward and avoiding eye contact, she turned quickly to leave Lucy in peace.

Lucy continued walking around the store picking up the items that she needed while Nicole went back to the till to serve a customer who just wanted some cigarettes. She was used to people being scared or intimidated around her, but not in the same way Nicole was reacting. She didn't like it.

Nicole watched Lucy as she pulled on the peak of her cap and adjusted her shirt before she strolled up the aisle towards the till. She was intrigued as to what kind of accident she had had, and she wondered if maybe they had anything in common, but the thought of asking churned her stomach. Because she had learned her lesson many times about questions that she had no right to ask.

"Will you be home late for dinner?" That was all she had asked, a simple question so she could plan their evening meal around him. The punch to the back of the head had given her a

headache, and she wasn't sure that he hadn't broken a rib as he screamed at her to never question him again.

"I-I-I wanted to thank you," Nicole stuttered when Lucy came closer to pay for her goods, still avoiding eye contact with each other.

"What for?" she asked, perplexed by the statement as she glanced around, fidgety and unsure where this conversation was going.

"Letting my daughter, Storm, hang around your place. I-if she bothers you just let me know and—"

"She's no bother," Lucy broke in while fishing in her pocket for a wallet. "Smart kid."

Nicole took a moment to assess her up close once again. She really was quite stunning. She had beautiful green eyes, wide and bright. She was tall too and slim, maybe too slim, in her ripped denim jeans and leather jacket that was open and allowed a glimpse of the tank top she wore underneath. And more scars. But, she was beautiful in a haunted kind of way. Nicole blushed as she realised that she was openly gawping.

It hadn't gone unnoticed by Lucy either, and a flush crept up her neck and hit her cheeks just as quickly. What was it with this woman constantly making her blush? She quickly put her head down and handed over the required amount. Grabbing her bags, she moved to the door as quickly as she could; she needed some air.

"Bye," called Nicole after her. She found herself smiling. She could do this.

Chapter Eight

The next time that Lucy went to her *spot*, she noticed Storm had brought her sisters with her. For a moment, she froze. Young kids were always the worst with questions. She watched as the twins ran around, screaming with excitement. Storm was trying desperately to quieten them down, but not having much luck.

"Sorry!" Storm called out, noticing that Lucy was hesitant to come any closer. "I'll take them home."

Lucy continued to watch them for a moment; they were having fun, not hurting anyone. They were kind of cute, so much life inside them just bursting to come out. She couldn't help but smile a little as she watched them run around and around with no particular destination. Such innocence yet to be marked by life's pain and sorrow. They were wearing matching clothes again, only one of them had a hat on covering her blonde curls.

"It's okay," she called back. Moving slowly, she limped across to her rock.

"Are you sure? It's not a problem to take them home, it's just Mom had to work on the house and they were getting under her feet," Storm continued to explain. She had a pained look on her face.

"It's okay," Lucy repeated as she thought about their mom, Nicole. She seemed like a nice woman. Too chatty, but nice enough.

Beautiful too. It was a strange thought for her; she had seen plenty of women over the years, but none of them had ever left any kind of impression on her like Nicole had. She supposed there must have been other beautiful women that she passed every day, and yet she never noticed them.

Just as if by thinking about her she had conjured her to appear, there she was, walking along the shore heading towards the girls. Her raven hair hung loosely around her face, and she was smiling as she caught sight of her girls. She had a great smile, thought Lucy as she watched her surreptitiously from beneath her cap. Nicole looked cool and fashionable as she strolled the path in loose linen white trousers paired with a long, flowing red top that seemed to float around her. When one of the twins noticed her, she ran and hugged her mother around the legs, and Lucy found herself unable to look away. The scene was heart-warming.

Nicole raised her left hand and waved to Lucy. Without thinking, Lucy waved back. She watched in slow motion as her hand retreated back down and into her pocket. Perplexed, she looked away and focused on a pebble at her foot.

As Nicole reached the other girls, Lucy could hear her telling them that she had to go to work. Apparently, Rita wasn't feeling very well, and the girls would have to come with her to the store for the evening, as she couldn't afford not to work the extra shift.

Storm protested. She didn't want to go, and Lucy could understand why. Sitting here by the lake, it brought more than peace to someone. It was somewhere you could just be. It seeped into your soul. Storm already felt it, that much Lucy was sure of.

"But Mom, it's so boring there," Storm pleaded. "I can stay here, I promise I won't do anything stupid."

"Baby, you're not old enough to be left by yourself yet, it's just out of the question, okay? Come on, get your things, we need to go," her mother urged, checking her watch again.

"But Mom," Storm continued to whine. Her sisters were still running around like mini-whirlwinds, and Nicole was finding herself becoming more stressed and frustrated with the arguing. She didn't want to go to work and drag them away from the fun they were having, but she had no choice. If she was going to be able to make this house a home, then she would need all the dollars she could get, especially when she needed to make sure they always had an escape fund, just in case.

"They can stay with me," Lucy piped up without looking up. Her own unexpected vocal outburst shocked her a little.

"Sorry?" Nicole said, unsure if she heard her properly.

"I said...they can...they can stay here, with me. I – if you want? If it helps?" stuttered Lucy, not quite understanding why she was offering to do this. It was so far out of her comfort zone. She had never looked after kids before.

Storm's eyes lit up in an instant as she looked hopefully at her mother. "Please, can we stay here with Lucy?"

"I...are you sure? They can be a handful," Nicole fretted, caught off guard by this unexpected offer and the decision she had to now make. Could she leave her kids with this virtual stranger that barely spoke to her? Would they be safe? What if Paul turned up?

"I'm sure I can cope, but if you think otherwise, I won't be offended," Lucy said solemnly, understanding completely the dilemma she could see Nicole going over in her mind.

"No, I'm sure you will do just fine." She smiled and tried to look confident about it. "If you're sure? It would be a huge help, thank you," Nicole said sincerely, deciding that maybe Lucy could be trusted. Rita had never had a bad word to say about her, and if Rita trusted her, then she figured she could too. She wouldn't be long anyway, just a couple of hours at most until she could close up and get back to them.

"What time will you be back?" Lucy asked as if she could read her mind. She had stood up and was looking at her now, trying to show the woman that she could be trusted with her most prized possessions.

"Around 8 I think, you can always bring them to the store if it's too long or if they get out of hand." They studied each other for a second or two, each of them sizing the other up to make sure this was definitely going to be okay.

Lucy concluded that it would and said, "It will be fine, what time do they have dinner?"

"Oh, I hadn't even thought about that, normally around 6, but they can wait until I get home."

"I can cook," Lucy said, walking toward her.

"Okay, so, okay." Nicole laughed a little nervously. "Then if you're sure?" she smiled again, giving Lucy a last chance to back out. "I'll get going then?"

"We will be fine," Lucy asserted, turning away towards her cabin, leaving Nicole to say goodbye to the girls.

"Be good for Lucy," she heard her tell them as she entered her home and closed the door.

When she came back out, the girls were sitting together on the shore drawing in the sand with sticks they'd found, and Nicole was nowhere to be seen. Lucy brought them each a drink and sat down with them. She took some calming breaths, a quick pep talk to convince herself she could do this.

Three little faces looked up at Lucy expectantly, waiting for her to entertain them. "So, what do you normally do to entertain yourselves?" she said to Storm, still a little unsure of herself around the twins.

"Well, I read, as you know, and these two make a lot of noise and mess, generally." She shrugged. The two smaller ones continued to just stare at her. She was surprised that they hadn't commented yet about her face.

"I see. Okay." Lucy thought for a moment and then, when an idea had popped into her head, she got up and went back inside again. The girls looked at one another, wondering where she was going to. Were they supposed to follow? but she returned minutes later with a box of empty plastic takeout containers under her arm.

"Right, I want you to go and find as many pebbles as you can, and fill this box up," Lucy said, placing the larger box on the floor between them. The twins immediately started to pick up tiny rocks and pebbles, bringing them back to Lucy for inspection. The ones she deemed to be good enough went in the box and the others were tossed in the lake. Storm wasn't quite so excited about the idea, but she helped her sisters anyway.

It took almost 20 minutes just to collect them, and when they were done they sat down next to the box, looking up at her wondering what she was going to do next.

"So, next you have to take one container each and flip the lid off," she said, picking up one of the containers herself to show them what she meant. "Now we have to put some pebbles inside, not too many though, we don't want to fill it up."

The twins grabbed a fistful and placed them in their containers just like they were shown, and when they had placed as many as they thought they needed into the boxes, they held them out for Lucy to inspect. Happy with them, they all put the lids back on. Lucy grabbed some tape from the box and taped the lids on tight. Storm was now very intrigued at what they were doing.

"Right, now we have some shakers," Lucy grinned as she turned the original box over, "and a drum."

"Yay!" The twins shouted and screamed in unison as they stood and shook their shakers making a god-awful noise. Storm laughed and sat down quickly in front of the *drum,* bashing at it with her hands in tandem with the girls. All three of them grinned from ear to ear as they made one hell of a noise.

"What about you, Luce?" Storm asked, smiling. Lucy noted the shortening and familiarity with which she now used her name. "What are you going to play?"

"I'm the audience!" she declared as she sat back with her book and listened to the racket. It had been a long time since she had heard such a lot of noise this close up. The twins were singing a made-up song; it was out of tune and made no sense, but it was endearing. They were happy, smiling and laughing. When she thought about it, she knew she was too.

Within an hour there were three tired out and hungry kids quietly sitting with their instruments laying idle in their laps. Job done, thought Lucy to herself. "Okay, inside then and get cleaned up so we can have tea."

"I'm not thirsty," Summer announced as they all walked back to Lucy's cabin together.

"Not drinking tea, tea is what we call dinner in England," Lucy explained, resting her hand gently on the child's shoulder. The contrast between the scarred tissue of her own skin beside the flawless cheek was night and day and yet, for once she didn't feel uncomfortable.

"Where's England?" Rain chipped in, looking up at Lucy with big expressive eyes.

Lucy turned towards her and answered, "It is where I am from, where I was born."

"Is it near Texas?" Summer asked as Storm sniggered, and even Lucy couldn't help but chuckle.

"Yeah, it's not too far from Texas," she said, smiling in Summer's direction once more.

~E&F~

They each took turns washing hands and faces at the sink in the bathroom and then sat quietly around the table as Lucy served them up some chicken and salad. It probably wasn't exciting to them, but it was the best she had, outside of crackers and cheese, which she didn't think was a very nutritious diet to feed someone else's kids. None of them complained, so she figured it must be okay.

When they were done, they all moved to the living room because it was darker outside now and a little cooler. Playtime was definitely over for today.

"You don't have a TV?" asked Rain, incredulous as she stared around the room with wide eyes.

"Nope," Lucy said, shaking her head for emphasis.

"Then how do you watch stuff?" Rain continued, her hands outstretched, palms up, a look of utter confusion on her face. Summer and even Storm waited for the answer.

"I don't."

"No SpongeBob?" Rain asked, her face scrunched up in more confusion. She was now seriously concerned for Lucy. Lucy had no clue who SpongeBob was.

"No, no SpongeBob."

"What do you do then?" asked Summer, completely perplexed as to what anyone did without a TV.

"Read, mostly."

The twins were silent and looking at one another as though this woman were completely bonkers. It was a silent conversation that only twins can have, and one that ended with both of them deciding sleeping was the only option left.

"I'm tired," announced Summer, followed by a nodding Rain.

"Hop up on the sofa then and I'll get you a blanket, you can take a nap." They both did just that, one at each end, legs and feet tangled together.

Lucy looked to Storm to see if she was tired and was greeted with a raised book in the air.

"I'm reading," Storm whispered so as not to wake the twins.

"Ok, me too," she said raising her own book and taking a seat on the floor opposite Storm. It was surreal for Lucy; her normal evening would be spent by herself reading as she was now, but she could hear the presence of her guests. She could hear the soft breathing of Summer and Rain as they slept peacefully, the gentle flutter of pages being turned as Storm read her book, grasping every detail as her eyes eagerly scanned each page. Lucy watched her for a while and smiled to herself; she liked having these kids around.

Just over an hour later, there was a gentle tapping on the door. She realised she had dozed off and woke to find Storm sleeping too as the gentle knocking became more insistent. Lucy got up as quickly as she could and stretched before limping across the room to the door.

"Hey, so sorry I'm late. We had a last-minute rush, some new tourists needing to stock up..." Nicole whispered, following Lucy's finger-to-lips instruction. Once again, she bowed her head as she spoke and didn't make eye contact. It was just for a moment, but Lucy noticed it. She didn't like it.

"Only by a few minutes," she noted, checking her watch. It wasn't a big deal. "Come in. Please." Lucy moved out of the doorway to make room for Nicole to pass her and enter the room before closing it gently and following her inside. She caught a trace of her perfume as she passed and breathed it in, enjoying the aroma of it. It was sweet and intoxicating without being overpowering. Lucy liked it.

Confident Nicole was back again, head held high as she looked around the room and tried to get a fix on this quiet woman and the way she lived. It unnerved Lucy to think about the possible reasons why this woman, this beautiful and kind woman, would be so afraid of her one minute and then relaxed the next. It also concerned her that she wanted to find out.

Nicole surveyed the room. Everything was beautifully restored and decorated with ornate carvings on the wooden posts and lots of beautiful rugs adorning the floors and walls. Lucy's cabin was nothing like her own. It too was sparsely decorated, but in a lived-in kind of way. It was homely.

There was a comfortable-looking brown couch and a chair that didn't quite match, her daughters sleeping on them, taking up all the seats available. The twins stretched out on the couch like they did at home in their bed, and Storm was dozing with her book rested on her chest, in the chair. From the way in which Lucy was stretching her back, she guessed she must have been sitting on the floor.

"Thank you so much for this, it was a lifesaver. I really can't afford to turn down the extra hours right now." Nicole honestly was grateful; every extra cent she could make meant her kids could have a better life, and that was all she wanted right now.

When Nicole had arrived at the store without the children, Rita had been concerned about them being left alone, so when Nicole explained that Lucy was looking after them, she almost passed out. "Lucy?" Rita had restated as she got her things together,

59

ready to go home and climb into bed to try and shift this bug she had picked up. There had been a moment of panic when Nicole actually thought about it. She hardly knew the woman, and what she did know of her made her seem a little weird. Had she been wrong to leave her kids with her?

"No problem." Lucy said, bringing her from her thoughts. "They were as good as gold."

"Well, thank you again, I'll take them home now and leave you in peace." she said, looking down at two sleeping 4-year-olds and wondering just how she was going to get them all home.

"It's okay, I can carry one." Lucy smiled shyly, swooping down and picking up Rain, who was closest to her. Nicole watched as this strange woman held her daughter with such care. Her arms gently wrapped around the small warm body as she held her close to her chest and cradled her with such tenderness. She picked up a small blanket and wrapped it around her; it wasn't cold, but she didn't want to risk waking her.

"Are you sure? I don't want to put you out any further." She waited for Lucy to nod in agreement.

"I've already got her, I'll be fine."

She gently shook her oldest child awake as she picked up her book and placed it into her bag. "Okay, Storm have you got all your things?"

"Yeah, I'm awake," said a sleepy voice as she pushed herself up from the chair and began to walk to the door.

Nicole looked around the room once more, checking to make sure her kids didn't leave any mess behind them, and then she picked up Summer just like Lucy had done with Rain. "Let's go then."

The walk back to the Grangers' cabin was quick and quiet. Storm opened the door and they all piled through. Lucy waited to be told where to take Rain.

"Just through here." Nicole pointed, speaking quietly as she walked towards a door to the right. Inside was a double bed and not much else. She placed Rain gently on the side of the bed nearest the door and covered her with a blanket, while Nicole placed Summer on the other side and covered her too. For a moment they both stood and watched the children wriggle and get comfortable before they left the room.

As she was about to leave and return to her own cabin, Nicole stopped her at the door.

"Would you like to stay and have a coffee or something?"

Lucy looked around, gathering her thoughts before turning her attention to Nicole. It was the first time she had really looked at her. She had charcoal eyes, not brown like she had assumed. They were darker, smouldering and sexy. And they were looking directly at her, studying her too. They were warm and deep and, in that moment, Lucy wasn't sure if she would be able to look away. She didn't feel any of the usual anxiety when someone new looked at her full in the face like that.

"No, thank you for the offer but I—" she pointed to her own cabin, "I better get back."

"Oh okay, well another time, maybe?" Nicole fidgeted, drawing attention away from her face to her hand that was gripping the fingers of the other in a wringing motion.

"Uh, yeah, another time." And with that, Lucy quickly turned and left to head home.

Closing the door behind her, Nicole couldn't help but wonder what had happened just now. There was a moment, between them, something she hadn't experienced before with anyone. And there was something about Lucy that was familiar. Like she had seen her someplace long ago, but she couldn't pinpoint it. All she knew was that the more time she spent with Lucy, the more she wanted to spend with her. If she would let her.

She turned and found Storm watching her. Watching them.

"So, did you have fun with Lucy?" Nicole inquired, wanting to double check that everything really had been as okay as it seemed to be.

"Yeah, she's pretty cool," she replied, pushing her glasses back up her nose. "We made instruments and played in our own band."

"Oh, that must have been fun!" Nicole exclaimed as she sat on the couch next to her eldest daughter. Storm leaned against her mother and snuggled in. It was still early really. She was often allowed to stay up after 8 p.m. now, but she was tired after all the running around she had done at Lucy's.

"Yeah it was, most adults get irritated when we make noise. But Lucy liked it," she declared quite adamantly.

"Well that's great, I'm glad you had fun." Now she knew Lucy must be nuts, liking the noise her kids made? It made her chuckle.

"She doesn't have a TV though; kinda weird." Storm giggled.

Nicole laughed before she answered. "Yes, I'm sure it is for you kids, I quite like it when the TV is off though. When you're older you'll understand more. Come on, let's get you to bed, huh?"

Chapter Nine

As April merged into May, Lucy found herself surrounded most evenings by three kids wanting to play on the shore. They had been here in the cabin a month almost, and it had become almost routine in the last two weeks that if Nicole had to work then the girls could stay with her. The twins, with their hair in bunches and matching outfits, thought it was immense fun to follow Lucy around everywhere she went; whatever she did, they did. At first, it annoyed her a little, but then she turned it into a game, and now she had fun with it. She would start off doing something normal and then she would do a funny walk or hop and skip. The twins would try and copy, and they always ended up laughing. Not once had any of them mentioned her face or any of her other scars that she knew must be visible from time to time.

She had gotten so used to it now that she had drinks and snacks ready for their arrival. Games she had bought had started to pile up around her cabin, and clothes that had been forgotten from the day before were scattered about waiting to be taken home again. It was messy and chaotic, but if she was honest, she loved every second of it.

Every day would start and end with questions, but not about her. Just questions that kids had, and she found herself looking forward to seeing them, so when they didn't show up that afternoon as she was expecting them to, she was concerned.

She paced around a little, picking up discarded toys as she considered all the reasons why they hadn't arrived. No matter what she came up with, it always came down to the fact that Nicole would have let her know, either by walking over herself or sending Storm with a message. Neither of those things had happened, and so she was now outside of her own cabin looking up and down the path that led between the two abodes. She was expecting Nicole to be working tonight, that was the plan, but maybe things had changed. It still came back to the fact Nicole would have told her. She was picking up her stuff to go back inside when she heard something she hadn't heard in a long time.

A scream. Not a kid playing kind of scream, she heard that every day with the twins, she was used to that kind of scream now. This was a scream of terror, and it sounded like Storm.

Dropping her things to the floor, she took off running as best she could towards the cabin. Her legs and arms pumped as she picked up as much speed as her broken legs would allow. When she ran into the clearing where the cabin stood, she saw nothing out of place. Nicole's old car was parked in its usual spot, the girls had a few toys scattered around, but that was normal. Nothing was out of the ordinary except the silence. Deafening silence.

Three kids made a lot of noise, Lucy knew this now; every day was filled with questions and talking, laughing and screaming. But not the scream that she had heard a minute ago. Her instincts told her not to call out, but to investigate instead. She moved as quickly as she could around to the back of the house and saw something that was peculiar. Another car, an expensive car. A bright red Mercedes soft top with private plates, NIX 1, sat gleaming in the sunshine that broke through the trees and dappled it. It was a nice car, that was for sure. She knew all about nice cars. In her old life she had several, all for show of course. The fast cars went with the big house. So, she knew this car was not supposed to be here, in the middle of the forest by a lake. No, this car belonged in a city, in a garage attached to a big house.

She walked quickly back to the front of the house and rapped her knuckles on the door, hard. Nothing, no response. So, she knocked again, louder this time.

She heard footsteps, then the door bolts as they slid across and the door opened just a crack. Nicole stood there half hidden by the door, only her right eye visible to Lucy. She looked upset, like she had been crying.

"Hi," Lucy said quietly, her head tilted as she tried to see behind Nicole.

"Oh, hello Lucy. Uh, it's not a good time...right now," Nicole stuttered, looking back over her shoulder for a second.

Checking to see what? Something was off; who else was in there with her? Who owned that car?

"Okay, I just wondered if the girls were still coming over?" she asked, trying to work out what was going on.

"Uh no, not tonight. We decided to stay in."

"Right, so Rita gave you the night off?" Her eyes narrowed as she asked the question.

"Uh yes, yes she did," she answered. Her head nodded, but her eyes, wide and fearful, said something else. "The night off, that's right." There was definitely something amiss here.

"Okay then," she said. Accepting the answer, she turned as if she was about to walk away. "Oh, I almost forgot, did I leave my jacket here?" Lucy asked, and then mouthed quietly, "Are you okay?"

Nicole shook her head, "No, you didn't leave it here." The wide-eyed look of fear still on her face was enough to tell Lucy all she needed to know.

"Okay then, don't worry about it, I'll work it out. Goodnight." She turned and walked away. Hearing the door close behind her, she moved out of view of the cabin and waited. Then she heard the scream again. The sound vibrated through her and ripped at her heart. She couldn't stand back and wait for the police to arrive. Out here it could take too long. She needed to do something and she needed to do it now.

Thinking on her feet, she went back towards the cabin and around to the back again to where the Mercedes was parked. She eyed it for a moment and then she saw what she needed.

Picking up an old axe handle that was left near the woodpile, she lifted it over her head and brought it down on the car headlight. The impact smashed it to pieces and immediately set off the car alarm. She then ran around the house the opposite way back around to the front and waited. A tall man with short, sandy blonde hair came running outside to the car. He was a big guy, muscular. He was red-faced and angry.

He had left the door open in his haste to get outside. The moment he was out of sight, she ran for it and flew inside, slamming it shut behind her and bolting the locks into place.

Breathing hard, she looked up and saw Nicole with a look of sheer terror on her face. She had a cut and swollen lip, with a black eye on the left side of her face. Three small tear-stained faces huddled together on the couch. Storm had a red handprint across her cheek.

"Who is he?" Lucy demanded as he pounded his fists against the door, shouting and screaming obscenities. She ignored him and concentrated on Nicole, who stood absolutely still, just staring at the door. "Nicole? Who is he?" Lucy insisted again, and this time the raven-haired woman turned slightly to look at her, flinching every time his fist connected with the door.

"My h-h-husband," Nicole confessed as she collapsed to the floor. Storm instantly went to her aid along with Lucy. She lifted her gently and helped move her to the couch, where the twins huddled against her immediately.

"Mommy, why is Daddy so mad?" Rain asked, tears streaking down her cheeks. Nicole didn't have an answer. She had never had the answer; he didn't seem to need a reason. Until now, she had managed to hide this side of him from the little ones, but now they knew. Now they could see for themselves just how mean a man their father was.

The banging on the door continued. He was still shouting and cussing. Lucy steadied herself, took a breath or two to calm her nerves, and limped towards the door. Her leg was aching, and it hurt with every step she took. As she reached for the bolt in order to open it and give this guy a piece of her mind, two voices screamed at her in unison. "No!"

She looked back at Storm and Nicole as they both shook their heads. Their eyes pleaded silently, terror and fear encapsulated in them both.

"It's okay. I'm going to get rid of him," she answered with such confidence that for a second Nicole actually believed her, but then the fear was back.

"He is crazy, please Lucy don't," she pleaded, and in that moment, Lucy understood everything about this woman. She looked from one to the other and made up her mind. She moved to where Storm sat on the edge of her seat, her bottom lip trembling as she fought to hold back her tears.

Lucy bent down to speak to the young girl on her level. "Storm, take your sisters into your bedroom, okay? And don't come back out here until Mummy says you can. Do you understand?" Storm looked to her mother for reassurance. Nicole nodded and Storm did as she was asked, looking back over her shoulder as she ushered the two younger ones to their room.

Lucy went towards the door again. She stood behind it, listening as his ranting decreased a little. He was still at the door, but the banging had stopped. Now, it was just a verbal assault, threats and promises of what he was going to do.

"You're not wanted here, Mate," Lucy called out. The new voice seemed to throw him for a moment and there was silence, but not for long.

"Bitch, you smashed my car. I should call the police and have you arrested!" he shouted back, a soft southern twang to his voice.

"Good, call the police," Lucy said, nodding at the idea. Nicole had crept up behind her and stood just a hair's breadth away from her back.

"What?" he shouted back, and she felt Nicole shrink away. Lucy reached for her hand and grasped it.

"I said, Dumbass, call the police. That will probably be the best thing you can do if you're not going to leave," she challenged, leaving Nicole to wonder what she meant exactly.

"Open this door." He banged once more, his voice filled with a venom and hatred that Lucy had never heard from another human being before.

"Sir, if I open that door then you are going to be in real danger." She continued to speak to him calmly; she was in control of this, not him. She wouldn't let him terrify her the way he had his family.

"What?" he said. "Open the door and I—"

"And you'll what?" she said defiantly. "What are you going to do? I ain't scared of you mister, you can't bully me! Who the hell do you think you are coming here and behaving like someone gives a shit what you think!?"

He went silent. She ushered Nicole over to the window, a finger to her lips to indicate quiet before she used her fingers to point to her own eyes and then back at him; watch him. She then thumped the door as loudly as she could with the axe handle and he jumped out of his skin.

Nicole stifled a giggle before hissing as her lip split once more. A small trickle of blood slid quickly down her chin. Lucy reached out and with her fingers, she gently touched her cheek and wiped the blood away from the lip that he had hit.

"What the fuck was that?" he shouted, confused now. He was unsettled. This was his domain, and here was some woman treading on his toes.

"You need to leave or I swear to any God you might believe in I will hurt you," Lucy shouted through the door. She didn't want to get involved in any altercation, but if she needed to, she would take him on and give as good as she could. She gripped the axe handle a little tighter.

"You're fucking crazy."

"Yes, I think if you asked most people around here they would agree with you, do you want to take your chances? I mean beating up on women and kids seems to be your kind of thing, but I'm pretty sure I could whip your arse given the opportunity, asshole," she hollered. She was absolutely livid now; how dare this so-called man come here and bully this family. How dare he hit this gorgeous woman and damage her, and what about those beautiful kids? He didn't deserve any of them.

"Fuck this, Nicole you get your ass home with my kids or else," he shouted before turning back to his car. They waited, staring at each other in silence until he drove away. He had been gone for a couple of minutes before Nicole pulled her eyes away from Lucy's and rushed back to the girl's room to usher them out. Lucy collapsed against the door and slowly slid downwards as the full impact of what had just happened began to sink in. She could finally admit that she was scared. Her heart pounded in her chest.

"Girls, get your things packed," Nicole said, grabbing bags and throwing them onto beds.

"Wait, mama no," Storm pleaded. "I like it here. Can't we just make him go away?"

"Baby, we need to leave." She had no idea how he had tracked them down, but she wasn't going to take any chances; they needed to leave now. Get as far away as possible. Change the car, maybe their name again.

Lucy watched the scene play out in front of her from her place on the floor, and she didn't like it. She had run away herself from a situation she couldn't deal with. She knew all about running and hiding, not from a monster like him, but from herself, and she knew it didn't end well.

"Y-you're leaving?" Lucy asked timidly as she stood and made her way toward Nicole.

"Yes, we can't stay here now, you saw what he is like," Nicole answered as she continued to move around the cabin, picking things up and throwing them into bags.

"You need to clean your face up," Lucy suggested, anything to stop her packing. They couldn't just leave. Not now, not when she had just gotten used to them. "Before you get an infection."

"No, it can wait."

"He won't be back tonight, come and sit here," she ordered gently, pulling out a chair and walking into the kitchen for a bowl of warm salty water. She needed to concentrate on something, anything rather than to think about losing them, because in the month they had been here, they had become important.

"Do you have any cotton balls?" Lucy asked the room, not really speaking to anyone in particular.

"Bathroom," said Storm. "I'll get some." And off she ran.

When Storm returned, Lucy set about cleaning Nicole's mouth and nose. She dunked the cotton into the warm water and squeezed it to remove the excess, deftly sponging the area and cleaning the dried blood that had begun to congeal around the small cut to her lip. Nicole watched her, their eyes holding briefly as Lucy held the swab against her lip.

When she finished, she found some ice and wrapped it in a towel for her eye. Nicole was reminded how gentle Lucy had been with Rain when she had carried her home just days before, and now, here she was again, such a contrast to the person that had been on the other side of that door a few minutes earlier.

"You're going to have a bruise, but you should be okay," Lucy said. Her voice was quiet as she stared into onyx orbs that were still wet with unshed tears.

"Thank you," Nicole whispered, gulping down the urge to sob. "For everything, if you hadn't turned up when you did I don't know—" She didn't finish the sentence, but Lucy understood. "You were so brave," Nicole whispered in awe. Without thinking, she reached her hand up to touch Lucy's face.

"I'm not scared of him like you are," Lucy said. She reached out and clasped Nicole's hand, stopping her from touching her face any further, but as she brought their hands down, she kept them clasped together. Nicole looked sorry, and Lucy shook her head at the unspoken apology. It wasn't necessary.

"He will come back," Nicole said, looking off to the distance, her memory stirring something unpleasant.

The room was dark and she had gone to bed. He was out, another game night around Jim's. It was cool in the room as she relaxed and began to drift off. Suddenly there was a weight on top of her. She couldn't move; her arms and legs were pinned under the covers. In the moonlight, she could see his face, contorted as he raged incoherently about not having anything to eat. She tried to get out. Twisting, she saw the clock and the time. 4:04 a.m., that was when she felt the first punch. They rained down, one after the other into her torso, until finally he stopped and leaned down. Nose to nose he sneered, "I always come back." To this day she never understood what had set him off.

"That doesn't mean you have to leave." Lucy's voice brought her back to the present, grounding her.

"I can't put the girls at risk. He hurt Storm already, and I can't let that happen again, or to the other two."

"I know, she told me," Lucy acknowledged sadly. She hated to think of any child being hurt like that, but especially Storm. She was a sweet kid.

"She only told you about her arm, there is more. He is a very vicious man."

"All the more reason to stand up to him?" Lucy questioned, raising an eyebrow.

"I don't think I can." Nicole spoke in a barely audible voice, her head lowered back to the Nicole of old.

"Don't fucking look at me unless I tell you you can, do you understand me?" His rage was so easily triggered. Another bad day at work, and she had looked at him the wrong way when he demanded to know why the dishes were still in the sink. *"You're not worthy of looking at me. You can't even keep the house clean, you disgust me."* She barely felt the slap, barely. When he pinched her arm and pushed her to the floor, she felt that. She felt the kick to her stomach too.

"Maybe not on your own, but with help?" Lucy said. She placed her palm on Nicole's arm but withdrew it the second that Nicole flinched.

"Who would help me? I've been in public places and he has hit me and not one person came to help." She kept her gaze on the floor, but when Lucy next spoke she looked up.

"I came!" Lucy countered, looking her in the eye and holding her stare.

"Yes." She nodded, "You did." And she had never been more grateful for another human being in her life. She had spent so many years hiding the abuse from Paul that it was almost refreshing to say it out loud to someone who wasn't making excuses or judging.

"And he left, not me, I stayed, I am still here," Lucy insisted as she pointed to herself.

"Why?"

"Why what?"

"Why did you come? Stay? You don't speak to people, you keep yourself to yourself and yet..."

"I came?"

"Yes, why?"

"I don't know," Lucy said honestly, and they both smiled at one another. "I just – your kids they – well they have – they just get me!" she chuckled, finally able to admit how much she enjoyed being around them.

The children were in their rooms packing their clothes and toys like they had been told to, but Storm had gone to check on her mother. Seeing her speaking with Lucy, she tried not to eavesdrop, but she couldn't help it. She heard Lucy and hoped she could persuade her mother not to leave. Storm liked it here. She liked her time with Lucy and the lake and her new friends at school. She liked how her mom looked when she spoke to Lucy. She was happier, they all were. She liked how she didn't get locked in a cupboard for asking questions, or smacked for being in the way when all she was doing was watching the TV. She liked it now that she didn't have to hear her mother screaming as he beat her. Everything was better here.

Nicole took a deep breath. "Ya know, I think that's the first time you've smiled at me."

"I think it's the first time I've smiled at an adult in a long time," Lucy admitted, now unable to stop smiling. "Kinda hurts my cheeks."

"You should do it more often, you have a beautiful smile." Nicole felt herself blush, and she looked away quickly. She couldn't understand what was going on with her lately. She had just left a marriage; she was on the run from him and about to flee once more. Getting interested in someone else at this point was just futile.

"Maybe I will, it will be a shame you won't be around to see it though," Lucy said matter-of-factly. There was a pause while they both took each other in, their eyes locking again for just a moment longer than was necessary. Lucy recognised it for what it was: an attraction. "I should get out of your hair and leave you to pack." Standing as she spoke, Lucy looked towards the bedroom door where a young girl stood looking as though she was going to cry. Nicole's smile dropped, and she too looked in the direction Lucy was currently staring.

"I wish I could be stronger for them, protect them and give them the life that allows them to just be kids," she confided quietly, not wanting Storm to overhear. She had already had enough to deal with in her young life.

"You can, you don't have to leave," Lucy maintained, training her line of sight back on Nicole.

"Oh God, I wish you could understand," Nicole hit back, brushing a hand through her hair and raising her face to the ceiling, looking for any kind of celestial help in making Lucy understand just how frightened she was.

"I do, I understand what it's like to run away from your life and never look back, never talk about it, and all you can do is think about it. I understand," Lucy argued, raising her voice a little. "I understand fear, of thinking you're going to die, of wishing you did die. How it would be easier not to have to deal with it? You're not alone in that!" Lucy spoke with an openness she hadn't felt in a long time, and she wondered what it was about this family that kept on pulling her from the depths of her own soul back into the world.

"How can you? Have you ever had an abusive husband? Have you ever lost everything you had?" Nicole threw at her.

Lucy's heart grew heavy as she contemplated those questions, reminded instantly of why she didn't do this, why she kept herself to herself. Because it hurt when you lost everything.

It was a hot day. The breeze blew through the trees and caressed her cheek like her lover's palm had always done, and yet, she stood alone, balanced on a crutch as her parents looked on from a distance. The marble headstone was perfectly smooth and shining until the first letter was carved into it, forever marking it as the place she lost everything.

"No, no I've never had an abusive partner." She answered almost inaudibly, closing her eyes and feeling her head spin. She had to take a deep breath to get her thoughts back under control. Images of Nicky flooded her mind and swirled around with images of the girls playing by the lake. She was losing everything, again.

"Then you can't possibly know what this is like, to have everything taken from you."

"I didn't say that." It was a whisper, a faint acknowledgment of something she didn't want to think about now.

"What?" Nicole answered. Finally looking at her, she could see that Lucy was crying.

"I have to go, take care of the kids," she urged before rushing out of the cabin.

Chapter Ten

On a football field, Paul Nixon was a star. As the quarterback of the team, it was his job to lead. He gave the orders and they followed his plays and that was how he liked it. He was in charge and in control of everything, including his wife. He dominated everything, and in his mind, he owned everything, including her, and she was his to do with as he pleased.

From the moment they married, he had made it clear exactly what her place was in his life, and at times he had been disappointed in her behaviour and had had to put her right. She was a beautiful woman; it was one of the reasons he had chosen her as his wife, and up until a few days ago he had rarely hit her face with more than a slap. He didn't want to have to look at something that wasn't beautiful, but she had needed to be taught a lesson. You did not walk away from Paul Nixon. And if you thought you could then you were going to be taught a very harsh lesson in life.

On the morning that they left, she had deceived him. He had been led to believe that she had a doctor's appointment with the twins, something she knew full well was her job to do. So, she had leeway on her movements that day. She had access to the car, and it had enough fuel in it for the return trip. He had given her enough cash to pay for the appointment, and she was required to call him on the hour, every hour. And he was pissed about the money; he needed that. He had debts to pay. His bookie was not a nice guy.

He left for work at 8:30 a.m. like he did every morning. Her appointment was at 10 a.m., and she would need to leave at 9.30

a.m. to be sure to park and arrive on time. But what she did was nothing of the sort. He had no idea what she really had planned, because if he had, then she would never have left the house again.

~E&F~

When she woke that morning, she knew they had to go, and all the plans she had been putting into action for weeks now came to fruition. The night before he had been the worst he had ever been, done things he had never done before, things she wouldn't allow to happen to her again or, god forbid, to Storm. She took the girls under the pretence of dropping Storm at school before heading to the clinic, but she did nothing of the sort.

"Girls, hurry up and get in the car," she yelled back down the hallway. The car was parked in the garage and she had the engine running. The twins came running, as usual, coats buttoned up wrong and shoelaces untied, but they clambered into the back and buckled themselves into their booster seats. "Storm, come on!" she called once more to her older daughter.

She lifted the trunk and from behind a large tool cabinet, she pulled out a bag, one of those material sports bags. She tossed it in the trunk before moving quickly to the other side of the room and doing the same from behind a bin. Her heart was racing. Her ribs were aching, but she had to do this. "Storm, now!" she called once more. Her daughter strolled in through the door as she pulled down a cardboard box from a shelf.

"Mom?" Storm was worried. She had seen her mother on many mornings frantically cleaning with bruises to her arms, but this was different.

Two bags and a box; that was all she had, all they had. Two sets of clothing each, plus the ones they were already wearing. She had managed to sneak three books for Storm and a couple of toys for the twins and hide them in the box. Her make-up, perfume and jewellery, what was left of it, was hidden inside her handbag, along with birth certificates and other paperwork she might need. The photograph of her parents and one of the three girls were the only things of her own that she took with her.

"What's all that?" Storm asked, watching as her mother moved around the car erratically.

"Just get in the car Storm, we need to go...now." Sensing that something big was happening, she did as she was asked and climbed into the back seat between her sisters. She looked in the mirror towards her mom and felt her heart swell with pride. They were escaping.

"Where are we going to go, Mom?" Nicole didn't answer. Instead, she ran back into the house and grabbed the box of small change where Paul had been collecting quarters and dimes. Every little bit would help!

When she climbed back into the car, Storm asked her again. "Where are we going, Mom?" She knew what it looked like, but she couldn't get her hopes up just yet.

Nicole pulled the vehicle out of the garage and onto the street, nice and slow. She would do nothing to draw attention to them. "I don't know sweetheart, I don't know."

She drove north, stopping only to make a call at 10 a.m. She lied to him and made out that the doctor was running late. He bought it, and she breathed a sigh of relief before tossing her phone out of the window into the hedgerow. Two hundred miles later and they were skirting the edge of Oklahoma. There she found a second-hand car dealer. She swapped out the almost brand-new SUV for a smaller family car, making some money on the deal. Probably not as much as she could have done, but she didn't care. The guy was willing to do the deal without the usual holdup for paperwork.

It was another one hundred and fifty miles before she pulled into a drive through and ordered burgers, fries, and milkshakes. The kids were beside themselves with excitement; this was something they were never allowed to have at home.

~E&F~

When she failed to call in at midday, Paul called her. It rang and rang and he assumed, stupidly, that she must be in with the doctor. But by 1 pm when she hadn't called in, he was livid and went straight home to find an empty house. Nothing was out of place, but something was off. He called the local sheriff to check for accidents that might have occurred, but there had been none reported. At 2 pm he made a call and she was being looked for.

She had a 5-hour head start. She had hoped he would assume she would head south or east, back towards where she came from. She was right.

Eight hours had passed as she headed west on I-40. She was getting tired, running on adrenaline. The twins didn't know what was happening, so they had been bored and acting up, but now they had finally fallen asleep, giving Nicole some breathing space. They all needed a rest. She was uncomfortable sitting for such a long period of time.

"Mom, do you think he will come looking for us?" Storm asked timidly, already knowing the answer would be yes. Her father was a monster.

"Yes baby, I think he will and that's why we have to be super smart and keep moving. You understand?" Storm nodded. "I am going to keep driving until we're as far away as we can be and then, we will find somewhere we can get some sleep, alright?"

She didn't stop until it was dark. Pulling off of the highway just outside of Flagstaff, she found them a small motel in the middle of nowhere. She booked them a room at the back of the block and as quickly as she could, she moved the sleeping children inside and into bed.

"Storm? I need to go and find a store. I need you to be a big girl and stay here with the girls. Okay?"

"Sure."

"I won't be long. I'll get us some dinner and breakfast for the morning," she whispered gently, not wanting to wake the girls. "Don't open the door to anyone, okay, baby?"

Storm nodded as her eyes filled with tears and her chin began to tremble. "Mommy." She ran to Nicole and threw her arms around her waist. She knew she needed to be brave, but she didn't feel that way. What if he found them?

"It's alright, don't cry. We're safe here, Storm. I'll be 20 minutes max." She guided the miniature version of herself over to a chair and flicked the small TV on. "By the time this show finishes, I'll be back." Her lips pressed a kiss to Storms hair. "Don't open the door," she reiterated.

It broke her heart to walk out of that room, hearing the whimpers as Storm cried gently to herself. Scared. She had been scared almost her whole tiny life, and that was why Nicole had to do this. They needed to eat, they needed toiletries and supplies for the following day, because she had no intention of stopping for anything longer than bathroom breaks and coffee.

That night had been the longest of her life, and she had had some awful nights previously during her marriage to Paul Nixon. They had all slept together in the queen-sized bed, something Paul would never have allowed – the children had their own rooms for a reason. He didn't want a child in the way when he wanted to have his way with her.

Nicole explained to the twins that it was an adventure that they were on and that it was going to be fun to hide and pretend to be someone else. She told them all that their new name would be Granger.

"So, as of tomorrow if anyone asks you your name, then what are we going to say?" she asked, her face smiling as they all huddled together.

"Granger!" the twins called out in unison.

"My name is Rain Granger, pleased to meet you." Nicole laughed. Her ribs still hurt when she breathed, so laughing was almost torture, but the medication and bandages she had gotten while out on her trip for supplies were at least taking the edge off, and hearing her kids laugh unhindered was medicine enough.

"What about you, Storm?"

The youngster rolled her eyes. She didn't need to play a game to understand that she was no longer going to be called Storm Nixon. "Same, my name will be Granger."

Nicole nodded and stroked a hand through her messy curls. It was going to be tough, so much change so quickly for them all, but there was no going back now. If he found them, he would eventually kill her. That much she knew.

Chapter Eleven

Getting back to her cabin had taken a lot of effort for Lucy. She had run and run, ending up much further along the path before her legs collapsed under and she fell to the ground sobbing, her leg stiff and aching. When she eventually managed to hobble back to her home, she threw herself on her bed and curled into a ball. She cried like she hadn't done in years, not since that awful day in the hospital when her mother had gently explained by her bedside that she had lost Nicky. Woeful sobs gave way to feral cries as her heart tore in two once more. Maybe it had never healed together in the first place and had now just cracked open a different fissure? It didn't matter; what mattered was that they were leaving and she would be alone again.

Sixteen years had passed and not one day had passed without her thinking about Nicky or Scott, Mike, Ben, or Sarah. She blamed herself for making Nicky get on the bus. Why hadn't she just gone along with what Nicky wanted and taken a cab later? She blamed herself for being late on the bus; had it set off on time, maybe it wouldn't have been hit by the car with a foreign driver who had gotten confused with which lane he should be in. But mostly she blamed herself for living. They had died and she had lived, and for what? She had lost everything: her lover, her friends, and her career. Her life ended that night with them, but she was forced to live on regardless in this perpetual hell on Earth.

She had considered ending it. Of course she had. Several times over the years she had thought about it; it would be so easy.

Nobody would miss her, but she had always ended up convincing herself that it was her punishment to continue living like this, to always be reminded that it was her fault.

And she was mad at herself for letting her guard down, for allowing the Grangers into her life only for them to have to leave. She should have known better. Why had she let them in? She had no clue; it wasn't like her. It wasn't as if people hadn't tried before. She kept people at arm's length for a reason, far enough away that they could never be hurt by her and she would never have to tell them her story, but sitting there with Nicole just now, she had almost said it. She had almost told her how she lost everything.

She had no idea how long she had been lying there for. Her eyes were sore and gritty and she needed to pee, so she got up and wandered to the bathroom. Crossing the room in the half-darkness, she almost had a heart attack. Storm was sitting on her couch, elbows resting on her knees, her shoulders hunched and her face held within her palms. She looked a sorrowful state.

"Storm? What are you doing here?" she asked gently as she moved across the room to sit with her.

"Hiding," she answered honestly. Her face was tearstained, her eyes red and puffy; she looked miserable.

"Is he back?" Lucy went into panic mode, ready to run and kick this guy right in the nuts.

"No, I'm hiding from Mom," she wept. She tucked her legs up and wrapped her arms around them, letting her face fall into her knees as she sobbed.

"Why?"

"I don't want to leave." She continued to sob. It was that simple.

"Oh." She didn't know what else to say, what could she say to the kid to make her feel better? It was a shitty situation all around. She went to the toilet as she had planned and when she came back out, Storm was lying on the couch holding a cushion to her chest.

"I'm going to go and tell your mum that you're here, okay?" she said softly, crouching down to her level. "She will be worried."

Storm didn't reply, and so Lucy pulled the blanket down and over her. Then she stood and began the short walk back to the Grangers' cabin.

~E&F~

"Is she with you?" Nicole shrieked. She was frantic as she saw Lucy appear along the path.

"Yes, I just found her on my couch. She's okay, but she says she is hiding."

Nicole sighed with relief. "Thank goodness." She ran her fingers through her dark hair in frustration. "Okay, I'll come and get her once we're all packed and loaded up, if that's alright with you?"

"Sure," Lucy agreed, turning to leave.

"Lucy?" Nicole called after her. Lucy turned to face her, frowning. "I'm glad I met you."

Lucy said nothing as she turned to walk away again. It was all she could do to just keep on walking; she couldn't afford to let herself care now, not if they were leaving.

~E&F~

Time felt like it was slipping through her fingers. It wasn't that long before Lucy and Storm heard the car pull up outside. It was dark by now. The world outside was silent but for the movement of the woman walking toward her up the path.

Lucy looked at Storm and they shared a quiet moment, a look that said their time was up. The knock on the door took Lucy's attention and she rose up unsteadily and crossed the room. Nicole ushered the twins inside quickly and followed. Lucy didn't bother to speak.

"Storm, it's time to go, baby, say goodbye to Lucy."

"No. No, it's not fair. I don't want to go, you lied to me!" She shouted at her mother. "You lied, you always tell me if someone is mean to someone I should stand up to them, but you're not, you're running away."

"I'm trying to keep you safe!" Nicole sighed. "Don't you understand that, baby? I can't let anything else happen to you."

91

Lucy watched the family discussion, feeling as though she were intruding and shouldn't be here. Storm just sat there, steadfastly refusing to acknowledge what it was that her mother was explaining.

"So what? You want to stay here?" Nicole asked her daughter. "You want to be here when he comes back? And what then? When he is done hitting me? And you? What about your sisters?" She knew she was being unfair, but Storm had to understand the severity of what had happened, what could happen again if they didn't go now and try to find somewhere else to hide.

"I want to stay here and stand up to him!" Storm shouted. "I want to tell him I hate him and to leave me alone. I don't want to be afraid anymore. I'm 8, and I want to be with my friends!" She reached up and took Lucy's hand. It took all of Lucy's strength not to drop to her knees and beg for them to stay. Nicole had tears streaming down her cheeks. This child had more courage than all the adults in her life put together. The twins, they didn't really understand anything. They were just scared, like she was, but Storm, she was the brave one of them all.

"Me too, Mommy." Summer tugged gently on her hand. "I wanna stay by the lake." Rain nodded in agreement with her sisters.

"Baby please, don't make this any harder than it already is," Nicole begged, taking hold of Storm's hand. She didn't want to force her, but she would pick her up and carry her to the car if she had to.

"Can I talk to you?" Lucy interjected. "Outside?"

Nicole nodded. She watched as the girls all huddled together with Storm. Her girls, precious and beautiful; they deserved so much more.

The cool air was welcome on Lucy's hot skin, but she wrapped her arms around herself protectively anyway. She couldn't believe what she was about to do. She watched as Nicole walked over to her and they both leant against the hood of the car. It was quiet. The moon was bright and there were no clouds. Stars dotted the night sky in their thousands.

"Why don't you stay here tonight and then in the morning once she has calmed down, you can leave?" She wanted to add, 'If you still want to,' but she failed to see the point in constantly getting her hopes up. They were leaving; she needed to accept that.

"Stay here? In your cabin?" Nicole repeated as she turned to look at Lucy.

"Yes!" Lucy said, nodding. "He won't come here and if he does, well I have a shotgun and I am quite happy to shoot him in the nuts!" She smiled conspiratorially.

"We couldn't impose on you like that," Nicole said, shaking her head.

"Why not? What do you have against people helping you?"

"I don't know, what do *you* have against it?" she threw back. *Touché,* thought Lucy.

"I'm not against it. I tried it, it didn't work, but my situation isn't the same."

"What is your situation?" She could feel Nicole's eyes boring into her and she looked away.

"You might not have noticed, but I don't talk about it."

"Well you might not have noticed, but my kids seem to think you talk quite a lot."

"That's because they don't ask the wrong questions."

"God, you are so frustrating!" Nicole said, throwing her hands up in the air. "You expect me to trust you but you have no intention of trusting me."

"This isn't about me, it's about your child that is hurting and needs to deal with her situation before she becomes me!" Lucy said, shocking Nicole with her admission. "Is that what you want? A child that withdraws into herself and hides from the world because she doesn't know how to deal with her fears and feelings?"

Lucy was right and Nicole knew it. Storm wasn't shy or slow to join in, but there were times when Nicole noticed warning signs of little walls starting to build. The more aware she became of her father, the more she pulled back. Nicole had been relieved to see the old Storm returning to the fore since they had arrived at the lake; since she had met Lucy. "How do I help her?"

"I don't have a fucking clue," admitted Lucy as she laughed at the absurdity of it all. "However, that kid of yours—" She pointed back into the cabin. "-has more courage than the pair of us put together and I don't think you should ignore that, but she is your child and you must do what you think is right."

Nicole nodded and pushed herself away from her resting spot on the car to walk back inside the cabin, hoping to goodness that the decision she had just made was going to be the right one.

Storm looked up at her, eyes wide in fear that she would be told to get in the car, and yet, still filled with hope that she wouldn't be. The twins were sleeping, one either side of their elder sister.

"Lucy says we can stay here tonight, and then in the morning we will come up with a plan," Nicole said, trying desperately to sound confident in her decision, more for herself than anyone else's benefit. He had found them with help from friends in high places, tracking their car to its new owner. He had soon worked out where she had sold it and what route she was on. He followed the trail once, he would do it again.

"You mean it?" Storm said. "We can stay?"

"For tonight, and in the morning, we will discuss it further, okay?"

"Yes, thank you, I love you, mom!" she cried, jumping up and throwing her arms around Nicole's waist. Looking up, she saw Lucy standing in the doorway leaning on the jamb. "Lucy! Thank you, I love you too," she said, running towards her and wrapping her arms around her. Lucy was taken aback by this sudden rush of emotion being pushed her way. She hadn't been held by anyone for a very long time; it was so foreign to her now. Slowly she reached her hand to Storm's back and patted gently, and with each movement, it became easier. Something lifted, just a little bit, but the darkness deep inside her moved and made space for something else to fill it, something lighter.

Chapter Twelve

When the girls were all tucked up in bed and drifting peacefully off to sleep, Lucy helped Nicole to move the car to the back of the cabin out of sight, just in case. She really didn't believe he would be back tonight, but to placate a fretting Nicole, she went along with it.

The cabin was quiet as she opened a bottle of wine and brought two glasses, placing them on the table in front of the couch. She poured a little into each and offered one to Nicole, who accepted it with a warm smile, then winced as she was reminded of the small cut to her lip as it stretched with the movement.

"Does it hurt?" Lucy grimaced, lifting a hand to touch her but realising quickly enough to stop herself. She forced her hand back into her own lap.

"Yes, a little, but not so bad really." Nicole, however, did raise a hand and touch a finger to the cut, imagining Lucy had. "I...I've had worse."

"How long?" Lucy inquired, looking at her and wondering just how or why anyone could do such a thing to another person, let alone someone you're supposed to love.

"Did he beat me for?" Nicole queried, completely void of any emotion. She could do that now, switch off from it. These weeks away from him had allowed her to see it for what it was, to remove herself from it and accept that it happened. What she needed to do was find a way to accept it wouldn't happen again.

Lucy nodded.

"The majority of our married life." Her voice broke as she admitted it to someone for the first time.

His face darkened. The smile on her face faltered as she saw the change. He had just been laughing and now, as he stared across the room at her, she realised he didn't like what he saw. She took a step backwards, away from his friend Jeff. His oldest friend had simply kissed her on the cheek in greeting, but Paul didn't like it, that much was clear.

When the last guest had left, she had forgotten all about it, but he hadn't. She hadn't even heard him enter the room until she felt the punch that hit the back of her head, knocking her off her feet. There was no time to react before he grabbed a fistful of her hair and dragged her upright, only to knock her down once more with another punch, this time to the stomach.

"Paul, please don't..." She never finished her sentence. The kick that came knocked the wind from her.

She shook the memory off and glanced up at Lucy, her face passive as she sat still, waiting for her to continue. "But then a year ago he started to hurt Storm. Not often," she was quick to interject when she saw the look of horror on Lucy's face. Continuing on, she explained, "She had got to an age where she knew what was going on and she stood up to him. That was when I knew we had to leave."

"That must have been a very brave decision," Lucy said, taking a sip of her wine.

"I didn't think about that. Hurting me was one thing, but I just knew I couldn't let him hurt my girls. So, I kept on his good side for as long as I could, gradually syphoning some money to one side without him noticing. I hid clothes and toys in a box in the garage ready for us to take off when the opportunity arose."

"Why couldn't you just leave him?"

"You don't know who he is, do you?"

Lucy shook her head and waited for further information.

"He used to be a football player, he is an idol where we lived and they all adore him; the homegrown kid made good," she mocked, shaking her head. "He is friends with the police chief, the judge. Anyone who is anyone knows and respects him and he can charm them all into believing I am just a troublesome wife that doesn't know her place."

"So, he thinks he can just hit you and that it's all ok?" Lucy responded, getting up and hobbling over to the fireplace. The air had chilled around them. She was unsure if it was the temperature or the atmosphere, but she felt cold to the bone.

"He doesn't think it, he knows it," Nicole answered, watching as Lucy struggled to bend down. She started to crumple old newspaper into balls, adding some kindling and a couple of small logs before lighting it up. The fire brought instant warmth with just the appearance of the flames.

"I have never understood why anyone would want to hurt the person they say they love, I can't imagine ever raising my fist to—" She stopped herself from saying Nicky, but she raised her eyes to the photograph as she grasped the mantle to pull herself upright.

"Can I ask you something?" Nicole said, tucking her bare feet up under herself on the couch.

"You can ask," she replied, looking back at the flames awaiting the questions she knew were coming.

"Do you miss home?" Nicole had noticed the accent a while ago. Mostly Lucy sounded American, but now and then she would say something and it was like Mary Poppins was in front of her.

"No, there's nothing there for me, this is where I live now." Nicole noted she didn't call here 'home.'

"So, you wouldn't go back?"

"Like I said, there is nothing for me to go back to."

"Was there ever?"

Lucy smiled wistfully and looked away as tears pricked at her eyes, threatening to spill over once more. She got herself under control and replied calmly, "Yes, many things."

"Like?"

"The usual," she offered up evasively as she moved slowly back to her seat on the couch. She wasn't trying to be obstinate; it was just too hard. She couldn't swim with those memories again, could she? Not without drowning in a sea of pity that she would find in Nicole's eyes.

"So, Lucy...What plans do you have now for moving forward?" the therapist asked her for the fifth time since Lucy had begun these sessions. "Have you thought any further about that?

"What's the point?" Lucy answered, her eyes content to just stare absently ahead.

"Well, there must be things that you miss, that you'd like to—"

"Miss? I miss everything. My entire life is gone...is there some kind of magic shop I can go to and find all the things I miss?" She would have jumped up in fury, but her body hurt too much with such a movement. "There is nothing for me now, not here anyway."

She was jolted from her thoughts as Nicole spoke to her again. "What was she like?" Nicole asked, the question taking Lucy aback as she stared into the eyes that searched her own.

"What was who like?" She was aware of who Nicole was asking about, and she was stalling, her brain scrambling to keep her emotions under control.

"The woman you loved...I mean I'm assuming it was the woman in the photograph," she said, looking towards the fireplace where Nicky's picture sat proudly in its frame. "She is very pretty."

Lucy sat silently for a moment. Did she want to share Nicky with this woman, with anyone? Maybe it was time. Maybe she needed to be a little more like Storm and say enough is enough.

"She was vibrant." Lucy spoke gently, but with pride. "She was alive and living life in the moment, we all were." She paused as she remembered and smiled. "She was simply everything to me."

"Come on Luce, we're going to miss it!" Nicky shouted out as she ran towards the bridge. It was New Year's Eve and they were in the middle of Paris. It was minutes to midnight. Onlookers and partying people clogged the streets, all waiting to see the fireworks that would go off announcing 2001 had arrived. Somewhere in the distance, she could hear the lyrics of Prince's song "1999." Lucy grinned and chased after her, dodging through the crowd until finally they were both on the bridge and she grabbed hold of her hand and pulled her closer.

"Happy New Year!" she said, leaning in to kiss her just as the first firework exploded above their heads. Loud whooshes and bright colours soared above them. They broke apart and stared upwards. "That's you," Lucy whispered in her ear.

"What is?" Nicky asked, turning in her arms.

"You, you're like a firework. Loud and bright and vibrant, soaring above everyone."

"I love you, Lucy Owen." Their lips crashed together once more.

"What happened?" Nicole asked, knowing she might be pushing too far, but she had a feeling tonight was going to be cathartic for all of them, including Lucy.

There it was, the million-dollar question. Lucy rubbed her hands over her face and poured another glass of wine. She didn't drink wine often, it was a drink to be drunk with others, not by herself, alone. She was enjoying it, maybe a little too much, and it had loosened her tongue, shaken her thoughts.

"I don't talk about her," Lucy said honestly, taking a long swallow of the sweet liquid.

"Okay, but maybe you should?"

"Why?" she answered sadly. "It's not going to change the outcome."

"Maybe it's just time, Lucy? Time to let it go and accept it?" she said softly.

"I'm not sure I'll ever be able to let it go, and I accepted it a long time ago; she isn't coming back, I know that, but I can't let it...*her* go." She found herself staring off into the distance, her mind swimming with images of the bus crumpled around her. Nicky's smiling face just moments before the impact. Waking up alone and confused in a bright hospital room surrounded by flowers and cards from people she had never met, all offering their condolences and best wishes.

"Relationships break up all the time," she heard Nicole say. The fugue of her brain cleared in an instant as she registered the assumption.

"We didn't break up. We would never have broken up, she was my life and I was hers. We were kids, but we adored each other."

"I don't understand then." Nicole was truly perplexed. She looked over at the photograph and then back to Lucy.

Lucy stood, paced the room a few times, and then walked hastily over to the photograph. She picked it up and brought it back to her seat, sitting closer to Nicole than before. They were touching, thigh to thigh, though she didn't notice. Her thoughts were only on Nicky and the truth. She handed her the photograph. Nicky deserved the truth.

"Her name was Nicola, Nicky, to everyone other than her parents. They didn't like her name to be shortened," she explained quietly as a small smile ghosted her lips for just a second before she added, "And she died."

Chapter Thirteen

She had finally said it out loud to another person. Her heart banged in her chest, and she felt like she might pass out. The walls of the cabin were pressing in on her. *Breathe, just breathe*, she told herself.

"Oh God, I'm so sorry, I just...well I don't know what I thought," Nicole rambled, feeling overwhelmingly out of her depth. She cringed internally as she remembered the accusation that Lucy had no idea what it was like to lose everything.

"It was an accident of course, but, it was my fault. If I had just listened to her instead of forcing her to do what I wanted to do then she would be alive today," Lucy continued, unable to stop now that she had started; it was like someone had twisted a faucet and everything was beginning to pour out.

"You can't know that, I mean maybe it was fate, like, we don't get a say in those kinds of things."

"But I'll never know because she is gone." She spoke to the ceiling, afraid that if she looked at her, if she looked into those dark, smoky eyes of Nicole's, then she would fall apart.

"And you've been alone ever since?" Nicole probed gently.

"Yes, pretty much. I tried to find my way again, meet new people, but all I did was end up hurting them. Nobody measured up to her. I compared everyone to her, and so I just stopped trying."

"How long?"

"Have I been by myself?" She watched as Nicole nodded. "The last time I tried to date someone was probably...ten years or more."

"That's just so incredibly sad."

Lucy studied her then, the way she was looking at her; there was no pity, just a sadness in her eyes. "Is it? Maybe it's all I deserve."

"Why would you think that?"

It was now or never. Nicole was probably leaving tomorrow, so what would it hurt? She could just tell her and it wouldn't matter after tomorrow. Then she could go back to being the weird Lucy that rarely spoke to anyone. Nobody would ever need to know she had bared her soul.

She went to her bedroom and came back with another photograph which she held out for Nicole to take: heavy silver-framed image of a group of people all smiling, professionally taken.

"You probably don't know who they are," she said as Nicole studied the photo some more.

"Solar Flare," she said, smiling at a memory. "I had their album."

Lucy blushed and laughed ironically. Of course she would have.

"What?" Nicole said, laughing now along with Lucy. "They were good."

"Look closer," she said, nodding at the photograph.

"What am I looking at?" And then she remembered something, something in the far reaches of her teenage memory. Solar Flare broke up because of a horrific traffic accident. The band were travelling together, on their way to the airport for a tour of the States, and several of them were killed when their coach overturned.

I was in an accident.

"Oh my God!" Nicole gasped, looking more closely now at the lead singer and pointing. "That's you, you were the lead singer in Solar Flare?" she stated, looking up at her and then back at the photograph. Her hair was blonde back then, not the mousey brown colour it was now, but there was no mistaking that it was Lucy.

"Yes," she said as a rush of air left her lungs. She hadn't told a soul since leaving England all those years ago.

"You were in that accident?" Nicole wanted to clarify.

"Yes."

"Lucy, I..." She was lost for words; what did you say to someone who had lost their lover and friends like that? Lucy really had lost everything. Now everything about her made sense. She sat back, the photo resting easily on her lap, and listened as Lucy told her story.

"Mike, Sarah, Ben...and Nicky were killed instantly. Scott died 3 days later in hospital," Lucy explained, pointing each one out in the photograph. Her eyes glistened with tears that had remained unshed.

"What about you?" Smoky eyes watered as they focused solely on Lucy.

"I was in a coma for a week and sedated for another two. I had multiple injuries. Jenna and Chris had broken bones and Sasha walked away without a scratch, the only one of us that had a seatbelt on. Rob needed surgery to relieve the pressure on his brain, but he never recovered fully." Her voice tailed off to almost a whisper.

"Jesus," Nicole said. It was unbelievable, and yet she recalled the accident being in the news. She had been sad about it; they were a good band and she was hoping to get tickets to see them.

Needing to change the subject, Lucy asked about Nicole's marriage. "How did you meet him?"

Nicole smiled, accepting the change of subject as a bargaining tool. Give a little, take a little was how this conversation was going to go, and she could live with that. She took a swig of her wine. It had been so long since she had shared a bottle of wine with someone and enjoyed it, been allowed to enjoy it.

He gripped her arm so tightly that she knew there and then there would be a bruise. Pulling her along with him, he smiled and joked with one of his friends as they passed each other in the hallway. He pushed her through the door and into the kitchen. She prayed there would be someone, anyone in there, but she wasn't that lucky. "What do you think you are doing?" he hissed, grabbing the glass from her hand and slamming it down on the worktop. The wine sloshed over the edge and formed a dark red puddle. "I didn't marry a drunken slut."

"It's just one—" His hand moved so fast, she didn't see it coming, though she always expected it now. His palm making sharp contact with her face. His fingers clamped roughly around her jaw, his fingers and thumb pressing into her cheeks. "Don't lie to me, I know what you're doing! I see you throwing yourself all over them. You're mine, remember that!" He released his hold on her. She was filled with terror as he turned to walk away only to spin around on his toes and put his face in hers. "Don't make me deal with you."

"I used to be a model, nothing fancy, just local stuff really, but I did okay." She blushed.

"I can see how you could be," Lucy remarked, admiring her. She noted the slight blush that rose on Nicole's neck and cheeks, and felt a slight blush of her own at that admission. Nicole laughed, and Lucy found herself wanting to make that happen again when the time was more suitable.

"Well, he apparently saw a poster campaign for an underwear range that I did and decided he just had to meet me. Being the star football player that he was, he was able to get himself invited to places he thought I might be, and eventually that paid off. We met at a charity auction. I was the prize, dinner with me!"

"And he bid for you?"

"Yeah, and that was that. We started dating. He was all charm and sophistication. He lavished me with compliments and gifts, took me places I had never been. It was hard not to fall for him. He was the good-looking all-American hero, and I was worth $2500."

They simultaneously sipped their drinks and observed each other for a moment, each of them finding it strange that until now they had never spoken about their pasts with anyone else, but they found a comfort in each other that allowed them to just open up. Just speaking out loud released some kind of valve that had been holding it all in.

"What happened after the...after the crash?" Nicole asked, deeming it a fair point in the conversation to switch it back.

Lucy sighed. "I was in the hospital for about eight weeks," she explained. "Broken bones and various other injuries. I was out of it for the first 3 of those. I missed all of the funerals." She spoke quietly, staring at the couch as she said that last part. It was the hardest part, the part that hurt the most.

"Including?"

"Yes, including hers. They couldn't hold on forever, nobody knew how long I would be in the hospital for, and so they had to go ahead." She wiped away a solitary tear.

"That must have been very hard for you," Nicole sympathised. She wanted to reach out and touch Lucy, hold her hand or just pull her into her arms and hold her, but she didn't dare move.

"I doubt it would have been any easier if I had been able to go," Lucy admitted for the first time, clasping her hands together. As if reading Nicole's mind, she sat back in her seat, putting distance between them. "Our relationship wasn't something her parents approved of, and the media would have turned it into a spectacle."

"No, I guess not, but it's closure isn't it...you didn't get to have that."

Lucy considered that for a moment, and it was true, she had never had 'closure' as the Americans liked to put it. How did you ever have closure with something that lived with you day in, day out?

"So when did he change?" Lucy asked, switching subjects once more.

"Once we were married it was a different story, but by then he had isolated me from my friends, moved us back to his hometown and taken away my independence. No wife of his was going to flaunt their body for other men," she said, imitating him. "Then I was pregnant with Storm, and suddenly he was nice to me again; all the time I was pregnant he never laid a finger on me."

"Why didn't you leave him before?"

"He convinced me that I had nowhere to go, I had no money of my own anymore. He used it all to gamble with. I wasn't working and I didn't know anyone unless they were his friends. I guess he wore me down. Constant comments about how ugly I was or how fat I'd gotten." She looked away with tears threatening to fall. It seemed to be the night for it.

"You don't still believe that, do you?" Lucy asked tentatively.

Nicole nodded her head as the tears streamed down her cheeks. She hadn't thought about this for weeks. She had been pushing these memories and thoughts from her mind as she concentrated on her girls and their new life. But now, as she looked up and into such empathy staring back at her, she couldn't hold it in. An emotional dam burst.

"Oh, you are so wrong, trust me. I am a lesbian, I notice these things," Lucy joked, trying to smile. "And you are far from ugly, and as for fat? Seriously, you're gorgeous." She said it sincerely, albeit rambling as she finally reached out and took Nicole's hand in her own.

"Ha, yeah right, I've got a black eye and a split lip and you want me to believe you think I'm gorgeous??" she laughed. Lucy surveyed her until she stopped laughing and returned the gaze, staring back at her and then down at her hands. At their hands, linked together so naturally.

"Yeah, because you are." The air stilled around them as they both continued to stare into each other's eyes for just an instant longer than was necessary. Lucy was the first to look away as she

112

reached for her glass. It was empty, and so she then reached for the bottle, but that too was empty.

With the bottle of wine finished, Lucy announced it was probably time for bed, and Nicole agreed. It was pretty late, and both had had an emotional night. She needed to try and get as much sleep as she could so she could be up early and ready to leave. As they stood, Nicole thanked Lucy once more for all she had done before doing something that Lucy hadn't expected: she hugged her. Two warm arms wrapped around her, the warmth of a cheek brushing her own as Nicole whispered good night in her ear. A shiver ran through her and she brought her own arms up and slowly hugged her back. It was the first time she had held another woman in a very long time, and she had to admit, she didn't dislike it.

~E&F~

Lucy wasn't sure at first what the noise was that woke her, but Lucy was very aware that someone in the house was in distress. Someone was crying out, pleading for help, and now that she was awake, she knew that it could only be one person. She got up and grabbed her robe and was still tying it around her waist as she left her own room in search of the turmoil. She found Storm standing outside the door of the room her mother was sleeping in.

"Hey Stormy, what are you doing up?"

"I heard Mom shouting, is she having a bad dream again?" she asked sadly, and Lucy considered just how often this must happen.

"Yeah, I think she is, I'm going to go in and check on her, okay? You go back to bed, she will be fine. I promise I'll look after her." She smiled and tried to look as confident as possible so that the eight-year-old would stop worrying and be able to go back to sleep. It wasn't something a kid should be concerned with at such a young age. Lucy felt her heart tug at the sight of her.

The little one seemed to consider it for a second before nodding. Then she turned and went back to the room she was sharing with her sisters, leaving Lucy to come through on her promise.

Her hand raised, and she hesitated just a moment before knocking lightly on the hard wood. Her palm wrapped around the handle, and slowly she pushed the door open. It took a moment to become accustomed to the darkness, and she waited for Nicole to tell her she was okay, or to get the hell out. But with no response from the brunette, she quietly made her way further into the room.

She could make out the sleeping form of Nicole as she tossed one way and then the next, the sheets tangling around her as she fought an invisible monster. Incoherently she mumbled, but the words 'no', 'help,' and 'don't' were quite clear, and it tugged at Lucy's heart to see her in such distress. Lucy wasn't sure what she should do for the best, but she couldn't just stand there, watching and doing nothing, so gingerly she made her way closer to the bed and knelt down beside it. She was sure she had read somewhere that you shouldn't wake people up when they were in the middle of a bad dream, or was it sleepwalking? She wasn't sure, but she had to do something, so she began to carefully stroke Nicole's hair in the hope it would soothe her. It was something Nicky had always done to her when she was in a foul or upset mood, and it usually worked. Gently she pulled the raven locks through her fingers and then began again, over and over. Gradually she could feel the woman begin to relax under her touch, her pleas becoming no more than whimpers. When she was confident that Nicole was going to be okay, she removed her hand, but as she stood and was about to turn to leave, she felt her hand being grasped.

"Don't go, please," Nicole mumbled, her voice laced with sorrow and sleep.

"Okay," Lucy replied. Swallowing down the anxiety that was forming, she bent down, ready to kneel back on the floor.

"Not down there, up here," Nicole said more coherently, pulling back the cover to reveal a space beside her. The curve of her breasts was outlined under the nightdress, pulled so tight across her chest where it was twisted from all the thrashing back and forth under the sheets. Lucy found herself drawn to look and felt the small tug of arousal that had not been present for the better part of ten years.

"I don't think—" She averted her gaze and was about to say that it wasn't appropriate, but Nicole cut her off.

115

"I just—" She paused, "I feel safer with you here. I won't touch you," she promised, although in her mind she considered the idea of being held by Lucy and she liked the idea.

Lucy considered her options. She could just refuse, go back to her room, and leave a woman in distress to face her nightmares alone, then possibly be awoken again later with another nightmare episode, or she could be a mature adult and share a bed with someone who was the closest thing she had to a friend other than Rita, someone who now knew her better than anyone else knew her. Somebody she wanted to stay.

Chapter Fourteen

Bright sunshine streamed through a window that wasn't hers. Lucy opened one eye and remembered the reason that she wasn't waking up in her own bed. She remembered she wasn't alone, and that wasn't her own arm wrapped snuggly around her waist as though it had every right to be there, or her hand that had crept under her top and rested just above her hip bone.

Nicole.

Lucy felt warmth and comfort. It had been a long time since she had woken up feeling so calm and at ease. It was a long time since she had slept so well too.

During the night Nicole had clearly gravitated towards her bed partner, subconsciously ignoring the promise not to touch. Their limbs had become so entwined with each other that Lucy was unsure where she began and Nicole ended. Her dark hair splayed out messily so that all Lucy could smell was the scent of her mixed with shampoo and sweat. It was intoxicating. Arousal again tugged at her at every nerve that made contact with Nicole's body. Lucy froze. Unsure what she should do, so she did what she always did. Nothing.

It took several more minutes for Nicole to sense her surroundings. As she began to stir, her fingers moved unconsciously and began to lightly stroke the bare skin beneath them as they gently tried to figure out where she was. It was almost unbearable for Lucy, and she held back a small gasp as the feather-light touches made her skin tingle, heat emanating from every pore. Gradually Nicole opened her eyes and as they focused fully, she looked straight at Lucy's face, just inches from her own. The bruising around her socket was now more pronounced, but her eye wasn't damaged enough that she couldn't see.

"Sorry." She flustered, quickly untangling herself and moving to the other side of the bed where the sheets where cool, indicating just how long she had been asleep on Lucy. "I didn't realise, I'm so sorry, Lucy."

Lucy remained silent, confused. She didn't know what she should say, but she knew one thing: she missed the warmth. Wasn't that what her life had become? Missing something; it was what she was used to, what she was comfortable with. But this loss was different; it was warm and alive.

She jumped out of bed muttering things like, "It's ok," "Not to worry," and "Seeing to the kids." And then she was gone.

Nicole sat up with a sigh, wrapped her arms around her legs, and rested her head on her knees. She closed her eyes and rebuked herself. Of all the stupid things she could have done. Throwing her legs over the side of the bed, she got up and dressed in yesterday's clothes. She would find time for a shower and some clean clothes later. Right now, she needed to get the kids ready to leave. And she needed a clear head to deal with Storm's opinions on the matter.

She headed out to the kitchen, where she found her three daughters already up. All of them sat at the table, messy-haired and sleepy as they ate some toast. She glanced around the room and realised that Lucy wasn't there. Something about that caused her shoulders to sag. There was something about the other woman that gave her strength, and she felt lacking in that right now as she caught her eldest daughter's eye.

"Morning babies." Nicole greeted her brood as she poured a cup of steaming hot coffee that she assumed Lucy had made. She was trying to be upbeat, trying to show them that everything would be okay, but deep down she wasn't so sure anymore. She had let her guard down, assuming that they were safe when they were far from it.

"Mom! I'm not a baby," Storm complained, and Nicole smirked as much as her split lip would allow. She added creamer to her drink, stirring slowly as she considered just how grown up her eldest was becoming. She frowned when she realised she was far too wise for her years, that her youth was being stolen from her.

"You," Nicole said, bending to kiss her eldest daughters head, "will always be my baby, no matter how old you are." Storm winced at that idea, but she relished the attention from her mom. "As will you." She kissed Rain. "And you," she added, turning to kiss Summer, who was already waiting with pouted lips for her kiss. "Where is Lucy?" Nicole asked casually as she stood and took another sip of coffee.

"Outside," answered Summer, tugging on a corner of her toast with her teeth. "Is Lucy your baby too?"

"Does she get a kiss?" Rain laughed.

Nicole blushed but ignored them, though she couldn't help the smile that she felt grace her lips. "Okay, you guys keep eating, and then we will talk," she said over her shoulder as she walked towards the door and towards Lucy.

~E&F~

When she reached the shoreline of the lake, she could see Lucy sitting by herself on the small jetty, her shoeless feet dangling over the edge, toes just skimming the clear water. The small boat that was tied to the dock bobbed gently up and down a little further along. It was another beautiful day at the lake; they had slept for much longer than Nicole had intended, and people were already out on the water in small boats and kayaks in the distance, enjoying the sunshine just like Lucy as she sat leaning backwards, her arms straight out behind her, all her weight on her palms as she gazed up at the sky. Her eyes were open, and she seemed to be searching for something way up high above them.

Nicole was about to turn and leave her in peace for a little longer, but something held her feet firmly in place. Her thoughts were jumbled. They should be on the road by now. She should be so scared and anxious that they would be a hundred miles away already, and yet, she wasn't; she was still here at the lake. Something about this woman in front of her made her feel calmer. She was so focused on her own thoughts, she barely heard Lucy speak. Her voice was quiet but clear, and Nicole noticed for the first time just how very American she sounded today.

"Hey, you can stay, ya know?"

Nicole smiled shyly. "I thought you might want to enjoy the quiet by yourself," she said as she closed the distance between them and sat on the deck with her.

Lucy looked to the sky again. "Sometimes, I feel like the noise is deafening, almost as loud as the silence."

Nicole chuckled. "I'll have them out of your hair just as soon as breakfast is over."

"That wasn't what I meant," she replied, turning back to the lake. It was a peaceful morning: barely a breeze, the sun was shining, and the water was like glass, so calm and clear that she could see right through it. She could hear the kids bickering over juice in the background and she had to admit, she had gotten used to them being around. She would miss the noise. But she could feel in her bones that something was changing within herself; she was less guarded, more open and more hopeful.

"I think my days of solitude are coming to an end," she stated, turning to look at her. "Don't you?"

Nicole nodded.

"Stay," Lucy whispered, not sure if she actually said it out loud or not when no reply came forth immediately.

"We can't," Nicole replied after some thought. She wanted to, she really wanted to. They had made friends here, they could have a life here, but she couldn't risk her children.

Lucy nodded, understanding the reasons why. But for the first time since the accident, she had seen an opportunity for something, what? Better? Happier? It didn't matter now though; Nicole and the girls were leaving and that was all there was to it.

"Well, I need to go into town so, I guess this is goodbye?" she said, standing quickly, the lump in her throat threatening to expose her like an open wound.

"Oh right, okay," Nicole said, unsure what else she could say. She didn't want to hurt Lucy or see her upset, but there wasn't another choice; they couldn't go back to their cabin, not now that he knew where they were. "Thank you, for everything." She meant it, and yet, it didn't seem enough. It didn't feel right.

"Sure." Lucy smiled sadly and walked past her back to the house

Chapter Fifteen

The girls were still sitting around the table when Nicole got back to the cabin. The twins were talking animatedly to each other and playing with dolls that Lucy had bought them, but Storm just sat staring at her empty plate. Her face said everything her voice hadn't.

Taking a breath, Nicole pulled up a chair and sat down with them. "So, we need to discuss where to go next." She glanced around at three faces that were now frowning.

Storm pushed her chair away from the table, its legs scraping loudly on the floor before she ran from the house. Nicole knew it was going to be difficult to have this discussion, but she had hoped Storm would understand. Sighing deeply, she dragged herself to her feet again, telling the twins to stay there while she retraced the same steps back out to the path she had just come in from and headed back to the lake. What was it with this place that drew everyone to the shore when they were emotional?

The short path led down and through some brambles before the small patch of rocky shoreline and the jetty came into view. Storm wasn't there. She scanned the area and couldn't see her. She called out loudly several times, but she didn't hear or see a thing. And then she felt her heartbeat race and her skin chill as noticed it: the small boat, the same one that had been tied to the end of the dock when Lucy sat here. It wasn't tied there any longer; it was out on the lake and Storm was in it, desperately trying to row herself away and further onto the lake.

"Storm!" she screamed, panic rising furiously as she watched her daughter moving more and more into peril. "Get back here right this minute!"

Storm shook her head and just kept rowing. "You said we could discuss it, but you already decided. I'm not going." She screamed back at her mother.

Nicole tried again, calling her and begging her to come back, but Storm just kept going. She was now either totally ignoring her or couldn't hear her. Either way, it terrified her. She didn't know what to do. Her thoughts swirled. The twins were on their own; she had to get back to them. What if Paul came now? He could just take the twins, he could just take her. But Storm was in more danger, alone and out on the water in a boat she didn't know how to control. She had never been in a boat.

~E&F~

Storm had smiled brightly as Lucy strolled back inside the cabin. Her little hopeful heart had been pounding inside her chest the entire time that her mother had been outside with Lucy. But now, as she looked at the expression on Lucy's face, she knew already that nothing had changed. They were still leaving.

Lucy stopped by her chair and dropped to her haunches. "You need to be good for your mum, okay?"

Storm remained silent. Tears that had welled and threatened now began to slowly slip down her cheeks. "I don't want to go."

"I know, but..." Lucy had to swallow down the emotion that had suddenly filled her throat. "When you're older...you'll understand." She kissed the child on the forehead and stood. Her wallet was on the sideboard, and she reached out and grabbed it, pushing it into her pocket. "Hey, Rain? Summer? Don't be afraid to keep having fun, okay?" They both looked at her and then at each other, neither of them quite understanding what was happening.

"Lucy?" Storm called her name and she turned instantly. "I wish you were...I wish he wasn't." And Lucy understood everything she meant.

"Me too. Take care, sweetheart," she said as she reached the door and left quickly. She needed to not be here. It would be difficult enough for Nicole; the last thing she needed was Lucy hanging around. Storm would be difficult as it was. But, she also needed some time to get herself together, to try and salvage what was left of her walls and rebuild them as best as she could. Though her fear was that she wouldn't be able to, she was going to need to find a way of dealing with her newfound want for company.

Life had been easier in many ways before Nicole and the girls had arrived, but she struggled to remember anything good about it. She felt conflicted though, struggling to know who she was anymore in this world she had created for herself. Somehow these three little girls had wormed their way in, and she didn't want them to go. But they weren't hers to keep, and so she had no choice but to say goodbye. It wasn't just them though; it was their mother too. Nicole, so vulnerable and beautiful, had managed to bring Lucy out of her self-imposed shell, and now, when she was raw and exposed, Nicole was just walking away. She scolded herself. Who was she kidding, to think that life could be any different?

Storm hadn't taken it well, not that she had expected she would. The twins were too young to worry about anything other than the doll they were playing with, but Storm understood. She knew that it meant they would never see each other again. This would just be a chapter in their lives, nothing more, and Lucy couldn't bear to be around to watch them leave, so she left. Cowardly, she knew.

She walked with no real purpose; it was more a ramble. She hadn't even really stuck to the paths or paid any attention to where she was walking when she heard Nicole from the other side of the lake screaming at Storm. The kid wasn't going to make things easy for her mother, that much was clear. She smiled inwardly as she considered the bravery of one little girl trying to find her place in the world. Lucy hoped that one day she succeeded, because the other possibility, her father, just wasn't an option.

But when she heard Nicole scream for the second time she knew something wasn't right. She was pretty close to the water's edge, but her view was obscured by bushes and trees, so she had to manoeuvre herself around them before she could get a clear view back across the lake. She could see Nicole on the other side, and she was waving. At first Lucy thought she was waving at her, but there was no way she would even know she was here. She scanned the area for the ex-husband, but he wasn't anywhere to be seen either. And then she saw it. Storm was standing in the row boat, gesturing, and now as Lucy concentrated, she could hear that Storm was also shouting something.

"Storm, what are you doing?" Lucy shouted. On hearing Lucy's voice, she began to turn around in the boat, but her movement caused the boat to rock and become off-balance, and she wobbled. "Don't move," Lucy called again, holding her hands up. "Just stay very still." Storm did as she was told; apparently, she didn't like the idea of plunging into the water either.

Lucy looked around for another boat anywhere, but there wasn't anything. She walked along the shore a little further, but still found nothing. And then she heard the splash, and the fear that raced through her at that moment was unlike anything she had ever felt before.

"Shit," Lucy muttered as she realised the only way to solve this problem fast was to swim out there. She stripped off her clothes down to her underwear and hopped as best she could across the rocks until she was clear of them and could wade in. It was more than cold. The water lapping against her skin was painful. It was freezing, but she pushed on, ignoring everything but the need to get to Storm before it was too late. As soon as it was deep enough, she dove in and began swimming for her life.

~E&F~

Nicole screamed. Her heart stopped and her stomach roiled as she watched Storm lose her balance and topple into the water.

127

She only breathed again when she saw Lucy wading in. The twins had come running out of the cabin to see what all the noise was about. They clung to her legs, one either side, not really understanding what was happening other than that Mommy was upset again. Nicole was torn between diving in or staying with them. Lucy was nearer, all she could do was watch as her friend swam powerfully through the water towards Storm, who was flailing about, screaming.

The water was so cold. It might have been sunny, but this far out into the lake was deeper, and the water was deceptively colder as Lucy ploughed on. She looked up and watched in horror as Storm slipped under the water. All that filled her senses was the ear-piercing scream from Nicole on the shore. Reaching the spot Storm had last been, she dove under, searching the murky water. Her long arm reached forward and grabbed at the flailing arm of the girl she knew she already loved, pulling her back to her. Swimming upward for all she was worth, she pushed Storm up and out of the water in one fluid movement. She reached for the boat, and as quickly and gently as she could, she pushed the girl up and over, back into the craft before climbing in after her. She rolled her over and checked her airways. Storm coughed and water vomited from her mouth as Lucy lifted her up and held her tight.

"Don't you ever do that again!" she scolded as tears ran down her cheek, but she didn't let her go, and Storm herself began to cry, the shock of what had happened sinking in. "You scared me," Lucy admitted. "What the hell were you thinking?"

"I'm s-s-sorry." She sobbed, her breath catching as she tried to speak between sobs. "I'm s-s-sorry," she kept repeating.

Relief suddenly enveloped Lucy and she realised she was freezing, her underwear no protection from the cold water that she had been in, the shock all helping to make her shiver more.

"I w-w wanted t-t-to s-stay with y-you."

"Let's get home. Sit here and d-d-don't move," she instructed the kid, who nodded furiously as she too began to shiver and shake. Lucy grabbed the oars and began to row them around and back to the shore, back to Nicole, who was already wading into the water to meet them.

Chapter Sixteen

Nicole helped Lucy bring the boat in and as soon as she could, she laid her hands on her child. She carried her into the cabin with Lucy following behind, dripping all over the floor as she shivered.

"Jesus Storm, what the hell?" Nicole admonished as she held her tight to her, water dripping from their wet clothes.

"We n-n-need to get her out of these w-w-wet clothes," Lucy stuttered as she stood there shivering, virtually naked. "And I need to g-g-go and g-g-get dry too, will you b-be okay?" Her teeth chattered as she spoke.

"Yes! I'll be fine," Nicole snapped, desperately stripping shoes and socks from Storm. "Lucy?" She sighed as she looked up and fastened her gaze on the other woman. "I'm sorry, thank you." She smiled quickly before her attention swayed back to Storm.

Lucy nodded, then turned to go and change into something dry herself. Her wet footprints left a path to her room as she padded half-naked across the area. She caught a glimpse of herself in the mirror. Every scar on her body stood out like a roadmap. The cold had made them more noticeable, every jagged line, every puckered piece of skin. It was all there, visible.

~E&F~

Lucy stood under the shower and let the warmth of the water wash over her. Gradually her skin and bones began to warm

130

as the water brought her body's temperature back up. She took her time getting dressed, giving Nicole time with Storm but also hiding out. She was scared to look in Nicole's eyes and see pity staring back at her. She grabbed a pair of warm sweatpants and a hooded top and felt much better, more herself again. Hidden.

She went to the kitchen and began the process of making some hot chocolate. First of all, it was warm, and Storm definitely needed warming up, but most importantly it was the best drink ever. She had half expected to find they had all left, but to her surprise, they were still there.

Storm was curled up on the couch with a blanket around her. The twins thought the whole thing was funny, especially that Storm had fallen in. They were too young to grasp the severity of the situation, that their sister had almost drowned. Nicole, though, was now starting to realise exactly what had almost happened, and she was shaking as she sat at the end of the couch.

Lucy placed 5 mugs of hot chocolate on the small table and then knelt in front of Nicole. The brunette was perched on the edge of the seat, her knees held tightly together as they bounced up and down, her face hidden in her palms.

Lucy reached out to her, and she flinched a little at the unexpected touch. "She's alright," Lucy stressed. She saw the scar on her hand and retracted her fingers, pushing her hands into the front pocket of her sweatshirt. "I know it was a shock and very frightening, but she is okay."

Nicole nodded, so at least Lucy knew she was hearing her. She continued on.

"It wasn't your fault, it was just an accident. She didn't mean to fall in, and she is alright." She kept reiterating that Storm was indeed fine. She was cold and a little scared, but she was fine.

"I know." Nicole finally spoke, rubbing a palm over her face. She looked up. "But if you hadn't been there? I feel nauseous." She sat up abruptly but kept her elbows on her knees as she rocked back and forth.

"Then she would have probably stayed dry," Lucy said honestly. "She only lost her balance because she tried to turn around to talk to me."

At that point Storm piped up. "You're the only one that listens to me."

Nicole closed her eyes as tears sprung and erupted. Did her child hate her that much?

"That's not true, Storm," said Lucy, defending Nicole. "Your mum listens to you, but sometimes adults have to make decisions that mean they can't do what you want them to do."

"We never do what I want to do," Storm said, sitting up but keeping the blanket wrapped around her tiny body.

"That's not fair, Storm," Nicole objected. "Do you think I want to leave?"

Storm looked away, knowing full well that the answer was no. She knew none of this was her mom's fault. But it wasn't hers either, and she was so over having a monster for a father.

Nicole continued to speak to her daughter as Lucy passed around the hot chocolate. "I don't, I don't want to leave here, but what choice do we have? If he comes back and he hurt you or the twins..." She shook her head, not even able to consider it being an outcome. "Thank you," she whispered, taking the warm mug from Lucy.

"So, what are we going to do, Mom? Keep running? Spend my whole life never having a home? friends? What about school, Mom?" Storm was on a roll with her argument now. "You always told me to work hard at school so I can be someone."

Nicole nodded. "Yes, I did, I know and I want that, I want you to work hard."

"For what, Mom? What is the point? If I will always have to be someone else. What's my next name going to be?"

The kid had a point, and Lucy found herself selfishly rooting for her to win this argument. Somewhere along the line, Nicole would have to stop running and deal with this situation, but the biggest thing that Lucy considered was that she too could maybe face some of her issues and deal with them if this family hung around.

Nicole stood up and walked to the window, needing to think. She knew her daughter was right, but she had to weigh up the options: take their chances and stay here, or move on and hope for the best. The only thought in her mind was what was best for her children. She had taken such a risk to leave him. Even now she couldn't believe she had actually done it. And she hadn't expected to find somewhere like this so easily to make a home in; she had expected to keep moving. Storm knew that, they had had the conversation about it, but she liked it here. She liked that her children were happy. She had a job, she had friends, and she had Lucy. Why did he have to find them? How did he find them? If he could find them here, then was anywhere safe? Would they ever be free?

"If we stayed here, we can't live in that cabin, he knows and will come back there," she said without turning, her focus on a small bird that was pecking away at the seed Lucy had on the table outside. *Even the animals, she cares for them*, Nicole pondered, *Lucy cares for all of them.*

Storm looked at Lucy and Lucy looked at Storm. They both had a little curve to their lips and a sparkle of hope in their eyes.

"You...you can all stay here," Lucy said, without thinking, not needing to think. It was obvious; it was the perfect solution. She had the room, and they were already here. It could work. Storm jumped up and moved to stand next to her.

"Please, please say yes, Mom," Storm implored. It was almost heart-breaking to listen to her.

Nicole turned around, her arms wrapped around herself, and what she saw made her burst out laughing: her daughter and Lucy, standing next to each other with the same expression on their faces. It was ridiculous. Paul would find them again, but somehow as she watched her daughter and Lucy, she knew she had to be braver. She had to give her children this chance.

"Doesn't look like I am going to get any choice now, does it?" She smiled as Storm rushed over to her and threw her arms around her waist. "There are going to be strict rules Storm," she warned.

"Okay Mom, I can live with that."

"Are you sure you know what you're letting yourself in for?" she said to Lucy.

"Nope, but I'm going to do it anyway." Lucy smiled.

Chapter Seventeen

Lucy and Nicole spent the remainder of the day emptying everything from the Grangers' cabin and moving it all into Lucy's. They wanted to make it look like they had just packed up and left in a hurry, so a few things were strategically left lying on the floor. Furniture that wasn't needed was moved and upended. They left it in disarray.

In some ways, Nicole was sad to see it back to the empty, unlived-in state she had found it in. She had spent a lot of time and precious money on trying to make it into a nicer home. But then she remembered Paul arriving, and how it was now just another thing in her life tainted by him. When she returned to Lucy's cabin and found the twins and Storm cleaning the spare room that would be theirs, she couldn't help but smile. This would be their home. Here, squashed in with the strangest woman in town.

Lucy had driven Nicole's car into town and found a car lot looking to buy second-hand cars. She sold it for barely anything. It didn't matter in the grand scheme of things, but Nicole was terrified that Paul would remember it and be able to follow them, so it had to go. Across the road was a car hire place. She strolled over and handed her driving licence over.

While she was in town, she figured there were a few other things she need to pick up, like a TV. Just because she didn't watch it didn't mean the girls had to go without. Driving around in the brand-new SUV, she realised she hadn't driven for a long time, and yet, it was like riding a bike. There was a huge store on the outskirts of town that sold electrical goods. Finding an assistant to help her had taken some working up to, but something had lifted within her, something that made speaking to strangers that little bit easier. There were three little girls who needed more than they had been given so far from the adults in their lives. So, with the help of a girl half her age, she filled her trolley with a widescreen TV and all the best equipment to go with it, including surround sound and a DVD player. She was bamboozled when the girl asked her about Wi-Fi and tablets, but in the end, she understood it all and bought a laptop and three tablets, all loaded with the educational tools the kids would need. She was having fun spending her money. She wasn't rich by any means, but the band had made enough in its heyday, and she still got royalty payments now and then. Living the way she was had meant it just sat in the bank, accruing interest. What better way to spend it than on others who needed it?

The last time she had gone on such a spree had been just before the crash, when she had spent hundreds of pounds on designer clothing. Now, she wouldn't even know who the designers were.

Remembering the sparseness of the children's rooms back in their old cabin, she wanted to make sure they didn't go without anymore, at least not while they stayed with her. There was a really nice furniture store along the way, and she figured in for a shilling, in for a pound. Forty-five minutes later and she had ordered three single beds, along with sets of drawers and a small wardrobe each.

She paid extra for it all to be delivered and set up in a few days. She had a new spring in her step!

They were kids, and kids needed toys to play with and books to read. They needed giant bears to cuddle and dolls to dress and blocks to build. Lucy found a toy store, and as she strolled around each aisle with her trolley, grabbing things for the twins and Storm, she thought about Nicole.

Nicole, who had left her life behind her; she barely had a case of clothes to call her own. She went from being a kept woman to a woman who worked all the hours she could to provide for her kids, and she never once put herself first. She wanted to do something nice for her too, and as she looked across the store and out through the window, she saw the perfect place to get it.

Toys all paid for and being packed, she quickly ran across the street and into the store opposite. It had been a long time since she had bought anybody a present, let alone a beautiful woman she was trying not to have feelings for.

She was almost done with her trip and just had to stop off at Rita's store to pick up some more groceries before she would be finished. And with 4 more mouths to feed, she was going to need a lot!

Chapter Eighteen

"Hello, Lucy." Rita greeted her, smiling like she usually did when the younger woman entered the store. "How are you today?" she asked as she always did, whilst she carried on doing what she was doing without waiting for the reply that never came.

"Hi, I'm good thanks, you?" Lucy replied. Rita stopped what she was doing immediately as she slowly turned and looked at her. Narrowing her eyes, she noticed something was different. She was still the same tall, skinny girl in jeans and sweatshirt, hair hanging loose with her cap pulled down, so that wasn't it.

"I am doing great also, thank you for asking." And there it was: Lucy had never asked her before. She studied her a little more. She had a cart; Lucy rarely used a cart. It was always a basket. There was something else though. Rita came out from behind the counter and walked slowly down the aisle on the pretence of looking for something, which of course she was. She was looking for Lucy, because the Lucy she had known for all these years wasn't quite there.

She was smiling!

Lucy Owen was standing in her store and she was smiling. There had been smiles before – well, they were more grimaces than smiles. A slight upturn of lips maybe, but not like this; this was a full on, happy smile. Lucy had dimples!

"So, it's a lovely day outside today isn't it?" Rita offered as a segue into further conversation while Lucy picked up items she didn't normally buy.

"Yes, it's beautiful outside," Lucy replied instead of her usual one-word answer. Rita was flabbergasted.

"Anything I can help you with over there?" Rita asked, noting that Lucy was trying to decide between two different brands of orange juice.

"Uh yes, which of these has the least amount of sugar?"

Rita had to seriously consider sitting down at this point. Sugar content in orange juice? What next?

"Oh, and are these yoghurts any good?" Lucy added, picking up the pack of four that she had in her trolley.

"Okay, enough, what the hell's happening here?" Rita exclaimed, looking around for candid cameras to jump out on her and let her in on the joke.

"Sorry?" Lucy questioned, not quite getting it.

"You have barely said more than one-word answers to me in 10 years, and now you wanna know which yoghurts are best and which orange juice has the least amount of sugar in it?" Rita said incredulously, one eyebrow raised.

"Yes, that sums it up." She smiled again, now realising she was messing with Rita's head a little.

"And now you're smiling at me?" she laughed. "Has the world ended? Did something happen while I was out back in the stock room?"

"I guess when you put it like that..." Lucy said, choosing a few bars of chocolate and bags of chips.

"So?"

"I don't know what you want me to say?" Lucy replied as innocently as she could.

"Well, we're already 50 words more than I've ever heard you utter, so let's go with that, huh?" She grinned, her eyebrow cocked quizzically.

Lucy thought about how her life had changed so much in such a short amount of time and how much she wanted her life to change. She was walking around a changed woman. She knew, and now everyone else was seeing it.

"Things change." She shrugged as she wheeled her cart to the till. Rita racked up her bill, all the while considering what could have changed so much in such a short time that Lucy Owens would be standing in front of her chatting away like a regular member of society.

"Lucy?" she called out to the retreating form. When Lucy stopped and turned to face her she said, "Welcome back."

Chapter Nineteen

"Mom!" Storm hollered as Lucy pulled up out front in a new car; a brand new, super shiny car that was filled to the brim with boxes and bags.

Nicole ran outside to see what it was that Storm was hollering so loudly about. What she saw in front of her made her gasp.

"Where did you get that?" Nicole asked, pointing to the car. Lucy had been given instructions to take her old car and swap it out for something similar, but this was not something similar, this was an upgrade of an upgrade on her old car.

"Well, I figured this made more sense." Feeling clever with herself, Lucy smiled to Nicole.

"Okay, but where did this come from? And how did we pay for it?" Lucy noted the 'we' in that statement but chose to ignore its connotations, even though she kind of liked them.

"I hired it, it's not that expensive," Lucy lied, smiling happily and hoping Nicole didn't ask too many more questions.

"Oh really? I might not know much about cars Luce, but I do know that that costs a lot more than the old heap of junk I just got rid of," Nicole argued, pointing at the new car for emphasis.

"Okay, but I...look, I have the money, so why not use it for once?" Lucy declared. "And...and if it makes you feel better, we can...we can share it."

Storm watched as her mother and Lucy went back and forth discussing who should or shouldn't pay for the new car. It wasn't that interesting to listen to, and her attention began to drift back to the car with more interest. It was then that she noticed that there was more than just a car to investigate.

"Oh my God, Mom!" Storm shouted, getting everybody's attention. "Lucy bought a TV!"

"TV, TV, TV," repeated the twins over and over as they danced around Lucy with the most adorable smiles on their faces. Their dark blonde curls bounced along with them.

"Alright, a word please," Nicole said to Lucy as she walked away from the kids for some privacy. Lucy followed as requested, with Storm giving her the 'you're in trouble' look. Lucy smirked and shrugged.

Lucy made the decision to put her defence in first rather than wait for a telling off from Nicole. "Before you tell me all the reasons why I can't or shouldn't buy things, can I please say something first?"

"Go ahead." Nicole motioned with her hand before crossing her arms and leaning her weight to one side. She didn't look happy, and Lucy coughed to clear her throat before she began.

"Alright, so it's like this." She smiled at Nicole and continued on. "I smiled and talked to Rita today." She paused, hoping for Nicole to understand what she was saying, but she looked perplexed and clearly needed more. "For the first time in all the time

I've known her, I spoke to her, asked her questions and behaved like a normal member of society, and do you know what she asked me?"

Nicole shook her head. She was intrigued as to where this was going. Who was she kidding, she was intrigued by everything about Lucy, so she listened, her stance softening a little.

"She asked me if the world had ended. She said I haven't said much more than one-word answers to her in all the years I've known her and here I was, asking her if one orange juice was better than another and which yoghurts where the best to buy." She couldn't help but chuckle at the memory of the conversation. "And I spent all morning visiting stores and speaking to assistants and asking for help so that I could buy all of this."

She sat down on a log that had been placed as a garden seat and patted the spot next to her for Nicole to sit down too. Which, after several seconds thought, she did. They sat side by side, thighs touching as Lucy continued.

"Having you here, with the girls has ended my world," she said softly, turning to look at Nicole, who momentarily looked horrified. "Because it needed ending. I was walking around with my eyes closed, and now, it makes me smile when I hear Rain sing that bloody annoying song, or when Summer screams like a banshee because there's a spider, and I live for the moments Storm asks me a question. When you said this morning that you would stay, I felt something lift within me. So yeah, I bought some stuff that will make you all happier. I spent my money on things that every kid should have."

"Finished?"

"Yes."

"Okay, thank you." She leant forward and pressed a soft kiss to Lucy's cheek, and with that, she got up and walked back to the girls and the car, leaving Lucy smiling and shaking her head. "Don't do it again," she called over her shoulder.

~E&F~

Rain and Summer ran around the cabin like mini tornadoes as Lucy carried the TV box into the main living area. Apparently tomorrow she was going to need to go and buy at least 20 movies on DVD that they had been calling out as essential viewing. Nicole raised a brow at that, but Lucy just grinned, and despite their conversation earlier, Nicole already knew she wouldn't win this argument with Lucy.

Once the TV was set up and the twins were settled down in front of it watching *SpongeBob SquarePants*, Lucy found Storm and asked her to follow her back out to the car.

"I got something for you," Lucy said, as they walked to the trunk of the car. When she opened it up, Storm could see several boxes and bags. Lucy reached in and pulled one out. Then she walked back around the car to the log she had sat on earlier with Nicole and patted it like before, only this time it was the mini version of Nicole that sat down beside her.

"I wanted to say thank you," Lucy said as Storm turned to her. "You make me talk about stuff and that's good for me." She smiled at the use of the word 'stuff' that Storm had used with her during their first conversation. "I never had anyone to just talk to before, and so I got you this as a way of saying thanks."

"I like talking to you Luce," she said, taking the wrapped box.

"I know, open the box though."

Storm took her time pulling the paper off the box, not used to being given things other than on her birthday and again at Christmas. Her father didn't allow them to have gifts at any other time.

She gasped as she saw what was in it. "You got me a laptop? Just for me?" she asked, unsure if it was really happening, Lucy nodded. "Thank you!" She threw her arms around her neck and hugged her with all she had. And Lucy hugged back.

"It's for schoolwork, you're going to need one soon," Lucy said, before reeling off all the information that the assistant had told her.

"Wow, but I can still play games and music on it too?"

"I guess, but no internet unless your mum says it's ok. We got rules, remember?"

"Yes, I know the rules. No talking to strangers, no walking near the old cabin, and no swimming in the lake without an adult."

"And no secrets or lies. No fighting with your sisters and no arguing over chores."

"Yes, Mom!" Storm said, sarcastically laughing along. "Thank you for my present."

"You're welcome."

~E&F~

While the girls were watching TV, Lucy began bringing all the other boxes and bags from the car into the house. She placed them all in the bedroom that the girls were sharing and piled them up in the middle of the room. Every item had been wrapped in-store and labelled for each child that it belonged to.

When Nicole was busy in the kitchen, she quickly sneaked the large boxed present she had bought for her into her room too and left it on the bed for her. Then she sat back on the couch and began her initiation into *SpongeBob*.

Rain was the first to get up and wander into her room to find her colouring book, only what she found meant she came running back out screaming with excitement as she babbled and rambled to her sisters that Santa had been there. Of course, Storm told her she was being silly, Santa only came at Christmas and that was months away. However, Rain was so insistent that both Summer and Storm followed her into their room to see what she was talking about. Lucy couldn't help the smile that cracked her cheeks as the shrieks and delight burst forth from three over-excited kids. When she looked up she could see Nicole staring at her with a smile on her own face as she heard her girls being happy. She mouthed a silent thank you just as Summer came running out to show her mom the new teddy she had been given.

Dinner had been enjoyed by them all as they sat together for the first time to share a meal, and it was not much later, when all three girls were exhausted and asleep, that Nicole said her own goodnight and went to bed herself. Lucy stayed up watching a documentary for the first time in nearly 12 years. TV had changed a lot in that time, and she was intrigued by all the different things she could watch.

She was so engrossed that she didn't hear Nicole's door open, or the footsteps of her new housemate as she made her way back into the room and over to the couch where Lucy sat. Nicole flopped down next to her, just staring. Lucy could see her out of her peripheral vision and quickly looked at her and then back to the TV again. Nicole didn't say a word; she just sat there and continued to stare at Lucy until eventually Lucy gave up trying to ignore her and put the TV on mute. She turned slowly in her seat and waited expectantly for Nicole to say whatever it was that was on her mind.

"Apparently Santa has visited me also," she finally said, tilting her head as she studied Lucy some more.

"Uh huh."

"Yes, there's this huge box on my bed filled with every kind of pampering product a woman could ever need."

"Is that so?" Lucy smirked and began to fidget.

"Yes, that is so." Nicole smiled. "Thank you. You didn't have to do that, you didn't have to do any of it Lucy, but I appreciate it, and one day I will find a way to pay you back for your kindness."

"I didn't do it so you would owe me anything, Nicole. I just wanted to do something nice for you all."

"Well, you better not complain when we find a way to do something nice for you," she promised as she rose up from the couch. And then, she bent down and kissed Lucy's cheek for the second time that day. "Goodnight Lucy."

When she was gone, Lucy reached up and touched the spot Nicole's lips had met. "Goodnight," she whispered back.

Chapter Twenty

The girls' room was organised three days later when the bedroom furniture arrived. It wasn't ideal that Storm shared with the twins, but she was willing to put up with just about anything if it meant they could stay.

Each of them had their own area of the room, with their bed pushed into a corner. A small drawer set was placed next to each one, and a night light was placed on top. Little mini wardrobes then stood at the bottom of each of the beds that were all covered in various Disney characters. Lucy had decided that she would gradually fill them with new clothes, if Nicole would let her.

What Lucy noticed was just how little they all had. She wasn't someone that viewed a life based on the things someone had collected, but they literally had left everything behind as they made their escape, and she wanted to change that and make life nicer. The problem was, Nicole was proud and had already been gracious in accepting the gifts she had bought so far, so she didn't want to push it. She didn't understand what the big deal was, but Nicole had been clear about it. She was going to have to be smart if she was going to find ways to get them things without denting Nicole's pride.

There had been a lot of change for Lucy too. She got to discover all about Disney, and to be fair, she kind of enjoyed it. She had to pick things up, toys and clothes that scattered the living room where they were abandoned for more important things. There was noise and talking all the time. And there was music, for the first time in a long time. She had even found herself humming along at times when the girls jumped around the room dancing and singing.

Right now, though, it was reasonably quiet. Nicole was at the sink peeling vegetables for that night's dinner. They generally took it in turns to cook and clean up, and tonight was Nicole's turn. She planned on roasting a chicken with some mashed potatoes and roasted vegetables. It was a simple, healthy meal that everyone enjoyed, which was pretty amazing considering how fussy they all seemed to be any other time.

"Coffee?" Lucy asked as she filled the machine with water and added the required amount of grounds to make the perfect cup.

"I would love one, thank you," Nicole replied as she continued to peel the potatoes.

"Do you need a hand?"

She smiled and turned to where Lucy stood holding a cup in one hand, the other shoved into her pocket. "No, thank you, I'm all good, but maybe you can get the girls to fix the table?"

Lucy turned and noted two very quiet little girls completely transfixed by a singing fish and another little girl at her desk finishing her homework. It was peaceful and tidy; she wasn't going to mess with the equilibrium.

"It's okay, I'll do it, let's enjoy the quiet a little longer, huh?" she chuckled, nodding her chin to the room in front of her, drawing

Nicole's attention to them. She watched them all for a moment. For once in their young lives, they looked like normal kids with nothing to worry about in the world.

"Yeah, that might be the best plan." She chuckled too. "So, listen, I wanted to talk to you."

"About?" Lucy asked as she grabbed another mug and got them ready for the perfect cup of coffee that she was brewing.

"We need to work out my share of the bills while we're living here."

"No, we don't," Lucy said, pouring two cups of steaming black coffee, the smell of which was wafting through the cabin.

"Can I have coffee?" shouted Storm.

"No," shouted Lucy and Nicole at the same time. They both smiled and laughed at their reaction.

"Yes, we do Luce, I am not going to freeload off of you."

"I'm not asking you to."

"Well, I would still feel better about it if you would let me contribute properly to the running of the house," Nicole argued. She put the last potato she was peeling into the bowl and grabbed the tea towel to dry her hands.

"Okay," Lucy said, more easily than Nicole expected.

"Okay? Great, so let's talk." She grabbed a mug and sat down at the kitchen table.

Lucy pulled out a chair and joined her at the table. "If you're going to insist, then you can chop the firewood and keep the kids' room tidy, and I'll organise the garden area and—"

"That's not what I meant, although I am happy enough to do that. I'm not sure how good I'll be at chopping wood, but I'll try. I meant financial, rent money."

"I know what you meant Nicole, but there is no rent. I own this cabin outright, no mortgage, and no rent. It's pretty much self-sufficient. I had a generator installed and solar panels to run it. We got water bills to pay, but they're pretty minimal so, $50 a month? You get a discount in Rita's store that saves us 30% off your food bills that I am now included in. So, tell me, what do you feel the need to pay for?"

Nicole sat for a moment just looking at her. She couldn't decide if she wanted to throttle her or hug her.

"You know what?" she finally said. "You are the most frustrating person I have ever met."

"I can imagine that I am," Lucy agreed, smiling.

"But thank you. I feel like I'm forever saying that to you lately, but I mean it. Thank you, Lucy."

"You're very welcome," she said, placing her empty mug down on the table. "So, I am going to drink my coffee outside and then go down to the store while you carry on with dinner, okay?"

"Sure," Nicole said, smiling as well now. "Get going, I'll call you when it's ready. Oh, and by the way," she shouted after her, "I'm not chopping the wood without help." She took a sip of her coffee and grimaced. "Did you make this with something other than coffee?"

Lucy turned to face her. Standing in the doorway, she sniffed her own cup before taking an experimental sip. "Tastes fine to me." She shrugged and continued on her path.

Nicole picked up her mug once more and took a sniff. Recoiling at the smell of it, she threw it down the sink and moved swiftly towards the bathroom.

~E&F~

Arriving back at the cabin an hour later, Lucy got out of the car and opened the trunk. She was aware of a vehicle pulling in behind her. She could see quite clearly out of her peripheral vision that it was Paul Nixon's red Mercedes. She continued what she was doing, lifting her bags out of the trunk and closing it just as she heard his car door slam shut. He wouldn't be terrifying her today, or any day, but she was wary.

Nicole watched through the window in horror as he neared Lucy. She was frozen to the spot. So far, he was keeping his distance from Lucy, but that didn't mean anything. He was a sneaky bastard. She could hear Storm speaking to her, but she couldn't turn away from the scene in front of her. Her mind was racing, making plans to leave. It wasn't safe here. Storm moved closer to her mother and looked out of the window to see what she was looking at.

"No, no, no, we're not leaving Mom, you said we could stay." Storm sensed where her mother's mind would take her the second she spotted him.

Outside, Lucy looked towards the cabin, her head high as she turned back to face him. He said something to her that she didn't quite hear, so she ignored him. His face started to get red as his rage built instantly. "Walk away Lucy," Nicole whispered to herself. But Lucy didn't, instead, she laughed at him and placed the bags down on the ground at her feet.

As he took a step forward, Lucy suddenly launched at him and punched him square in the face. His nose bloodied. He staggered as his hands flew automatically to his face.

Nicole grabbed a hold of Storm and held her tight. There was no way he would let a woman hit him like that. But Lucy didn't give him a chance to think about what had hit him, because she threw out her bad leg and kicked him in the centre of the chest. He hurtled backward and landed on his ass. She wobbled a little, but she managed to stay upright and got herself steady before she moved towards him.

Now she was the one doing the talking and he was scuttling backward, away from her. He was the one running now.

He lay there on his ass as Lucy stopped talking and walked away, dusting herself off. She picked up her bags and brought them inside. The atmosphere in the room was surreal. The TV played Disney tunes in the background, happy and cheerful as the twins continued to watch, unaware of anything else going on around them. Nicole and Storm stood together rooted to the spot, both fearful and panicked, but for wholly different reasons.

Storm ran across the room and wrapped her arms around Lucy's waist, clinging to her and sobbing. "Is he going away?"

She put the bags down and then reached down to pick Storm up, carrying her across the room to the couch. "You don't have to worry about him anymore. Keep an eye on your sisters for me?" Storm nodded and watched in awe as Lucy moved back across the room to Nicole. "He's gone," she said, her voice as calm as she could make it. Adrenaline was starting to wear off, and she could feel the tell-tale signs of her own fear working to the fore. Fear of what he could have done, but more so, for where Nicole could have run.

"What did you say to him?" Nicole asked. She still hadn't moved. Her eyes were firmly on the spot where his car had been parked.

"I told him that if I ever saw him on my property again, I had the legal right to shoot him. And then I told him that this was the last time I wanted to see him near you or the kids and that if he chose to ignore me, then next time it would be worse than a punch to the face." She sucked in the breath she had barely used while speaking.

"And he just went?" Nicole finally turned away and towards Lucy. Smoky eyes filled with tears and disbelief.

"He just went." Lucy nodded. "Bullies are cowards, Nicole. I'm not frightened of him and he knows it."

Nicole nodded, but she wasn't wholly convinced that he wouldn't be back. He would just be more furious now.

Chapter Twenty-One

Nicole knocked lightly on the bedroom door and entered without Lucy speaking. She wore a long white t-shirt and not much else. As she moved into the room, she was lit only by the light of the moon as she stood in front of the bed, almost glowing. Lucy sat upright needing to see what she wanted, thinking she may have had another nightmare. Without a word, Nicole moved closer, and in one swift fluid movement, she was able to straddle Lucy's thighs, settling herself as she looked deeply into her eyes and lifted the hem of her shirt, pulling it up and off over her head. Her full and perfect breasts were within inches of Lucy's mouth. She leaned forward, and Lucy gently tugged a nipple between her lips. Her fingers reached up to touch soft skin, anchoring the woman against her as Nicole threw her head back and moaned in ecstasy. Her hands moving to Lucy's hair, she tugged her gently closer to bend down and whisper against her ear. "I want you to love me," she whimpered, grinding down against Lucy.

The loud, incessant banging on the door woke Lucy abruptly from the dream. She could still feel the soft fingers in her hair as she shook herself awake. She felt confused, more confused than usual when thinking about Nicole.

"Yes, I'm awake, what's up?" Images of Nicole and then Paul Nixon clashed in her mind. She sat up instantly, feeling apprehensive.

"Lucy, you have to get up, Mom said you are supposed to go to town."

She sighed and relaxed at the sound of Storm's voice and ran her fingers through her hair. "What time is it?" Lucy shouted back. The dream had completely thrown her for a loop.

"It's 6:20."

"6:20?" Lucy mumbled to herself as she got up. She stretched her leg, bending her knee a few times to loosen the joint before she walked to the door in her PJs. Pulling it open, she found an adorable grin staring up at her. "Storm, it's not even 7 a.m. Where is your mum?"

"In bed," she answered thoughtfully, still smiling adoringly at Lucy, who was unable to be angry with her for waking her up so early, not to mention in the middle of that dream. Maybe that was actually a godsend. It wasn't a good idea to start developing a crush on her new roommate. It wasn't a good idea at all.

"So why are you waking me up at this god-awful hour?" she asked, rubbing the sleep from her eyes.

"Well, I was up and—" She was cut off as Lucy broke in.

"You were bored and thought I would be fun to play with?"

Storm smiled and nodded.

"You do know I am going to be grumpy all day now, don't ya?" Lucy threatened, but she couldn't help smiling. She felt pretty good; how many 8-year-olds thought an adult was so cool they had to wake them up to spend time with them?

"I made you breakfast," Storm said sweetly.

"You did? What ya make? It might earn you some bonus points." Lucy reached for her robe and pulled it on as they wandered out into the living area.

"Toast, with peanut butter and jelly."

"What flavour jelly?"

"Grape."

"Good choice," she said, moving to the kitchen and struggling to wake herself up properly. It amazed Lucy how resilient kids were. Here was a kid who, until just a few weeks ago, wouldn't have dreamed of waking anyone up in the house she lived in through fear of what her father would do. She wouldn't have even attempted to make anyone breakfast or even smile the way she was right now. In just a few weeks this little girl had come a long way, as had her mother, Lucy thought; as had she. There were still times when Nicole flinched or apologised when she had no need to, but on the whole, she was more confident and happier than Lucy had ever seen her. And Lucy was forgoing her hat now in the house. She spoke openly and easily with Nicole, and she made more effort with people when she was in town. Life was changing for the better.

They sat together, quietly eating their toast while the twins and Nicole continued to sleep. Storm talked about her impending day at school and Lucy offered to help her with any homework she had later. It was a nice moment, just the two of them. Lucy tried to remember if she had ever wanted kids. They were too young to have even thought about it, but she was sure maybe one day, Nicky and herself would have talked about it. Now though, she sat with someone else's little girl and she liked it, a lot.

She made a pot of coffee ready for when Nicole did eventually wake and got some juice and cereal organised for the twins while Storm washed up their plates. They made a good team as they worked around each other in the small kitchen.

"Lucy?" Storm's voice was quiet and unsure as she spoke.

"Yes, Storm?" Lucy answered gently, expecting a question with a difficult answer.

"Who is the lady in the picture?" She turned to face the mantle, making it clear she was speaking about Nicky. But Lucy didn't need to turn to know who she was talking about. There were no other photographs in the room.

"Her name is...was Nicky."

"Was she your girlfriend?" Lucy looked at her, an eyebrow raised at the question. "What? I'm 8, I'm not a kid, I know about stuff." There was that word 'stuff' again. The all-encompassing word for everything.

"Uh huh. Does your mum know about the stuff you know about?"

Storm shrugged. "So, was she?"

"Yes, Miss Noseypants."

"I thought so, she's pretty." She nodded, more to herself than Lucy.

"Yes," Lucy agreed, sipping her coffee and moving to sit on the couch.

"Do you think my mom's pretty?" came the next question, which caught Lucy by surprise considering what she had been dreaming not more than 45 minutes ago. She took a moment and considered the young girl before she answered. Storm was standing in front of her, the picture of innocence. She couldn't lie to the kid.

"Of course, she is very pretty, don't you think so?"

Storm took a seat next to Lucy before she answered.

"Yeah, I think so, but I wanted to know what you thought," she said, moving about on the couch until she was facing Lucy.

"Why?" Lucy asked, unsure as to where this conversation was leading, but it was certainly leading somewhere.

Storm shrugged again. Lucy narrowed her eyes at her and gave her the stare, which Storm only managed to throw back at her. But then, she seemed to come to a conclusion of her own and asked, "Do you like my mom?"

"Of course I like her." Lucy could feel the heat of a blush appearing and wished she had her hat to hand.

"No, I mean, do you *like* her!"

"Storm... okay, look...your mum she is..." She had a flashback to her dream, the t-shirt rising up. She shook her head and pushed those thoughts from her mind. "Not everybody likes each other that way, ya know?"

"I know, but I think my mom likes you," she said, causing Lucy to cough and take a deeper breath than before to calm herself. This was not the way she had envisaged this morning going. However, she was now intrigued.

"What makes you think that?" Lucy probed, trying to look and sound nonplussed and feeling as though she were failing considerably.

"I dunno." She shrugged again. "Don't you ever see her look at you?" she offered like a wise old sage who couldn't believe nobody else had noticed what she had. It wasn't like it wasn't obvious, as far as Storm was concerned.

"No, can't say I have," she said, picking up a book and pretending to be extremely interested in the first page.

"Uh huh, and you definitely don't like her that way?" Storm asked once more, for clarification.

"Uh huh."

"Hey, what's all the noise?" said a sleepy Nicole as she walked into the kitchen in her dressing gown, picking up a coffee cup and filling it with the hot delicious brew that Lucy had made. She thought she would be forever grateful to wake up to such delicious, freshly brewed coffee, but lately just the smell was enough to put her off completely.

Lucy decided to throw caution to the wind and end this idea of Storm's right there, fully expecting Nicole to clarify for her daughter just how wrong she was about this so that the subject would be dropped.

"Storm thinks you like me," she explained, without looking up.

"Lucy!!" Storm shrieked, absolutely horrified that she would be so open about their private discussion and embarrassed that she had told her mom. Lucy grinned at the reaction.

"What? We don't have secrets in this house," Lucy reminded her as Nicole stared wide-eyed for just a second before getting herself together. It hadn't gone unnoticed by Storm, or Lucy.

"Yes, and I think Lucy likes you too," she said to her mom before pulling a face at Lucy and watching as they both blushed and pretended to do other things. Jeez, it was so obvious, why wouldn't they just admit it?

"Right, so are you going to wake your sisters up?" Lucy said, trying to change the subject and noting that Nicole was yet to deny anything.

"Yes, are you going to turn that book the right way around?" Storm asked, pushing her glasses back up her nose as she jumped up to go and wake the twins. Lucy looked at the book and then put it down.

Storm poked her tongue out, and then she laughed as she went running from the room and into her own bedroom to wake up her sisters, singing K-I-S-S-I-N-G.

Lucy and Nicole looked at each other, neither knowing quite what to say to the other with regard to Storm's little outburst, so Lucy solved the awkwardness by departing to get dressed, leaving Nicole to take a seat at the table in the kitchen, wondering where the heck that had come from, and to actually contemplate what her daughter had just said, and why it was that every cup of coffee made her feel violently ill lately.

~E&F~

Neither woman mentioned that morning's conversation as they both sat quietly together on the shore watching the girls play. However, they were both thinking about it.

Lucy had to admit she found Nicole attractive, but that didn't mean she was attracted, did it? Nicole was a good person, fun and easy-going, and it didn't hurt that she had a particularly nice backside. But so did a lot of women Lucy noticed, and she didn't want to sleep with any of them. So why had she had that dream?

Just thinking about the dream and the way Nicole sauntered into her room was enough to make her blush and feel a stirring in a region where she rarely felt anything these days. She told herself that it didn't mean anything; it was just a dream, and lots of people had dreams like that, didn't they? They were spending a lot of time together, and so it was obvious Nicole would invade her subconscious thoughts; she just hadn't expected them to be quite so vivid or so intimate. She glanced across at Nicole. She was sitting with her face to the sun under a ridiculously large sunhat that she had gotten from Rita. Lucy chuckled internally; even in a stupid hat she was gorgeous.

Nicole had also spent the morning considering if her daughter's comments had any validity, and worryingly, she had to confess to herself that they possibly did. It had never occurred to her that she might be attracted to Lucy like that. But now that Storm had said it out loud, she had to confess, to herself anyway, that she was. Lucy was...what was she? Nicole wondered. She was just Lucy, and there was something strangely adorable about her. She was strong and contemplative, but she was also kind and chivalrous; she was everything she had thought Paul was, and look how that had turned out, she reminded herself. When she knew Lucy wasn't looking, she risked a fleeting glimpse of her. She was frowning, but somehow serene. Yes! It was just a crush, she decided. Jesus, she had been a pop idol of her teenage self; it was just a crush, nothing to worry about.

But, what if? Lucy thought. *What if I really do like her? Then what? What about Nicky? Would she understand? I'm not meant to love again, that's not in the stars for me! I can't allow it.* She was frowning, concentrating on trying too hard to understand her feelings. *This wasn't supposed to happen. I wanted them to stay for the company and because I like the children. I wasn't meant to fall for her, and I'm not going to, it's just out of the question.*

A sudden thought entered Nicole's mind. *I feel like I want to kiss her and then... Why am I even thinking about sex with Lucy? This has to stop, right now. She is your friend, and she has been good enough to allow you and your three noisy and messy children to invade her home, her life, and Oh God I love her for that, that's what it is, I am grateful and my feelings are confused because I am lonely and she gives me warmth and understanding.*

Storm was sitting in her spot holding a book in her hand. To all appearances she was reading, and she really was, only not the book. No, she was reading the two women in front of her, both sitting together in silence and giving each other quick glances. She shook her head and smiled to herself as she went back to her book.

Chapter Twenty-Two

With the onset of June, a lot more of the cabins nearby were full of tourists and vacation homeowners arriving for the summer sun. A lot more people were milling around the forests and lakes, the shops were fuller, and restaurants and bars that were closed during the winter or on shorter hours were now in full swing. It was usually the time of year that Lucy dreaded the most: inquisitive people with nosier kids finding their way onto her property while they rambled around. Going into town had become almost a no-go zone until the very last minute before Rita closed up. But things were changing rapidly for Lucy now that she had responsibilities.

Nicole was halfway through her shift at the store. For several days since Paul's visit, she had been on edge. Lucy had done everything to make sure that she and the girls where never on their own.

When the girls all strolled into Rita's, it was with a squeal as the twins ran straight past Nicole to the candy aisle. She always felt better when she had eyes on them, even though she trusted Lucy to keep them safe. She watched them run straight past without a hello or a wave, and had to chuckle at the sight of them so excited.

As usual, they had managed to convince Lucy that they absolutely had to go to the store today and get some chocolate. It was chocolate after all, and who could deny three smiling, adorable little faces the taste of something as wonderful as chocolate? Not Lucy! Getting to see Nicole just three hours after she had dropped her off at work wasn't the reason for going at all.

"Oh, seems like I am not required for hello kisses then?" Nicole laughed at the retreating figures that now sat huddled together on their haunches discussing which bar was the best to get.

"Hey Mom, Lucy said we can have chocolate, and they've been kind of excited about it the whole way here," Storm explained, giving her mom a quick kiss on the cheek as she too passed on her way to join Rain and Summer in choosing some candy.

"Uh, I think it was more a case of you all demanded chocolate and threatened to ruin my peaceful afternoon with noise if I didn't bring you here and buy you all chocolate." Lucy winked and laughed at Storm.

"Yeah, well that too." She smiled back from her spot by the Hershey bars. "Anyway, you said chocolate was the cure for everything."

"Uh huh, I did, however, what do you need curing of?" Lucy asked, narrowing her eyes and waiting expectantly for something cheeky to pop out of Storm's mouth.

"I'm too shy," she said with a shrug, walking back toward Lucy with her chosen item.

"Shy?" Lucy scoffed, "Are we talking about the same person? Nicole, did Storm get taken by the Pod People!?"

"Shut up, I *am* shy!" She laughed and playfully slapped at Lucy's arm.

"What are you shy about, baby?" Nicole spoke gently to her daughter, who was blushing slightly at the topic of conversation. Lucy was right; Storm was definitely not shy at home.

"Ms. Arnold wants me to sing at the pageant when we go back to school after vacation."

"Yeah, so?" Lucy said, not seeing the problem.

"I can't."

"You can't? Sing?"

"I don't know, but I can't do it in front of other people. And she wants me to sing in front of the whole school and I just can't do that," Storm said.

"Oh sweetie, you'll be fine, and once you've done it you'll wonder why you were so worried," Nicole said, clutching her daughter to her as two overly excited 4-year-olds scampered back down the aisle to them.

"We got it!" they shouted in unison. "Mommy, we gots chocolate." Their small arms were filled with bars of different delicious chocolate.

"Oh wow, so I see, that's so nice of Lucy to bring you here to see Mommy too."

"No Mommy, just to get chocolate, we can see you later," Rain said. The sight of her smiling her big cheesy grin up at her would be one of the images Nicole would store forever in her memory.

"Ah, well I guess you told me!" Nicole laughed and smiled at Lucy. Her eyes had a sparkle about them today, Lucy noted. They were usually warm and maybe a little distant, but today they held something else. Hope?

"Your teeth will rot if you eat all of that," Lucy joked with the twins. "Maybe you can put some back for another day?" They stared up at her with raised eyebrows before scurrying back down the aisle and putting everything back except for one large bar each.

Nicole turned back to Storm and added quietly, "We will talk about this later when I get home. Try not to worry about it."

"Right, Gale Force, let's see what you all got!" Lucy said to the girls as each of them placed a chocolate bar on the counter.

"Gale Force?" Nicole asked inquisitively.

Lucy blushed at the question. "Uh, yeah...well. Summer, Rain, Storm. They kind of all fit together, so I call them Gale Force, ya know, it's all weather-related, and well, they are kinda like a hurricane once they get going."

"I see, I never thought about it that way, we – well I just liked the names," she said with a smile, but the sparkle that had been shining brightly now left her eyes as she thought about her husband. "But you're right, they do fit," she said, suddenly realising something special about them that she hadn't put together before.

"Yeah, good strong names, and especially when you add your name in too," Lucy added.

"My name? How does that fit?"

"Well, it means 'victorious people.'"

"Really? And how do you know that?" Nicole asked, smiling more now, the sparkle starting to return as she watched Lucy's cheeks redden at her admission.

"Uh well, I looked it up. Storm was showing me her laptop and how to use it, and so—"

"So? The first thing you did was look up the meaning of my name?" she asked. Lucy wasn't sure, because it had been a long time since it had happened, but she thought maybe Nicole was flirting with her.

"No, the first thing I did was look up the meaning of my name." She smiled warmly. And now, she was flirting back, a little anyway.

Nicole laughed at this admission; it was quite sweet how Lucy had no qualms about telling the truth even if it embarrassed her. Just another aspect of Lucy's personality that was attractive. Paul Nixon was a liar from start to finish in their relationship. From his pretence at being the perfect husband and perfect father, to his addiction to gambling and God only knows what else. Her life with him had been a spiral of deceit, but not with Lucy. With Lucy she had openness, she had shared her darkest moments. With Lucy, there was fun and laughter, but most importantly, there was honesty.

"So, what does your name mean then?"

"Lucy just means 'light,' pretty boring I suppose, but my middle name is Alexandra and that means 'defender.' As in protector of man." She beamed.

"Well that is pretty impressive, it's not quite as impressive as my victorious people, but it's still pretty good. I wonder what my middle name means."

"What is it?"

Storm watched this conversation go back and forth with interest. Surely they could see it. She looked over to Rita, who was also watching, captivated by the pair of them, and when Rita turned her gaze on Storm, they both raised an eyebrow.

"Amanda, I am sure it won't have any exciting meaning though." Nicole laughed, continuing on with their conversation without regard to Rita and Storm's silent exchange. Her fingertips reached out and touched lightly against Lucy's arm. Rita had never seen anyone touch Lucy before, not in all the years she had known her.

"I'll look it up when we get home. Do you need me to do anything?" Everything was so simple, the way they worked well together. It was so domesticated.

"I should be home for dinner. I was thinking of doing something simple like lasagne or spaghetti? Is that okay?"

"Fine by me, did you want to watch a movie? I can pick up a DVD on the way back," Lucy offered, her smile growing by the minute. Someone else entered the store and Lucy instinctively turned her face away and brought her hand up through her hair to bring it forwards. Nicole reached out and touched her arm again, giving reassurance that she wasn't alone and it was all okay.

"Sure, sounds like fun, get two. One the munchkins can watch with us and one for when they go to bed," Nicole continued. The twins were excited about that news. They loved nothing more than watching films. Lucy always bought popcorn, and it was so much more fun than when they lived with their Dad. They could talk through it and ask questions and Lucy never got mad. They went to bed at night happy now.

Chapter Twenty-Three

Nicole got home to a quiet house. The girls were tidying their things in their room, and Lucy was in the kitchen mixing up a salad. In the oven was a lasagne that smelt out of this world. There was even garlic bread warming under the grill.

"Wow, I thought I was coming home to do the cooking," Nicole said, eyes wide in wonder. The smell of garlic, basil, and onions wafting through the home had her salivating.

"Don't be silly, you have been to work, that means you get the day off from chores," Lucy said, smiling. "And anyway, it wasn't difficult. Storm found the recipe online and I followed it." She was getting the hang of all this new technology now, though she often needed Storm to show her how to use it. She wondered what else she had been missing out on in her self-imposed exclusion from society.

Passing by Lucy, she let her fingertips skim across the small of her back. "Well it smells amazing, thank you."

Lucy felt herself aroused again at the close proximity. "Okay, so you have got about 10 minutes if you want to go and change or freshen up. Wine?" she offered, stumbling to the fridge, putting distance between them both.

"You read my mind. Please, I would love a glass." Nicole was a little dumbstruck at how thoughtful Lucy was. Even when she was pregnant and Paul was being nice to her, she had still had to do all the chores and cooking. It was so foreign to her to put her feet up and have someone else wait on her. And she had to admit, she quite liked it.

She wandered into her room and quickly stripped out of her work clothes and grabbed a towel, wrapping it around herself. Remembering she had a carton of milk in her bag, she hurriedly exited her room and crossed the living room to where she had left her bag on the countertop. She grabbed it, pulling the carton of milk from inside and placing it inside the door of the fridge before heading back across the room to the bathroom.

Lucy had to stop what she was doing. The sight of a semi-naked Nicole strolling across the lounge in just a towel that, although covered her perfectly, hugged every curve and allowed for plenty of uncovered skin to be on view, had momentarily frozen her to the spot. Placing the knife down on the chopping board, she put her hands on the counter either side and focused her vision on the half-chopped onion. She steadied her breathing and, in that instant, she was completely aware of just how attracted to Nicole she was becoming. It was a feeling she wasn't sure she knew how to cope with. She hadn't been attracted to anyone for such a long time; it was foreign, it was unwanted, and yet she couldn't stop it.

~E&F~

Dinner though, was a great success. Lucy was very pleased that everybody was enjoying it. It wasn't that she was a bad cook, but after living alone for so long, she had just gotten used to eating meals for one, or frozen dinners and takeout. Before that, she was on the road for months on end, and dinner was always supplied, so she was enjoying these moments now that she had...what exactly did she have? Friends? Guests? Family? Whatever they were to her, she had them, and she wanted to cook and make life easier for Nicole.

"Lucy this is amazing," Nicole enthused, taking another bite of the piping hot lasagne. And it really was; the flavours were perfectly blended. The sauce wasn't too sloppy, and it was full of tomato and just a hint of basil.

"Thanks," she blurted, not used to compliments and attention coming in her direction much anymore. Her cheeks immediately flushed, or was it because Nicole was looking at her like that, like she was the most important person in the room?

"So, what did we all do today?" Nicole asked, changing the subject quickly. The twins were making a huge mess on their plates with bits of food that had escaped their forks. Storm rolled her eyes at them while Lucy seemed to find it endearing.

"How do they make so much mess?" the elder of Nicole's girls asked incredulously. It never failed to amaze her just how messy her sisters could be with food.

"They don't make any more mess than you used to, Storm," Nicole said, laughing gently. "You used to get it all over your face, I took so many pictures—" She stopped laughing and her face took on a melancholy look as she realised they had left all of those memories behind. So many times she had thought about that day, when they had escaped, and wished she had taken just a few minutes longer to grab more of their things.

Lucy, who was sitting beside Storm at the table, saw the sadness that instantly appeared to mark the features of what had been a beautiful smiling face just seconds ago. In a moment of absolute madness, she knew what needed to be done. With the meal virtually finished anyway, she scooped a piece of lasagne up in her fingers and threw it at Storm, hitting her on the cheek. She stared and waited as it slid off, leaving a long red tomato sauce streak in its wake. Storm turned and looked at her, startled, not believing she had just thrown pasta and sauce at her, while Nicole sat wide-eyed.

"Might as well make new memories, huh?" Lucy said, picking up another piece. This time she actually smeared it across Storm's nose. The twins howled in delight, and even Nicole had to stop herself from laughing out loud. It took a moment, and Lucy was still unsure whether Storm was going to fall into a giant tantrum or not, but just as she was about to get worried, Storm's face broke out into a huge grin as she too grabbed a handful of food and threw it at Lucy.

"I suggest you find a camera if you're going to start capturing more memories," Lucy shouted over the squeals and giggles of three children throwing their food at one another.

Nicole grabbed her new phone, something Lucy insisted they both have now just in case anything happened to the children or each other, and clicked on the camera app, snapping away, all the while laughing hard at the antics until one of them threw something at her, and well, it would be rude not to join in.

~E&F~

With the clean-up in progress, Lucy was feeling pleased with herself. Nicole was putting the girls in the bath, and then they were going to watch a movie. In the meantime, Lucy had been given the job of clearing the mess. Well, she had started it, as Nicole had pointed out, and it was a fair point. She took her punishment and scraped food off of what seemed like every surface, but she smiled to herself for making such a great decision. Nicole was happy. The kids were happy, and in all honesty, so was Lucy.

Nicole soon returned with two sleepy 4-year-olds and Storm, all fighting to keep their eyes open for the movie. Lucy pressed play and started the film. Within minutes, Rain was snoring lightly on her momma's lap. A few minutes after that and Lucy had the pleasure of a dribbling Summer in slumber on her own lap. They looked at one another, and without a word, both stood to carry them to their beds. Lucy took a moment to just look at Summer as she slept; she was so peaceful, so unaware of all of life's hardships. All that was important to her was playing and chocolate. She felt the soft touch of Nicole's palm against her shoulder and turned, a half-smile on her face. "I wonder what they dream about," Nicole said quietly.

"It must be something nice, they never wake up grumpy," Lucy replied as they both turned to leave the room. She left the door ajar and followed the raven-haired Nicole back into the living room.

179

"Oh," she giggled as both sets of eyes landed on the sleeping form of Storm, stretched out across the couch with a cushion tucked beneath her cheek. "I thought she would have lasted at least another fifteen minutes."

"I'll take her," Lucy said, bending to scoop her up. "You change the movie, there is no point us watching the rest of this as they are only going to make us watch it 15 times tomorrow."

"You they might, I have to go into town," Nicole said, with a wink that sent an immediate shockwave of desire throughout Lucy's being.

She lifted Storm and felt her arms wrap around her neck; it was familiar, and Lucy adored this child. She adored all of them, but she and Storm had a connection that went deeper, and although Lucy couldn't explain it, she really felt as though she was meant to come into her life.

Nicole had poured two glasses of wine while Lucy was gone. It was nice to have these moments. In her old life, she never had the chance to just sit and enjoy a glass of wine by herself, let alone enjoy it with someone else. She wasn't allowed to drink unless they were entertaining people, and even then, if she had more than two glasses she would feel his glare. Of course, he could and would drink as much as he wanted. It was nights like those that she feared the most. Nights like the one before they had left. She shivered at the thought and then concentrated her gaze on Lucy, needing to ground herself in hope.

"I like the way you are with my kids," Nicole stated while continuing to stare at Lucy. She yawned. "God, I don't know why I feel so tired all the time," she laughed, feeling a little embarrassed at her statement.

"Well, they are great kids," Lucy replied with a smile.

"Yes, but they haven't had very good role models in their short lives, and you, well I think you're good for them."

Lucy blushed at the compliment but didn't say anything further, and Nicole didn't push it. They just sat and enjoyed their wine, watching the movie.

"Lucy?"

"Yeah?" she said, not taking her eyes off of the screen. For someone that had gone years without a TV, Lucy was now understanding what she had been missing out on.

"Do you think Storm will be ok?"

"Sure."

"I mean, at school, with the stage fright issue?"

"Oh, I guess so," Lucy said, turning her attention to the brunette. Big mistake! Nicole was sitting with her legs curled up underneath herself, leaning on the arm of the couch with her head tilted towards Lucy. She was biting her bottom lip nervously, and she looked stunning. No make-up, no fancy clothes or jewellery; her hair was messy and wild.

"Do you think – maybe..." She stopped to reconsider what it was that she had been planning to ask, and then decided against it. "No, it doesn't matter."

"What?" Lucy turned fully now, bringing her own legs up on the couch, bending them at the knee as she hugged and rested her chin on them.

"It's ok, I can't ask you to do—" She was cut off.

"Just ask. If I don't want to do it then I'll say no." Nicole considered that; Lucy wasn't shy in saying no. Lucy was staring at her and waited for a response.

"I just wondered if you could give her some tips on how to perform, to an audience, ya know on a stage?" She managed to get it out, and she prepared herself for being turned down, ridiculed, but then she saw those green eyes staring back at her and she remembered, this wasn't Paul. It was Lucy.

"Oh." That wasn't what she had expected to hear. She hadn't performed on a stage herself for so very long, was she even the right person to offer advice?

"See, I said I shouldn't ask. I'm sorry," Nicole apologised, looking away, back to the television and the film they were watching.

They sat like that for a while, the movie playing on in the background as they took sips of their wine. Lucy took the opportunity to glance across at her a few times. She was still sitting with her knees tucked up, facing Nicole.

"I guess I could show her a few things," Lucy offered.

"Really?" Nicole beamed, turning back to face her again, a huge smile on her face. "That would be so great, I mean she already looks up to you. In fact, I think she sees you as a parent."

"I'm sorry, I didn't mean for that to happen, I'll talk to her."

"What? No, I'm not unhappy about it, I think it's sweet she has you to go to when she can't or won't come to me. That's why I thought maybe you talking to her might help," Nicole said openly, pausing the film so they didn't miss it. In reality, this was a conversation she felt they needed to have. Storm was attached to Lucy, Nicole could see that. She needed to make sure that Lucy was comfortable with that too.

"Oh, I thought you wanted me to talk to her because, well ya know, what I used to do."

"It doesn't hurt that you know what you're talking about, but if it's too difficult then don't worry, I'm sure we...I can find another way," Nicole said, feeling a little awkward. She hadn't meant to bring up any unwanted memories for Lucy, or worse, make Lucy feel as though she had to take on parental responsibility for her kids.

"Nah it's fine, I probably can help her," she said, and then added, "I want to help her." The truth was, she would do anything for that child, if she could.

They switched the film back on and filled their glasses once more. The characters on the screen were being murdered one by one by a rather gruesome killer. Lucy was getting a little more than frightened with each grim scene, though she would never admit it, but Nicole wasn't deaf or blind to the squirming and gasps that were coming from the other end of the couch. It was yet another endearing part of Lucy to love.

But the tables turned moments later as one character was beaten to death. It was Lucy's turn to now be concerned at the whimpering coming from the other end of the couch. She silently cursed herself as she looked towards Nicole; she was crying, big fat tears rolling down her cheek.

Lucy reached for the remote and switched the film off, but it made no difference. Nicole's gaze was unfocused on the TV. She was just staring ahead, flashbacks of her own beatings came flooding back.

"Nicole?" Lucy spoke gently, not wanting to scare her further. "I'm going to move, okay? I'm gonna move to sit beside you." With no reaction, she edged a little closer. Nicole just stared off into the distance. "So, I was thinking maybe...can I hold your hand? Would that be okay?" Her hand hovered near Nicole's, and her fingers shook as they closed the gap. Ever so gently, she let her forefinger touch the soft skin on the back of Nicole's hand. With no flinch or movement from her, Lucy let all of her fingers touch. "It's okay. You're safe now." Lucy kept her eyes firmly on Nicole's face, watching intently for any sign that she was making things worse. "You're safe now," she repeated. Slowly, Nicole closed her eyes.

"I'm sorry, I just..." Her eyes opened, and she turned slowly to face Lucy.

"It's okay." Lucy tried a smile. "Do you want to..." She wasn't even sure what she was asking, but Nicole seemed to know and nodded, a half smile of her own before she leant forward into Lucy's arms.

Lucy held her breath, let her arms raise up and wrap around the trembling shoulders, the fingers of her left hand cradling the back of Nicole's head as she held her against her own chest and rocked them back and forth while she cried.

After several minutes, Lucy realised that Nicole had cried herself to sleep. With one hand, she reached behind and pulled down the old crocheted blanket that she had picked up at a craft fair years ago when Rita had dragged her out to the community market. She felt Nicole snuggle in, her head buried into the crook of Lucy's neck. Breath, hot against her skin, reminded Lucy just how close Nicole was. She breathed her in, the smell of her hair; the peach shampoo she used was intoxicating, and she found herself placing a kiss to the top of her head. Nicole murmured something unintelligible in her sleep, and then Lucy drifted off too.

When the morning light filtered through the windows, only Storm was awake. She wandered sleepily out from her room and was going to put the TV on while everyone else slept. She gasped with surprise when she found her mom and Lucy cuddled up together on the couch under a blanket. She giggled to herself and grabbed her mom's phone from the table, snapping a couple of pictures before she put the phone back down and slipped quietly away and back into her room.

~E&F~

The last time Lucy had woken with Nicole using her for a mattress, she had panicked and been frozen to the spot. This time, though, she found herself grinning. She lay there quietly and waited patiently for Nicole to wake. It didn't take long. It was as if she could feel that Lucy was awake and waiting for her to join her. The look of confusion on her face as she registered she wasn't in bed and wasn't alone was amusing. Then the blush that appeared when she realised she was laying on Lucy yet again was adorable.

"Hey," Nicole's sleep-laced voice said quietly as she looked up into the greenest eyes she had ever seen. If fresh grass could melt, then that would be the colour of them, with flecks of gold leaf peppering them to add a sparkle that contradicted everything about her.

"Hi, sleep well?"

"Apparently so, you?"

Lucy smiled, and that sparkle changed to something watery, glistening in the sunlight as she replied. "Best I've slept in a long time."

186

They both stayed that way for a little longer, until Storm could be heard rather loudly telling the twins to be quiet or they would wake them up. Lucy couldn't help but chuckle and was soon joined in her mirth by Nicole.

"I'm going to teach her about vocal levels today I think," Lucy said, grinning some more.

"I'm sorry about last—"

"It's fine, don't worry about it, I should have checked what kind of film it was...I...I didn't think, I'm sorry."

"Don't be silly, it's not your fault, Lucy," Nicole said. As she tried to use her hand to help push herself up into a sitting position, she realised it was trapped slightly under Lucy's torso, and her other hand she now realised was on top of Lucy's torso, under her top. "Oh, sorry," she said quickly, removing her hands and readjusting herself.

Lucy, in her usual straight-talking, no-messing way answered simply, "I quite liked it." This, of course, summoned a blush to appear, dappling her cheeks and neck with a faint pink hue. "Sorry, I shouldn't have said that."

"No, that's okay," Nicole said hurriedly "I...I liked it too." And she did; Lucy's skin had been warm to her touch, soft, and it felt right to be lying here with her so close.

Not wanting to confuse things any further and unsure where this was heading, Lucy let her stomach make the ultimate decision for them as it announced quite loudly that it was wanting breakfast.

"I guess that's our call. Bacon and eggs okay?" Lucy said quickly, but she moved slowly to extricate herself and stand up.

Chapter Twenty-Four

Lucy drove, dropping Nicole at the store for her shift, along with the twins. She then headed over to the school to get Storm to classes on time. Once she was alone, she began to consider how best she could help her new pupil.

Firstly, she had to discover if the kid could actually sing, because putting her up on stage if she couldn't would be horrific for her self-esteem. Having her humiliated in front of the entire school was not an experience Lucy wanted to create.

She found the store she needed and wandered inside. There was a certain smell that came with a music store. Wood and oil. She let her fingers dance across the smooth surface of the violins. They plucked at the strings of the guitars, the chord sending her memories hurtling backward.

"You can never find a better instrument than the guitar," Mike argued, having just played a sweet riff.

Ben did a double take before beating his drumsticks down against his tom-tom several times and then crashing the cymbals to make his point. "No chance, the drums are the best."

Sasha giggled and decided it was her turn to match the boys, fingers deftly flying across the keys of the board as she played an exquisite piece of Beethoven. "In your dreams, boys. The piano is by far the instrument of choice."

She hadn't even realised she had moved, but she had, across the room and past the drum kits. She found herself in front of the keyboards. Her fingers clenched into fists. She hadn't played in years, wasn't so sure that she even could.

"Can I help you?" A smart middle-aged man appeared from nowhere and was now standing by her side. "It's a beautiful model."

"I'll take it," Lucy said.

"You don't want to try it first?" he asked. Most people did. It was the bane of his life actually; people would come in and want to play around with all the instruments with no intention of ever buying one.

"No, it's the instrument of choice, isn't it?" she remarked. "I know it will be perfect."

~E&F~

Back at the cabin, she had a few hours before she needed to go and collect Nicole and the twins. Rain and Summer had been promised an afternoon by the lake if they managed to behave all morning at the store. It was highly unlikely they'd make it through; they found mischief in everything they did. Lucy smiled to herself, their antics often giving her reason to chuckle. But right now, she had something to think about, and it sat like a giant weight in her guts.

The keyboard was still in its box. The box was still sitting in the middle of the room, on the floor. She looked at it. Just a box, but what was inside of it was anything but just anything.

For the first 2 or 3 years of her life, she was much like the twins. Toys and chocolate were the most important things, but when she was 4, her uncle Rupert arrived. Everybody called him Strawberry, due to the colour of his fair hair and so, he became Uncle Berry. He had been away, working on cruise ships mainly, and he played the piano. Her parents had let him move in with them when he finished his last trip, and he never left.

Lucy woke up to the sound of music being played somewhere in the house. She loved music and would often be found singing and dancing to it. She wasn't a shy kid by any means, and it didn't matter where they were, if she heard a song that she knew then she would start bellowing.

Wandering down the stairs, she was intrigued as to what this music was. She hadn't heard anything like it before. Her tiny hands reached up and pushed the door open to reveal Uncle Berry sitting in front of a big wooden box, and he was pressing his fingers down on to shiny black and white blocks.

He grinned at her as his fingers danced away on the blocks and the music became more upbeat. Lucy began to bounce on her short little legs.

"Hey Luce, wanna play?" he said, not giving her a chance to answer before he reached down and pulled her up and on to his lap.

"Go on, touch the keys." He urged her on and so she did, clanging away, much to Berry's delight.

From then on, every day he would show her how to play a tune - as he called it. Bit by bit she learned how to play the piano until one day when she was about fifteen, he announced, "I think you're better than me now, Luce."

She wiped away a tear as she thought about Berry. He had died the very next year and it had devastated her, but in some ways, it had inspired her too. Because she played for him. She carried on with her lessons and she started to write her own music and perform her own songs, and eventually it had all paid off.

Finally, she opened the box and lifted out the long keyboard. It wasn't a piano and would never sound as good, but it would do for now. She had purchased a stand to go with it and had already set that up. Placing the keyboard on top of it was a little cathartic. She actually felt her fingers begin to itch, wanting to caress the keys.

When it was all plugged in and set up, she found a chair and sat in front of it, just staring. She reached out, her index finger extended, and gently pressed the 2nd octave G. Her middle finger and ring finger followed up with A and B. Tentatively she moved up and down the scale until, without even realising it, she was playing.

She was rusty. She could hear Berry laughing and urging her to keep going. So she did, her finger joints loosening with every sweep of the keys. Tears trickled, and yet she couldn't help but smile as she played her music for the first time since the accident.

Chapter Twenty-Five

At two in the afternoon, she arrived promptly at the store and was set upon in an instant by Summer as she ran from behind the counter and jumped straight into Lucy's arms.

"Hey, Juicy Lucy." She grinned. Lucy's eyebrow raised in surprise. She had been called many things before, but that was a new one.

"Okay...where did you get that?"

Summer laughed and snuggled into her neck. "Mommy told Rita that you was a...juicy Lucy."

"Oh, she did, did she?" She swung around to find Nicole frozen to the spot and staring right at her like a deer caught between the headlights of an oncoming juggernaut. "Juicy Lucy?"

"Okay, now that wasn't quite...I mean, that's not..." Lucy couldn't stop herself from laughing out loud. Nicole was flustered and it was cute, that much she had to admit.

Rain saved her blushes, however, when she came hurtling out from the back room and promptly fell over, sliding along the aisle. When she stopped moving it was only to let out an almighty scream. Shock more than anything had caused the scream, the friction burns to her knees caused the tears to follow, and only a hug from Mommy was going to make it better. So, Lucy took them all home.

~E&F~

Storm got the school bus home and was met at the top of the hill by Lucy. They walked back down the small road that led down to the two cabins, and as they broke off to the right and headed towards home, Lucy stopped walking.

There was a fallen tree, and Lucy sat down on it.

"Why are we stopping here?" Storm asked, looking around. There was nobody else here, just the two of them.

"Because I want you to sing for me." Storm's eyes went wide as saucers when Lucy announced that. She shook her head vehemently. "Why not?"

"Cos you might laugh at me," Storm admitted, flopping down beside her.

"Hmm, have I ever laughed at you before…I mean, when I'm not supposed to?" Storm shook her head, Lucy had never laughed at her or been mean. "So, why would I do that now?"

"Because…because I…what if I can't sing?" She felt Lucy's arm snake around her shoulder and pull her into a hug.

"I tell ya what, if you can't sing then I promise you, I will be honest and tell you, and then I will go and speak to Ms. Arnold and tell her that you can't do the pageant."

"You would?" Storm looked up at her with those big brown eyes.

Lucy nodded, "Yep, but…" she held up a finger, "if you can sing, then I will teach you how to perform on stage. Deal?"

"But...okay but, you can't look at me."

"I can't... Okay. I'm going to turn my back and then you're going to sing something for me, right?"

Lucy swivelled around and got herself comfortable and waited. She closed her eyes and listened. Birds tweeted and flew between branches. The breeze rustled the leaves and plants and then she heard it, the tiny trembling voice singing quietly a song that Lucy didn't know.

There was a lot of work to do, but the main thing was, she could hit a note.

~E&F~

The keyboard was a big interest to everyone, especially the two tiny terrors that wanted to play on it. Lucy wondered what Berry would have to say about that!

"Wow," said Storm, an expression of awe evident on her face. "You can play this?"

"Well, it's been a while, but yeah, I can play it. Might be a bit rusty though," Lucy said shyly. Nicole could tell that this was a big step, no a huge step, for Lucy, and there it was again: that little tug that kept nudging her heart open to this woman.

Lucy took a couple of deep breaths and wiggled her fingers. She went to touch the keys, but then pulled back at the last minute unsure, uncertain of herself and of what this meant. She hadn't played the piano on stage very often, that wasn't her job, so she figured she could do this. This wasn't Solar Flare, this was showing Storm that she too could face her fears. But how could she teach the kid that, if she couldn't face her own?

She felt a hand on her shoulder and knew without looking that it was Nicole. She looked up and found the darkest eyes just looking at her, not with pity, but with understanding. She knew how difficult this was going to be, and she was in awe that Lucy was doing it anyway.

"I might cry," she whispered to Nicole. It was one thing playing this on her own, but now with an audience, it was a different story.

"Me too." She smiled back. "But it's okay."

She never noticed the tears that streaked her cheeks, or the awe in which Nicole watched her, or how Storm sat open mouthed and scrutinised her fingers intently, trying to imagine how thrilling it must be to be able to play the piano. Instead, she focused on the music and let the emotion wash over her.

Nicole took out her phone and began to take more photos of them all. She took a moment to go through the photos already on her phone, smiling at the ones she had just taken. Then as she flicked back further she found the ones that Storm had taken of them asleep, together. She had her face buried in Lucy's neck, their arms wrapped around each other. They looked like a couple. She looked up then to listen to Lucy talking to the girls. When she caught her attention, Lucy just smiled at her and carried on talking to the children. That was the moment, the moment she realised Lucy was more than a friend, and she was rapidly becoming her person, the one she had longed for as a younger woman, the person who would be everything.

It was another one of those moments where they just fixed eyes and nothing else seemed to exist until Summer hit a key and tried to play. The spell broken, Lucy picked her up and showed her how to touch the keys properly.

"Lucy?" Storm said tentatively as she pushed her glasses back up her nose.

"Yes, sweetheart?"

"Can you, I mean, would you teach me?"

"If you want me to, then sure." Lucy nodded, it would be fun to teach someone else the joy of music at your fingertips. Just like Uncle Berry had taught her. It could continue to be passed on through the generations.

Storm beamed a smile that could have ruptured even the coldest of hearts, and for Lucy, it just confirmed how much she loved these kids, and when she looked up and found Nicole smiling exactly the same way, she realised something else too.

~E&F~

Supper was a simple meal of pizza from the local delivery/takeout place in town. It was nice; everyone was chatting and laughing. Lucy sat back and took it all in. In just a couple of months, her life had changed so much that she didn't even recognise herself anymore. She glanced at Rain, who was currently shovelling pieces of tomato from her salad into her mouth. Summer was stealing fries from Rain's share. Storm wasn't eating as she was too busy talking about wanting to watch a YouTube video on how to play the piano. Lastly, she glanced to Nicole, who was already watching her. She realised that Nicole had been watching her watch the kids, and she blushed, but she didn't look away; instead she kept her eyes right there and held her gaze.

"Mom?" Storm said, smiling at them. "Mom?" she repeated when she got no reply the first time. "Mom?!" she shouted louder.

"Huh? What?" Nicole said, tearing her eyes away from Lucy and looking at her daughter. "What's up, Storm?"

"Nothing, I was just asking for some juice, but you were in a trance with Lucy," she said, not quite understanding why Lucy and her Mom both blushed at the word "juice."

Chapter Twenty-Six

Lucy was lying on the couch. It was warm, and she could feel a summer breeze flowing through the window or an open door. She moved her head and surveyed the room, her eyes landing on the photo on the mantle. Nicky looked down on her, a smile fixed in time like always. She closed her eyes, and when they opened again the picture had changed. It wasn't Nicky any longer; it was Nicole.

She stood and limped towards it, picking it up gently and feeling the weight of the silver frame in her hand. Hearing a noise behind her, she turned to find Nicole standing there. She was speaking, but she couldn't hear her. She shook her head to tell her and Nicole repeated it, louder this time, but she still couldn't hear properly. It was muffled, like being in a pool underwater and hearing the sounds above. She walked closer and Nicole kept repeating it over and over until finally, she heard her, loud and clear. "My middle name is Amanda."

Waking from her dream, she called out for Storm. The youngster came running like her life depended on it. Her youthful exuberance and general need to impress her made Lucy smile to herself.

"Yes?" she called to Lucy as she ran into the room, skidding to a halt in her socked feet.

"Can I borrow your laptop for a minute?"

"Of course, I'll get it." And off she ran again. She was back in less than a minute, carrying the rectangular computer in her arms.

"Thanks," Lucy said, taking it from her and opening it on her lap. Storm clambered up onto the bed besides her.

"You're welcome. Mom is making breakfast. I'll tell her you're awake now, shall I?"

"Ok, thanks, sweetheart." She grinned. While she was waiting for the computer to load, she had the feeling she was being watched. Looking up, she found Storm was smiling at her. "What?"

"Nothing, I just like when you call me that," Storm said, and then she jumped off the bed and ran off.

Lucy shook her head, smiling at the way Storm was just, well, a sweetheart.

As the laptop finally loaded, she typed in quickly what she wanted to look up. *Amanda*. When the page changed, she clicked the various links until she got what she needed.

"Worthy of love," she read aloud to the empty room.

"What is?" Nicole said from the doorway. Storm had left the door open when she ran out a minute ago.

"Oh, you are," she said without thinking, but on seeing Nicole's cheeks redden, she quickly added, "Your middle name, I was looking it up, that's what it means." She felt her own cheeks flush now and quickly closed the laptop and reached for her dressing gown as she got up.

She was thrown for a bit, with the dream and then the meaning. Now, looking up and seeing Nicole leaning against her door, it was all just so natural, like it had always been this way, and yet she couldn't help but feel – what did she feel? Guilt? Guilt for what, though? She kind of felt like she was cheating on Nicky in some way, but then she also felt guilty for wanting to enjoy her life in a way that her friends no longer could.

"Well, it's nice to know that I am, sometimes I think people forget that part," Nicole said sadly as she turned to allow Lucy to follow for breakfast. "I was just going to tell you that breakfast is almost ready."

"Nicole, wait," Lucy called, stepping closer to her as she turned back around. "Your husband is an asshole and a bastard, don't judge your worth on anything he said or did."

Nicole thought for a moment. Her eyes met with Lucy's and she contemplated how she rarely even thought of Paul now, unless something triggered a memory. The person she was thinking about now was standing in front of her looking forlorn and unworthy. She quietly said, "I'm not."

These moments of time stopping for them both while they stared at each other were becoming a habit. Lucy took a second to glance away and down to Nicole's mouth. She had a nice mouth, soft lips that pouted a little when her face was relaxed. Kissable. She felt her breathing deepen as she realised what she was thinking, and when she looked back up to Nicole's eyes, she found them open, clear and watery, staring back at her hopefully.

"I... God I just want to kiss you right now," Lucy admitted, her thoughts spilling out from her in her usual candid manner.

"I'm not stopping you," Nicole replied honestly, finally allowing herself to admit she wanted that too. In fact, she really wanted it; she wanted to feel Lucy's warm lips upon her own, her hands on her skin. But Lucy just stood there, silently working through something in her mind that Nicole couldn't fathom.

Lucy didn't say anything; she couldn't, the words she needed just wouldn't come. She didn't know what the words were.

"I can't compete with a ghost, Lucy," Nicole said. Finally giving up, she turned around and walked back into the kitchen, leaving Lucy to stand alone with her thoughts – thoughts about how things needed to change, but she just wasn't sure how to do it.

Chapter Twenty-Seven

When Lucy was dressed, she didn't go to breakfast; instead, she took her photograph of Nicky and slipped out of the house. She walked to the end of the little wooden jetty that extended from the shoreline out into the water. It was her favourite place to go and sit when she needed to think, and today was a beautiful day to do just that. Nicole watched her through the kitchen window as she strolled slowly like a woman being taken to her execution. Her head hung low as her arms swung gently, carrying something that caught the sun off it.

Lucy must have sat there for 30 minutes, just thinking. It was a beautiful day, as was typical for this part of the world and this time of the year. The sun was high in the sky and warm against her skin. The water was cool on her toes as they skimmed the water's surface. It felt like today was a day for something new, something fresh, and something that had been in the air for a while was now forcing its way into existence.

"I've loved you for nearly twenty years now, Nicky," she said aloud while holding the photograph in her hands. The beautiful features of her lover stared out at her, smiling. "And a part of me is always going to love you, I promise you that. But, I've met someone, and I think you would like her. She is someone that I think might be good for me. No, she is definitely good for me, and I want to be able to tell her that I think she is worth it but," she smiled a tight smile and swallowed down the lump constricting her throat, "I can't while I have your ghost with me. I need to let you go now. I need to let you be free and in peace, and you need to know you don't have to look out for me anymore. I'm going to be okay." She wiped her eyes with her sleeve. "Can you forgive me?"

And just like that, a light breeze blew across her face and caressed her cheek like a loving palm. She reached up to touch it and, in that moment, she knew she had her answer.

~E&F~

Lucy walked into the cabin with purpose and placed the photograph back on the mantle in its usual position. The twins were watching a movie, something about a snowman and a princess. Storm was on her laptop, and Nicole was in her room. She knocked lightly on the door and felt eyes on her as the kids turned to watch. The atmosphere in the room had changed, and they'd all noticed it. It took what felt like a lifetime before Nicole opened it.

There were no words. Lucy smiled shyly and let herself fall into those watery onyx eyes that seemed to bore into her anytime she caught their observation. Her gaze drifted lower to the plump lips she had been imagining kissing for so long, lips that curled into a smile just as she leaned closer and closed the gap to meet them. It was a gentle kiss, one of liberation and initiation. A first and hopefully not the last. Lucy was well aware of the three small faces watching them, so despite her longing to deepen the kiss, she pulled back. Her palms still gently cradled Nicole's face, but she had no recollection of doing that, nor did she have any clue just when Nicole's own hands had reached for her and settled perfectly around her waist.

"I'm...you terrify me. I've spent so long just...and then you come along and I can't..." Lucy's palms slid slowly from Nicole's face to take her hands and place them over her heart. "I can't breathe when I think about you leaving. I don't want to be alone anymore."

~E&F~

The children were in bed, the twins asleep, but Storm was far too excited about the kiss and wanted to know if they were in love and getting married and would Lucy be her other mom now. Lucy was happy to let Nicole deal with all the questions. Instead, she made herself useful and opened a bottle of wine, collected two glasses, and found a box of chocolates she had hidden from the greedy little fingers that managed to snaffle anything good around here.

She sat upright on the couch and poured the wine, not quite knowing what to do with herself while she waited. It had been a long and emotional day. She was fidgety and moved about the couch, trying to get comfortable and look calm and collected. Finally, she found a spot that felt right and thought back to earlier while she waited.

After the kiss, all hell had broken loose with Storm running around screaming and singing K-I-S-S-I-N-G for half an hour. The twins didn't really seem to understand what was going on, but they thought that Storm was very funny and joined in anyway.

By the time it came around to lunch, they had thankfully settled down, and after eating a light meal together, they all piled outside to spend some time along the shore and in the water. It was a warm day, and the twins ran back and forth chasing each other. Storm sat on Lucy's lap, leaning against her chest. She was calmer now, but still smiling.

"I knew you loved Mommy," she said, sounding more like a child than she had ever done, and Lucy was pleased about that. For an eight-year-old she had seen and been through way too much, so to hear her now, being like a kid and enjoying herself, it melted Lucy's heart.

"Yeah okay kid, don't go getting a big head." She felt the smile on Storm's face more than she saw it.

"I think Mommy is gonna be happy now."

"I hope so, that's kinda my intention," Lucy said, kissing the top of her head. "What about you? You gonna be happy now?" The child looked up at her, studied her face and stroked a finger down the scar on her cheek.

"Yeah, you let me touch this," she said softly. "You've always loved me." This child seemed to understand things way beyond her years, and she had managed to wriggle her way inside Lucy's heart way before even Lucy had recognised it.

"Well, that might just be true," Lucy whispered, and Storm sighed, leaning back against her chest again. Nicole watched from *the shore and smiled at the scene. Her child was loved. She was loved.*

Bedtime for the little ones came quickly as tiredness worked its way through them after the fun of the afternoon. Storm decided she would watch a film while sitting in between the pair of them, asking her numerous questions. They had barely had two minutes to themselves. They had held hands for a while, and Lucy had managed to steal a few discreet kisses while they made dinner, but they needed to talk and spend some time alone. That time was coming now as she heard the door to the girls' room close.

"Hey, I poured you a glass," Lucy said, looking up as Nicole rounded the couch and flopped down.

"Thank you." She took a sip. "Mm, that's good." She twisted to lean against Lucy. comfortable as she felt an arm wrap around her. She felt safe here in these arms.

"So, you kissed me, finally," Nicole said to her, the corners of her mouth lifting into a smile. She felt so at ease with Lucy, and it was fun to tease her a little.

"Yeah, I did. I'm sorry that it took so long." Lucy felt the blush rising slowly like she always did around Nicole lately.

"Is it going to take as long before you do it again?" Nicole asked, her head tilted to one side as she looked up at her, confidence growing by the minute.

"Oh, I'm sorry, am I the only one allowed to initiate kissing?"

"No, but I figured you might need some time to adjust," Nicole replied, her heart leaping at the playful banter between them. It was this that she had always longed for: someone to not take things so seriously with, someone who would tease and unwind with her after a long day.

"Uh huh. And how many other women have you been kissed by, may I ask?"

"Uh, a few," Nicole replied, then almost laughed out loud at the look of shock that registered on Lucy's face. "What? Did you think I didn't have a little fun before I married a pig?"

"No, I just...I guess I just assumed that you were...ya know."

"Straight?" She twisted around so she was more or less lying on top of Lucy.

"Three kids and a husband from hell? Yeah, I thought you were straight."

"Well, I've never actually slept with a woman, but yeah, I've fooled around some."

"Some people are just sneaky," Lucy said with a grin. She closed the distance between them and this time, with no audience to hold her back, she got the kiss she had been waiting for.

There was no rush to it. It was a slow build-up of nips and pecks. "Stop thinking so hard," Nicole whispered against her lips. Pressing more firmly, she urged Lucy to relax and let go. Lucy felt her heart beat rapidly as she succumbed to it, letting Nicole take charge. It was a kiss full of promise, a kiss that was everything Lucy remembered it would be and yet, so different. Even though kissing Nicky had been so long ago, she had always remembered how it felt to kiss her, to be kissed by her. Kissing Nicole was so different, but just as wonderful. It asked questions and it found answers, for both of them.

She felt the tizzy of excitement in her tummy when she sensed Nicole's fingers glide up her back and pull her closer. Her own fingers tangled in Nicole's raven locks, touching her face, it was all so sensual.

When the kiss finally broke, Lucy rested her forehead against Nicole's just like she had earlier. They were breathing heavier now, and she needed to take a moment to process. "Okay, so that was a kiss to remember." She chuckled.

~E&F~

As they lay together watching a movie that neither had any real interest in, Lucy let her fingers skim up and down the side of Nicole's torso. There were tiny goosebumps appearing on her arm as Lucy's finger pads enticed and teased the area of soft skin they could reach.

They lay like the proverbial big spoon, little spoon with Lucy behind Nicole. Her left arm lay under Nicole's neck and wrapped around her upper chest, holding her close. The right hand was the one that was doing the wandering, just lazily up and down with no real purpose or design.

"I like you holding me," Nicole said quietly. "When I woke up in your arms that first morning I felt...at home."

Lucy smiled, pressing her lips against her shoulder. "I felt the same way."

"Can we take this slowly?" Nicole asked, twisting around to look at Lucy. The long scar that weaved down her face seemed so out of place. She traced a finger down it and watched as Lucy stiffened slightly, but she allowed the touch. Nicole kissed it, just above her top lip, on the cheek, and felt Lucy relax again.

"Yeah, I think that's probably for the best," she agreed. "Not that I don't want to ravish you because, quite frankly you are stunning, but," she noticed the blush that crept up Nicole's neck and face, "well it's been a long time since I have been intimate with a woman and I want to do it right. This isn't something I want to rush."

"God, when I first met you, what, just two months ago? I had no idea you were so," she searched for the word, "romantically adorable."

"I hide my many attributes well," she said, laughing and leaning down to kiss her gently once more. It was all so second nature, and yet just a week ago it was so very different.

"Do you think maybe we can get to second base and then take it slow?" Nicole asked as her cheeks reddened and dimples appeared with a grin.

"You'll have to tell me what that is," Lucy said seriously. Baseball references weren't something a girl from England grew up with.

"I'd much rather show you," Nicole teased, seizing her by the neck and pulling her down again. She was amazed at just how quickly she had grown in confidence. With Lucy around, she felt as though she could do anything. She could speak without fear, go anywhere without restriction. Her life was finally starting to feel like it was hers.

As they began kissing again, she reached for Lucy's hand and brought it slowly to her breast. She held it there until Lucy got the message that she was allowed to explore. Lucy felt the air leave her lungs as for the first time in so many years she was able to connect with another human being, to be emotionally and physically in the moment with someone who left her breathless. Someone who she could actually see past tomorrow with; a future.

The soft moans and whimpers of both women as they discovered parts of each other through clothing was arousing to both of them. Who knew having your neck kissed by Lucy could be as thrilling and as much of a turn on as it was? And how the hell did Lucy not know that she liked having her ears licked and nibbled, kissed and sucked until Nicole found a lobe with her mouth?

The film had finished some time before either noticed. The light grey screen illuminated the room just enough to see each other.

"We should hit the hay," Lucy whispered in her ear.

"Yes, the girls will be up early, especially Storm."

"She is a little lark, isn't she?" laughed Lucy as she climbed off of the sofa and helped Nicole up. The brunette placed her own hands on her breasts and squeezed. Lucy raised an eyebrow.

Laughing Nicole added, "Sorry, they just feel...tender."

"Oh, well maybe we should leave second base to another time," Lucy answered, concerned that she might hurt her.

"It's fine, my period's probably due."

Lucy reached for Nicole's hand, eyes holding her gaze. "I want to sleep...with you?" she asked.

Nicole's chest rose and fell with every breath she took as she calmed herself. "I would like that too."

"Will the kids be okay about it?"

"I think so, the twins won't take any notice, and Storm, well she wants us to get married and call you Mommy, so I think we're safe to assume she won't have a problem with it." It really was that simple, this whole situation that had encapsulated Lucy was just so unassuming. The last 15 or more years had been so difficult to manoeuvre through, like walking through chewing gum. The constant thought that she was never destined for anything more than her sad lot in life had held such a tight grip on her that she had never assumed this kind of life could be hers. She followed as Nicole led them to the door of her bedroom.

"So, I am going to go and get changed then," Lucy said, pointing over her shoulder with her thumb to her room.

"Okay, I'll do the same in my room, then meet you in bed?"

"Sounds like a plan to me." Because she really wanted to enjoy waking up wrapped around Nicole this time.

Chapter Twenty-Eight

The one thing sure enough to wake you without fail is the sound of a 4-year old who has found the switch to turn on your electric keyboard and believes in their heart that they can play the thing just as well as you can. And it was to that exact scenario that Lucy and Nicole were both pulled from their slumber with a shocking awareness of noise infiltrating their ears.

Lucy stirred as the racket got louder. "Oh my God, really?" Nicole laughed into the crook of Lucy's neck. They were nestled together with arms and legs entangled. It was better than before. It was comfortable and Lucy wanted to stay this way, together. "I bet it's Summer." Lucy chuckled at the idea of the youngster banging her tiny fingers and fists across the keys. Her lips found solace against the soft raven hair that tickled her face. She kissed gently and sighed at the thought of having to leave this nest they had built during the night.

"You're going to have to start their music lessons and get them to a standard where they can at least play a tune." Nicole smiled as she climbed out of bed and grabbed her gown. She took a moment, all the noise in the background swimming out of focus as she stared down at Lucy, her hair all sleep-mussed, her eyes still sleepy. She looked different, lighter. Nicole bent, and with one knee resting on the bed, she kissed her. "I'm sorry, good morning."

"I don't mind if they all start like that, with a kiss." Lucy smiled up at her like a kid at Christmas. She reached up and slid her hand behind Nicole's nape. Raising up, she found the warmth of soft lips waiting for her.

The noise increased as it became clear that there were now two small people playing on the keyboard.

Nicole raised up and smiled. "I can't believe Storm is putting up with that." She moved off of the bed and towards the door. Looking back over her shoulder, she warned with a grin, "Don't move, I am coming back."

~E&F~

The noise ceased and Lucy breathed out the breath she was holding. She gave herself a little pinch to make sure she wasn't dreaming. As the door opened, she looked up expecting to see Nicole, but instead it was the mini version. Storm.

"Hey sweetheart, you're awake then?" Lucy said.

"Yeah." She lingered at the door. In her old life she wouldn't dare enter her parents' bedroom without permission.

Sensing the youngster's hesitation, Lucy put her fears to rest instantly. "You can come in ya know."

So she did. At lightning speed she was on the bed, bouncing with excitement. "Are you and Mom getting married?" she asked, kneeling in the space Nicole had vacated.

"Uh, not right now," Lucy answered, watching a small frown appear on Storm's face, the little crease between her brows in evidence. "Why?"

"Well...If you and Mommy were married then Mommy would sleep in here with you all the time, right?"

Lucy nodded, a little unsure where this whole conversation was headed, and wishing desperately that Nicole would reappear any minute to save her from whatever the next question was.

"Then, can I have Mommy's room?" She grinned, and Lucy breathed a sigh of relief. Was it really going to be this simple?

"I dunno, you might have grown up and moved out before that happens." Lucy giggled at the wide-eyed look of horror on the young girl's face. "Mummy might not want to marry me, and then what?"

"She will." She nodded her head furiously, an all-knowing grin appearing. "People that love one another get married," she stated matter-of-factly. "Everybody knows that, Luce."

"Is that so? Well, I think it might be a little while, so don't go getting your hopes up, okay?" Lucy explained. The little one spent a moment considering something before she smiled, grabbed a pillow, and threw it at Lucy. Laughing, they spent a few minutes in a pillow fight while Nicole stood at the door watching them.

"Don't just stand there woman, help me! I'm being attacked by a munchkin!" Lucy called out to Nicole as she bounced a soft pillow against Storm.

Nicole had no choice but to come to her rescue. Grabbing a spare pillow, she joined in too. Before they knew it, there were two more small munchkins joining in on the action as Rain and Summer came bursting through the door too.

"Okay, truce!" Lucy shouted while laughing too hard to even lift a pillow. "Truce."

Rain and Summer had no idea what a truce was, so they continued to bash pillows and giggle until they noticed everyone else had stopped. There was a lot of smiling going on lately, and it felt just the way a family should feel. Happy.

"Wow. So, what started that?" Nicole asked, out of breath and flushed from the unexpected exertion as she flopped down onto the bed and into the crook of Lucy's arm, an arm that instantly wrapped around her shoulder to pull her closer.

Both Storm and Lucy pointed to each other.

Chapter Twenty-Nine

The afternoon was flying by as they spent some more time just hanging out by the lake. It was a hot day, so hot that the twins were stripped off and running around half naked, and Storm was in her swimsuit, reading in her spot.

Lucy looked down at herself. She was wearing skinny jeans and a long-sleeved top. An outfit for autumn, not summer. She stood up and limped her way back to the cabin. Stripping quickly, she found an old bikini and slipped it on, amazed that it still fit. She pulled on her robe and just as casually strolled back outside to the same spot next to Nicole.

Only the lower part of her legs was visible. A long pink line drew down the length of her left leg, tiny dots on either side of it where the staples had held her skin together. She had red marks either side of her knee from where the metal cage rods had held her bones in place. It wasn't pretty. She stood there for so long that Nicole looked up at her, concerned.

"I...I'm gonna..." She looked at Nicole. Her eyes were sad, but determined, and she drew courage from the woman staring back at her. "I want you to see. I want you to know what you're getting."

"I know what I'm getting, Lucy." Nicole's eyes never left Lucy's. "We both have scars sweetheart, yours are just visible. They don't change who you are or why I am attracted to you." She reached out a hand and gently squeezed Lucy's arm. "But I understand how difficult this is for you, so you do what you have to."

Lucy nodded. "I just want to prepare you, ya know, because it's not...it's everywhere, okay? When I was on the bus and it flipped...I was trapped, and the glass, the tarmac, it all....and I don't want..." She blew out a breath. "I don't want...the first time, ya know, I don't want that to be the first time you see me."

"It's ok. Just show me." The kids were sitting quietly playing with pebbles and rocks. Storm was still reading her book. It was just Nicole looking at her. Looking at her with love, not pity. Looking at her with admiration and tenderness. She took a deep breath, preparing herself for the look of horror she was sure would imprint itself on Nicole's face when she finally saw Lucy and the full extent of her injuries. Nicole held her gaze as she slipped off the robe, and only when she thought Lucy was ready did she allow herself to look lower and take in the body on show to her.

Lucy wore a black bikini. The scarring that marked her shoulder went much lower, under the bra and out again at the bottom, down her torso to her hip and further still along her thigh. There was a crisscross of lines that smattered her torso area, her stomach. She turned slowly to allow Nicole's eyes to rake over the back side of her body. More and more marks and scars scattered across her soft skin in lines of pink. It was horrifying, not to look at per se, but because she could tell just by looking at them all of the pain that Lucy must have suffered. Her left arm from the elbow upward and across her shoulder blade looked as though she had been dragged across the ground (which she had). Her skin was puckered and torn where pieces of grit and tarmac had embedded themselves.

When Lucy had rotated all the way around and Nicole had seen all she needed to, there was a silence that Lucy expected. What she didn't expect was for Nicole to lean forward and place her lips against the rough patch of puckered skin that peppered her side. Her fingers traced the thick lines as her lips moved softly against her skin.

"Okay?" Lucy asked. It was a rhetorical question rather than an actual one. She was okay. That was her biggest issue right now. She had shown Nicole almost everything, and she was okay with it. Lucy was used to it; her scars didn't bother her anymore to look at them. That was never her problem, well not for years anyway. Her issue had always been dealing with other people's reactions to them. The questions and the pitying look she would get.

"Oh yeah... I am fine. Enjoying the view," Nicole said, smiling against her skin.

Lucy was lost in the feeling of being home. Nicole hadn't run from her, and she was still enjoying the feeling of being touched for the first time in many years. She barely noticed when little fingers touched her hand. Looking down, she found the little blonde head of Rain looking up at her, her eyes wide as saucers.

"Can we play in the water?" she said quietly. She hadn't even noticed. This small child had looked at her, and yet not seen anything other than Lucy. To Rain, there was nothing to be frightened of.

"Yes, come on then." She let herself be led to the water. Summer ran across to join them, and the three of them splashed around, squealing at each other. Storm looked up from her book and smiled at them before putting her nose back into the pages and carrying on. Everything was just perfect.

Chapter Thirty

"You're not hot? It's boiling out here," Lucy said, drying herself off with the towelling robe she had used previously to hide behind. Laying it down on the floor, she plonked down on top of it and got comfortable next to Nicole, the only one of the group still in clothes.

"I'm good," Nicole replied, but she didn't look at Lucy as she spoke. Instead, she bit her lip and looked away, an air of discomfort about her.

"What's up?" Lucy probed gently.

"Nothing, I'm good," she said, quickly glancing over at the woman she loved. She smiled shyly and looked away again, her line of sight focusing out across the lake.

"No, you're not. I'm going to touch you," Lucy warned before reaching out to her. Fingertips gently pressed against her cotton-covered thigh. "It's a beautiful day, there is nobody around but us, and it is really hot, so, why don't you want to enjoy it?"

"I am. This is me enjoying." She sat back and took Lucy's hand in her own, her fingers squeezing gently.

"Alright, I'm not going to push, but I think you like looking at me in my bikini, it's only fair I get to see you," she said with a wink, kissing her hand just as Rain shouted that she had found a fish.

It turned out it wasn't a fish at all, it was just a candy bar packet that some lazy tourist had discarded without a thought for the environment. Lucy fished it out anyway and found the girls some nets so they could try and catch real fish, which they thought was one of the best ideas ever, especially when Lucy told them they could keep any fish they caught as pets.

When she turned around again, Nicole wasn't there. Her lips tightened into grimace and she really hoped she hadn't overstepped the mark when she had suggested changing into something cooler. It wasn't a surprise really that Nicole might have some issues with her own body image; she was married to a complete arsehole after all.

She sat back down on a towel in her customary pose of face to the sun and relaxed. It wasn't very long until she registered a presence next to her. She glanced sideways and saw Nicole sitting there very still, in her bikini.

"Wow," Lucy blurted out. "Where have you been hiding?" She continued looking Nicole up and down. Nicole blushed but smiled shyly at the compliment. "You really have no idea, do you?" said Lucy, astonished. Nicole sat there looking blankly at the ground; she really didn't. "Nicole, you..." She paused and leaned closer. "You are beautiful, stunning I mean... God, you're just gorgeous."

The dark-haired woman continued to stare at the ground, not knowing what to say. Compliments had been something few and far between these past few years, and when they had come, they had come in the shape of a drunken fumble, or when he wanted to show her off to his friends. Then she would be beautiful, amazing, such a wonderful mother or wife. Behind closed doors the compliments were less than appealing.

"You don't believe me, do you?" Lucy asked gently, watching as Nicole shook her head slowly. "It's okay, I am going to show you. Bit by bit, day by day, I am going to make you believe what I am saying because you are gorgeous, sweetheart."

"I am far from perfect, Luce," she said, her hand rubbing over her rounded tummy.

"Who wants perfect? I am not perfect, look at me," Lucy argued back, swivelling around to face her.

"Your scars are because of an accident, I am just..." She stopped speaking as tears threatened to overflow.

"You're what? What were you going to say?"

She shook her head and looked up to the sky, trying to ward off the tears. There were moments when she felt on top of the world. She felt like a normal, healthy part of society again, but then, there would be something that always pulled her back. Back to the life she had with Paul, where she was worthless.

"Tell me what you think is wrong with you."

Nicole swallowed hard; it was difficult to explain, but she wanted to. After everything that Lucy had put aside for her, she knew she had to try. "I...I'm not in the best shape, since having the kids I mean. I...I...need to get back to the gym, but..."

"Woah. Wait up." She reached over and caressed Nicole's face with a scarred hand. "You think...you're under the impression that you're overweight? That somehow the way you look isn't good enough?" She shifted onto her knees.

Nicole nodded furiously, glad to have finally gotten it out into the open so she could deal with Lucy agreeing with her and start working on shifting the pounds.

"Babe...god, no! No, sweetheart that is so wrong, so wrong!" Lucy said, cupping her face with both palms now so that she had to look at her. "That's just what he told you to make himself feel better, to keep you from leaving him. I promise you he is a liar."

"He said I am fat. That I was gross and not worthy of him, that he only slept with me out of duty." She sobbed now and fell into Lucy's arms. Storm looked up and was ready to run to her mother, but Lucy smiled and nodded at her. She had this. Storm nodded back and went back to reading her book, one eye still on them.

"Its ok babe, let it out." She held her close, knowing that she needed this to start the healing that she needed to do.

Chapter Thirty-One

Now that Lucy was finally re-emerging back into the world around her, she found that she was looking forward to doing things that before she would have shied away from. She would do the school run and not think twice about saying good morning to the other parents dropping their children off. People would now say hello to her as they passed by in the street rather than cross the road or stare at the woman they found difficult to understand. There had been a couple of pitiful looks or questions from inquisitive children, but she dealt with them and held her head up rather than hiding underneath her hat.

The agreement to take things slowly had seemed like the perfect idea once upon a time on a couch not that long ago. But now, as the days turned into weeks and the end of June was almost upon them, moments of intimacy were becoming a battle. Kissing was now a given, at any opportunity. With the heat holding, bikinis had become the norm on days that Nicole didn't have to work, and with the kids at school or with Rita, they had plenty of time to fool about and get to know one another more closely.

And now, with her confidence growing, Lucy was very keen to take Nicole on an actual date. She had spoken to Rita and she had readily agreed to look after the girls that night so that they could go out and have some fun. Nicole dropped them off at Rita's place around 7 p.m.

"Well, don't you all look cute?" Rita said as the girls filed through the door. Shouts of "bye Mom" and "see you soon" were hollered over shoulders as Summer and Storm made themselves at home in Rita's house.

"Mommy and Lucy are going out," Rain said, not understanding that Rita knew already.

"They are? Well, it's a good thing you're staying here with me then!" She smiled down and received a big grin in return.

The girls loved Rita; she had become like a surrogate aunt to them all. "You have a wonderful time with Lucy, we will be fine," she said to Nicole. "We have ice cream and that movie you've all been talking about," she said to the girls.

"Thank you, we shouldn't be too late in the morning to collect them."

"Don't you worry about it. Enjoy the freedom." She winked, and Nicole blushed before kissing her girls and making a hasty retreat.

~E&F~

Lucy was nervous. In her younger years, she had been the kind of woman who dated with all the confidence a pretty, happy-go-lucky girl in her prime should have. She was witty and cheeky, often trying her luck with girls who were out looking for a boyfriend. When she met Nicky though, everything changed in a heartbeat, and she no longer even looked at anyone else. She didn't need to; Nicky was all she wanted to look at. They had fun, going out to bars and clubs. When the band took off and Lucy became famous, it barely changed anything, they were just more discreet.

Now, as she waited for Nicole to return, she could feel the butterflies fluttering in her tummy. She couldn't sit still. She paced the room and checked her image in the mirror more than once. She had promised Nicole she wouldn't hide behind her hat, that if the people in town couldn't deal with her scars, then it was their issue, not Lucy's, and if people stared or asked questions then they would deal with it together because Nicole was proud to be seen out with Lucy.

Nicole arrived back from Rita's and wandered into the cabin to find Lucy waiting for her; she looked dashing, dressed simply in dark jeans and a red shirt, her long hair pulled up into a ponytail.

"You look great," Nicole said, walking up to her and kissing her quickly on the cheek, so proud that she wasn't hiding herself.

"Thanks, you look stunning though," she replied, taking Nicole in. She was wearing the customary little black dress, with legs that seemed to go on forever. She was a sight for anyone's sore eyes, but especially Lucy's. "Are you ready to go?"

"Yes!"

~E&F~

They shared a meal that was simple and yet, just perfect. And apart from a couple of people who stared at Lucy for a few seconds, nothing spoilt the time they were spending together. There was a time when anyone staring at Lucy would have had her running for the door to hide, but here, with Nicole holding her hand across the table and glaring at them, she actually found the whole thing quite funny. She had scars, she could deal with it; if it didn't put Nicole off, then she could deal with other people staring. After all, she liked it when Nicole stared at her.

They strolled through town back to the car hand in hand, sharing jokes and conversation as they went. It couldn't be more comfortable.

"So, Juicy Lucy?" she asked, smiling. "I never did get to the bottom of that."

Nicole blushed and tugged on her hand. "Okay, okay...I admit that I might have been telling Rita that I liked you."

"Uh huh, and why was that?"

"Because she asked. Apparently, it was obvious to more than just Storm, but she wasn't going to ask you in case it sent you scurrying back under your hat again." She giggled and felt herself being tugged to a halt. Just for a second, she zoned back to a time when she wasn't allowed to laugh or make fun and tease, but it was gone in an instant. The moment she looked at Lucy and into those honest eyes, she felt safe again.

"You okay?"

"Yes." She leaned in and kissed her.

The ride home was quiet as they each contemplated the next step in their relationship. For each of them there was a nervous outlook; for Lucy it had literally just been so long that she almost felt like a teenage virgin again. For the first few years after losing Nicky, she had concentrated only on getting better. Her recovery was slow and painful in every way, and the thought of ever having another relationship hadn't even entered her mind. Eventually, she considered it. She went on a few dates with women her friends set her up with, but she didn't feel any spark with them. All she could think about was how she was disrespecting Nicky. And then she met Megan. They were both using the same physiotherapist. Meg had fallen and damaged her knee ligaments. She was also blind and couldn't see the scars that covered Lucy. She was sweet, and Lucy had been able to enjoy spending time with her. It was fine until Lucy realised that she could see, just not with her eyes. Right then, Lucy knew she wasn't ready, and she hadn't been until now.

For Nicole, having been with someone as vile as Paul for the best part of the last decade meant that sex had connotations attached to it that she never wanted to think of again. To contemplate intimacy with anyone else had been unthinkable until these last few weeks. She knew though that being with Lucy was not going to be anything like being with him; it would be gentle and intimate, special. She knew Lucy would take care of her and she wanted it. Even though she had declared the need to go slowly, it had been a real difficulty to keep her libido from racing ahead. She could only hope that tonight would be the night.

"Do you want a drink?" Lucy asked as they entered the cabin. She moved around the room flicking lamps on, trying to calm herself. It wasn't that it was decided already that things would progress, and it might have been years since she had been in this situation, but she wasn't blind. She recognised all the signs of arousal in herself and in Nicole, and she was ready for this to go further. Scared, but ready.

Nicole watched her for a moment, noticing she was just as nervous, and decided to just take the bull by the horns. She moved closer to her, her eyes never leaving Lucy's. As she reached her, she placed her palms flat against her chest, sliding them up over her shoulders and around her neck, fingers tangling in her hair.

"No, I have everything I want right here," she whispered, leaning in for a kiss. A kiss that was instantly reciprocated.

"Everything?" Lucy asked, smiling and placing her hands around her waist, tugging her towards her.

"Mmm hmm," Nicole replied, smiling into the next kiss. Her fingers slid further into Lucy's hair, keeping her lips in place. "I think we should take this to the bedroom," she all but whispered, taking Lucy's hand and leading her to the room they had been sharing these past nights.

Nicole reached the bed and then turned to face Lucy, reaching her hand up behind her and pulling the zipper on her dress down. The dress loosened around her shoulders and she shimmied out of it, letting it fall slowly to the floor, leaving her standing clad in just her underwear, her almost black hair matching perfectly.

"You're so beautiful," Lucy whispered as she closed the distance between them and captured her lips once more. "So very beautiful."

Her touch was tender; everything about Lucy was loving and giving, and although apprehensive about being this vulnerable in front of her, Nicole knew she would be in good hands, and she wanted those hands to touch her, to caress her and to pleasure her in every way that was possible. She wanted to finally know what it felt like to be loved by someone so fully like she knew Lucy would love her.

"You can be loved by me, Lucy," she said solemnly. "And I know I can be loved by you."

Lucy brought her hand up to Nicole's cheek and stroked her skin. Once upon a time, that action by someone would have made Nicole flinch, but not now, not here, and not her.

She covered Lucy's hand with her own and kissed the palm. "Love me tonight?"

Feelings began to overwhelm Lucy. Her heart ached, but in a good way; a way that felt like it was mending. Her fingers tingled, and the need to touch Nicole made her tremble. Her fingers slid effortlessly through raven locks, inching ever closer until they were kissing. Their lips, like always, were so soft and pliable as they moved with ease against one another, parting slowly to deepen and bring forth a murmur of need and want.

"I will love you *every* night," Lucy whispered reverently. There would be no other option for her. She loved this woman, she knew that much now.

The buttons that held Lucy's shirt together were small and fiddly, but Nicole's deft fingertips worked quickly to release them from the security of their cotton cradle. She slid her palms beneath the soft material, her left hand skimming over smooth skin that was soft and yielding to her touch. Her right hand felt a polar opposite: flesh that was rough and hardened. Nicole used the back of her hands to slowly reveal Lucy as she pushed the scarlet material off of her shoulders. It caught on her biceps, but Nicole wasted no time in pushing the material down until it fell by its own volition to be forgotten on the floor. Lucy's eyes followed every movement, captivated by the way Nicole could spark such a desire within her. Every touch sent a shockwave of excitement and longing through her every cell.

She kissed Lucy along the scar that marred her beautiful face, down her neck and along her collarbone. Her lips, like her fingers, felt the change of smooth to rough skin. It didn't faze her. She was pulled upward, back to waiting lips that felt like home.

Breaking the kiss, Lucy took a moment to study Nicole. The swell of her breasts encased in lace, the soft roundness to her tummy all added to the beauty of her. She couldn't envisage ever thinking of her as anything less than beautiful.

Lucy climbed up onto the bed and then reached out her hand for Nicole to take, leading her to the centre of the mattress. On their knees, pressed thigh to thigh, breast to breast, they kissed once more as confidence began to surge through them both. Urgency bubbled beneath the surface, held back with a need to explore and enjoy this moment that they would never get back.

It wasn't difficult for Lucy to let her fingers explore, a skill long ago learnt; her instincts wouldn't fail her now. They stroked slowly down Nicole's tummy before dipping inside the band of her underwear, and when she heard the low, sensual moan that came from Nicole at her touch, she decided that it was unequalled by anything she had heard in a long time.

Their kiss deepened. Lucy felt the arc of electricity that shot between them as she slid gently inside of her, feeling Nicole's fingertips grip her shoulder with one hand as the other began its own search of skin to touch and stroke: a breast, her waist. Nicole couldn't think; all she could do was feel, feel the way in which Lucy was adoring her, touching her with tenderness. They were making love, that was the difference. That was what had always been missing: someone to make love to her. Someone who wanted her to enjoy the experience, to participate with her as they found pleasure together.

They collapsed side by side on the bed, smiles adorning both faces as they continued to caress and kiss, teaching one another in ways that until now either had barely considered possible.

"Are you okay?" asked Lucy, wanting to be sure that Nicole was comfortable with everything they were doing. Her eyes had misted over, and it had unsettled Lucy a little.

"God yes," Nicole gasped as she felt Lucy's fingers find a particularly sensitive spot along her torso. Her tears began to overflow as she shook her head. "Happy tears." They both laughed. "Nobody has ever..."

Lucy's smile widened as she understood what Nicole was trying to explain. She pulled her in tighter and hugged her closer, enjoying the feeling of this intimacy, the familiarity of it. "I will always treat you with care and respect," Lucy said gently into her hair as she sobbed quietly. "Always."

Nicole looked up and found Lucy's vibrant eyes. In them she saw everything she hoped Lucy was seeing in her own. Want, need, lust, love. She moved to kiss Lucy again, gently pushing her onto her back so she could show her how she felt. If it was indeed possible to show someone that they adored them and wanted them in every way possible, if there was a way to show Lucy just how much she was attracted to her and aroused by her, then she would find it.

Lucy's legs parted and allowed Nicole to settle her own trim thigh neatly between them. She was no expert, but she wasn't naïve; she knew what women could do together, and her imagination was in overdrive right now.

She kissed a path downwards, following the pattern of scars and mapping the areas that caused a whimper or a gasp from Lucy.

She wanted to find every way she could to give Lucy what she had given her. Using her knee to nudge apart Lucy's thighs further, she settled herself between them and used her mouth to bring pleasure so irrefutably immeasurable that Lucy could do little more than give herself over to her. Lucy felt lighter, as though she were floating and yet she was anchored, safely sheltered in the harbour of Nicole's love, an enclave that only she would ever bear witness to.

In the hours that followed, between bouts of sleep, they made love again, effortlessly slipping into each other's arms, healing together. When the sun began to rise and peak in through the window, Lucy found herself captivated by the woman sharing more than just her bed. Raven locks shone in the sunlight, a smile lazing on her sleeping face, and for once, everything felt right with Lucy's world.

Chapter Thirty-Two

She tried to disentangle herself from Nicole. Slipping her arm from around her waist was easy enough, but as she was just about to slide her other arm out from under her neck, Nicole tugged her back against her and sighed dreamily.

"Don't go anywhere, coffee can wait," Nicole demanded, her voice sleepy and gruff as she wrapped her leg around Lucy and held tight.

Lucy chuckled. "How did you know I was going to make coffee?"

"Because you can't live without coffee." She grinned and burrowed in, her arms wrapping around Lucy limpet-style.

"Ah, so you know my weakness already?" Lucy laughed and snuggled deeper under the covers, content to just lie there in this woman's arms for eternity if need be.

They lay together like that for a few minutes, just looking at each other, stroking arms and faces. Tender kisses spoke so much more than words could.

"Thank you," Nicole whispered, her tone suddenly serious.

"There is no need for thank you unless we're both saying it," Lucy replied in all earnestness. She hadn't woken up feeling this light and happy in so many years; it was all so foreign to her. She felt like she wanted to jump out of bed, climb on the roof, and shout it out to anyone that could hear.

"Okay, you can make your coffee now," Nicole said, kissing her shoulder and moving to allow her out of the bed.

"You want one?"

"No, I dunno what's wrong with me lately, but the smell of it just makes me feel nauseous." She grimaced even at the thought of it.

"Oh, well I won't have one then." Lucy smiled, turning so she could snuggle back in.

"Don't be silly, it's your morning drink. Go on, I'll have a glass of orange juice, and can you bring me some of those peanuts?" Lucy jumped out of bed and padded naked to the kitchen. It was a little bit weird not having the kids here, but it was nice to have that moment of freedom like she used to have, of just being able to stroll around butt naked if she wanted to.

"Peanuts?" she mumbled to herself with a quiet chuckle.

She made the coffee and poured the juice. Searching the cupboards, she found the peanuts that Nicole wanted and placed them all on a tray. Carefully she carried it all through and placed it down on the bedside table beside Nicole. The brunette suddenly lurched upwards and ran to the bathroom, where she promptly threw up.

Lucy followed in after her and aided her in her distress, holding her hair out of the way and stroking her back.

"Oh god, I am so sorry," Nicole said between bouts of vomiting.

"Hey, you can't help being unwell, though I am not sure what could have caused it."

"So embarrassing, I am really sorry," she said, sitting up. She instantly felt much better. Lucy passed her a washcloth to wipe her face. "It's the coffee, I took one sniff and..." She closed her eyes and tried to fight off the need to vomit again.

"I'll go get you some water, why don't you lay down for a moment?" Helping her to her feet and back into bed, Lucy disappeared quickly before she returned with a glass of cool water from the fridge and watched as Nicole took a long sip and thanked her for it.

"Feeling any better?"

"I'm not sure, I was fine and then the smell, it just hit me." The colour had returned a little to her cheeks, but she still looked a little peaky in Lucy's opinion.

"Might be a 24-hour bug or something. Why don't you stay in bed and I'll go and get the girls, then if you're up to it we can have some breakfast." Pulling on some sweatpants and a t-shirt, Lucy readied herself to make a quick trip.

"Okay, I don't really feel up to arguing," she said. Suddenly she went pale again and rushed back to the bathroom.

"Maybe I should just call Rita and ask her to keep the girls for a little longer?" Lucy suggested as she soaked the washcloth in cool water again and wiped it across the back of Nicole's neck. "I don't want to leave you."

"Aww, you're so sweet, ya know that? I'll be fine, I promise, I'm a mom, I'm used to sickness." The smile was genuine, but Lucy still felt torn.

"Are you sure?" Lucy looked so concerned that Nicole thought it might be the sweetest thing she had ever witnessed. Paul would never have sat with her and helped her like this. He would have screamed at her, told her how gross she was and to clean herself up before she came back out. Her eyes closed at the image of her husband looming over her, his face contorted, red and angry. She shook the image away, focused on the warmth of the hand that was rhythmically stroking down her spine. When she opened her eyes again, she found love staring back at her with apprehension.

"I'm okay, I promise. Get the girls and I'll grab a shower and be right as rain by the time you get back."

Chapter Thirty-Three

Arriving at the store, Lucy found Rain and Summer sitting on their haunches down the middle aisle placing tins the right way up along the bottom shelf. Lucy had never seen the shelves look so neat.

"Child labour back?" Lucy joked as she rounded the counter to find Storm at the till. Pushing her glasses back up her nose, she looked up at Lucy and grinned.

"Rita said I can have a job when I'm old enough."

"Oh, right...well that's good." Lucy glanced around and found Rita smiling over at her from the deli counter. She finished serving her customer and then headed straight for Lucy, wiping her hands with a cloth that she dropped into a trash bin.

"Hey, have a good time?" she asked, smiling as the blush rose easily on Lucy's cheeks.

"Uh, yeah," she answered. She reached up and rubbed the back of her neck as embarrassment crept across her skin. "So, the uh...they behave?" She jutted her chin in the direction of the twins and changed the subject, much to Rita's amusement.

"Sure did. We had a great time. Wanna cup of coffee while you tell me all about your night?" She was already moving out back to put the kettle on.

"Actually, I need to get back, Nicole isn't feeling well."

"Oh, what's the matter with her?" Rita asked before Storm chipped in too.

"Is Mommy okay?"

Lucy reached out a hand and stroked her hair. "Yeah, she's fine...just a little upset tummy I think." And then to Rita she added, "She was sick this morning."

"Maybe something she ate?"

"Maybe, but we mostly ate the same things, so..." She shrugged her shoulders and scratched her head. "Anyway, thank you so much for having them."

"Anytime, Lucy," Rita replied. "Grab some chicken soup, that'll help settle her stomach I am sure."

~E&F~

The girls were super excited. They talked non-stop all the way home about the fun they had had with Rita, and Lucy couldn't hold back the smile at their exuberance.

"Can we go outside when we get back?" Storm asked from her seat between the twins.

"Sure, I just want to check on Mummy and then we can go for a walk maybe, how does that sound?"

Thankfully, Nicole was up and dressed and looking much healthier when they all piled in through the door. Lucy's eyes searched her out in an instant. Her skin was back to its natural golden glow, and she was drinking some orange juice while standing at the sink.

"Hey beautiful, how ya feeling?" Lucy placed the back of her hand against her forehead to check for a temperature, but she felt fine.

"Much better, thank you." She smiled up at Lucy.

"You don't feel hot, so that's good, right?"

"Yeah, I think I'll be okay. You want some bacon and eggs?"

"I do, but I am going to make it, and you are going to sit down over here with the munchkins." She laughed as she guided her to a seat next to Storm. The girls were very excited to tell her about the fun they had had with Auntie Rita, as she was now being called by all three of them.

"Are we having pancakes?" Summer asked hopefully, her little face all lit up like a kid at Christmas.

"Well, I don't know," Lucy said in all seriousness. "Have you been good while you were at Rita's?"

"Uh huh," she said nodding her head furiously.

"Then you can have pancakes!" she said, placing a finger on the child's nose. She watched with delight as Summer smiled the biggest smile back at her.

"Yay!"

Lucy got all the ingredients out and started to whisk up the pancake mix while the bacon cooked under the grill. She poured more coffee and got the girls some juice, and then Nicole sprinted to the bathroom again.

"What's wrong with Mommy?" asked Storm, concerned.

"I think she has a bug." Lucy replied.

"Ew, Mommy been eating bugs?!!" Rain shouted, to which Summer also started making grossed-out noises.

"Girls, can you be a little bit calmer today while Mummy is unwell?" Lucy asked them quietly as Nicole walked back into the kitchen.

"Sorry, God I haven't felt like this since I was...." She stopped mid-sentence and covered her mouth with her hand.

"Since when?" Lucy said, chomping down on some toast as she turned back to face her. She looked ghostly pale again.

"Since I was..." Nicole tried to speak, but the words wouldn't come. Her mind was going around in circles as she tried to fathom out what was wrong with her.

Lucy turned the gas down and was about to close the distance between them. "Nic? What's wrong?"

Nicole shook her head to shake the thoughts out from it. "Oh, I'll tell you later," she said trying to cover her anxiety with a smile. Lucy worried and watched her for a moment as a frown slowly appeared, but the girls all started talking at once and Nicole's attention was drawn back to them.

~E&F~

Lucy spent the rest of the morning trying to keep the girls entertained, making sure that Nicole rested and drank lots of fluids. Storm had been practising her singing for a little while and was getting quite good now. She had a nice voice, and with a little help from Lucy, she had managed to correct the few issues she had with projection. By the time the girls went back to school, Lucy was sure that Storm would be confident enough to sing the song her teacher had planned for her.

After lunch, while Nicole took a nap, she had then taken them all for the promised walk around the lake, pointing out flowers and birds to them. The twins were intrigued by all kinds of things, and Lucy loved their inquisitive little minds and all the questions they came up with, often making her giggle at the simplicity of it all.

Storm was unusually quiet as they walked, so when the twins were occupied with picking Mommy some flowers, Lucy broached it.

"You're very quiet."

Storm looked up at her and shrugged.

"Anything you wanna talk about?"

She shrugged again. Lucy became concerned then that maybe her relationship with Nicole wasn't going to be quite so easy with the eldest as they had thought, even if she had been so excited about it to begin with. There was a small bench coming up and she guided them all towards it, sitting with Storm while the twins continued with the task of searching out things.

"So, what's up?" Lucy said. There was silence for a moment before Storm finally opened up.

"I wanted to know something, but I don't know how to ask," she said, her little nose scrunched up as she thought about it some more.

"Oh, well firstly, do I have the answer?" Lucy asked, and Storm nodded slowly. "Then you can ask me anything."

"I know I can, but I don't know how to."

"You just say it. That's the easiest way," Lucy stated simply. She waited and knew eventually that Storm would find a way. But it wasn't anything she was expecting.

"I know you said you had an accident." Lucy nodded. "And that's where you got the scar on your face." Lucy nodded once again but kept quiet, letting Storm get to her point. "But...how? What kind of accident?"

Lucy took a breath and considered how to answer that appropriately. "Well, a long time ago I used to be in a band."

"Like a pop band?" Lucy nodded, and suddenly Storm's eyes widened in surprise, "Cool...are you famous?" She grinned, and Lucy couldn't hide her own grin. Images flashed in her head of a time long ago, on stage: the lights, the noise from the crowd.

"A long time ago I was, yes." Storm's eyes lit up even more at the news, but Lucy continued before more questions threw her off her train of thought. "So, one day we came off stage and we had to get on the tour bus and head to the airport." Storm sat quietly, listening to every word. "Well, as we were travelling really fast on the motorway, there was a car that was being driven by someone who got confused about which lane he should be in and we swerved to avoid him, but...we ended up in an accident." She didn't feel the need to go into details, but Storm wanted them.

"So, how did you get all the other scars?" Lucy had always thought it too good to be true that none of the kids had mentioned them that day on the lake. She was unsure exactly how much she should divulge to an eight-year-old.

"When the bus swerved, it toppled over and...I was injured when the bus slid along the road on its side." Storm thought for a moment before asking her next question.

"Did it hurt?"

"I don't remember. Sometimes when things happen a long time ago we learn to forget the pain. I suppose it probably did, but I was in a long sleep while I healed, so that helped," Lucy explained, adding a small smile to lighten the mood. When Storm spoke next it almost broke Lucy's heart.

"Do you think when I am old, what Daddy did won't hurt me anymore?" Storm stared at her feet, dangling back and forth in the air. Lucy lifted her up and onto her lap, her arms wrapping tightly around her.

"I think that we will find a way to make sure that he doesn't hurt you ever again. You're safe now, you know that, right?"

Storm nodded. "But what if he comes back again, like last time?"

"Then Mummy and I will make sure he goes away again," Lucy said, squeezing her a little harder. Every fibre of her body wanted to protect this child, this family.

"But... he always hurts mommy."

"I won't let him. I promise you right now. Your daddy will never lay another finger on you or Mummy, okay?" Storm smiled, nodding her head.

Chapter Thirty-Four

Nicole took advantage of them all being out of the house and instead of the planned nap, she had popped into town. She picked up some sickness relief and got the makings of dinner. Rita had been insistent on her sitting down for a cup of coffee so she could fill her in on all the details from their date, but that just made her feel ill again.

When they returned from their walk, the twins were virtually falling asleep on their feet, so Lucy tucked them into bed for a quick nap, while Storm settled on the couch to watch some TV.

Nicole was in what had rapidly become *their* bedroom.

Lucy knocked lightly on the door before entering. The curtains were closed and she could see the shape of Nicole lying on the bed facing away from her. So, she backed out quietly and left her for a little while longer.

"What ya watching?" she asked, flopping down beside Storm on the couch.

Without looking up she said, "A re-run of *Into the Night.*" Lucy said nothing and watched along with her for a while. It was a cop show. After a while, Storm decided to fill her in on some of the characters. "That's Andi Stark, she's my favourite."

"Yeah? Why's that?" Lucy asked. The actress that played her was a little like Nicole. Dark hair and tanned skin, tall and quite frankly, gorgeous. Lucy became more interested.

"I dunno, she's just tough and she always helps people that are in trouble. I wanna be like that."

"I think you already are," Lucy said, kissing the side of her head. "I'm going to go and check on Mummy again, okay?" Storm just nodded, her eyes not leaving the screen.

~E&F~

"Hey gorgeous, are you awake?" Lucy whispered as she closed the door quietly behind her. She sat down on the edge of the bed. With no response from her lover, she laid herself behind Nicole, wrapping an arm gently around her. There was nothing she loved more than being able to do this, to pull her close and hold her in her arms. "Are you okay?"

She could feel the telling signs of crying, Nicole's shoulders twitching lightly as she sobbed quietly.

"Nic, what's wrong? Are you still feeling unwell?"

Nicole turned suddenly and burrowed into Lucy muttering how sorry she was.

"Come on now, there's nothing to be sorry about when you're not well."

"I'm not ill," she sobbed, her voice cracking with emotion as her grip tightened.

"Okay, well whatever it is, it won't last forever," Lucy countered as Nicole sobbed harder.

"It will... oh god," she wailed. Her fingers tightened around the material of Lucy's shirt as she pulled her closer, feeling the need to have a firm hold on reality because right now, it was like living in a nightmare that never ended.

"Nic? It's just a bug, that's all," Lucy said, pushing her hair away from her face. She swiped her thumb across her cheek and wiped the tears away. Nicole's eyes were filled with fear before she hid in the crook of her neck once more.

"I'm pregnant," Nicole whispered against her flesh. Lucy froze.

"Say that again, you're kind of muffled down there," she said, laughing it off because her hearing was clearly playing tricks on her.

Nicole sat up and tried to quell her sobs. Wiping her eyes and taking a deep breath, she repeated what she had just said. "I'm pregnant, Lucy."

"Okay, I know last night was pretty great, but even I can't get you pregnant." She laughed as Nicole sobbed once more. "Sweetheart, talk to me. Why do you think you're pregnant?" If it wasn't for the fact that Nicole was so upset, she would assume this was a prank.

"Because this said so," she said gravely as she lifted the plastic implement: a pregnancy test.

"Alright, but they can be wrong."

The brunette reached behind her and pulled out a further two from the bedside drawer, and all of them had the same blue line indicating she was definitely pregnant. To say Lucy was shocked would be the understatement of the century. Those words were not ones she had ever imagined hearing from a lover, but she *had* just heard them and now she felt, what did she feel? Sick? Saddened? Hurt?

"H-how?" Lucy asked as her face fell and her heart broke a little bit. How could she be pregnant unless Nicole had...no. She couldn't even think that during all this time of them becoming closer that she had been seeing someone else.

"No, don't you think that! I haven't cheated on you," Nicole cried out, reading Lucy like a book. Not that it would be cheating per se, but the last few weeks they had definitely been building towards what happened last night, even if nothing had been said between them until recently. She could see the hurt in Lucy's eyes as she imagined just how she had become pregnant.

Nicole sat up. "Then how? How do you become pregnant without...?" Lucy couldn't even say it. She couldn't even begin to imagine it.

"I can't, I don't want to talk about it." Nicole shut down, closed her eyes and wrapped her arms around herself, hugging her knees to her chest.

"Really?" Lucy stood up and paced the room. "You tell me that you're...." More pacing. "After last night!" she said incredulously.

She pushed the fingers of both hands through her hair and sagged against the door. She felt empty, heartbroken. Her world was crashing around her and she couldn't understand why.

"Please, Lucy!" Nicole begged while sobbing. "Please don't make me tell you."

His hands were touching her as he hovered menacingly above, fingers gripping her thigh as he roughly shoved them apart and forced himself lower. "You'll do what I want, when I want." His breath stank of stale beer as he breathed all over her. She couldn't move. The stench of his cologne mixed in with the beer and sweat made her nauseous. His weight held her in place until he rose up, flipping her over. She was trapped.

"I shouldn't have to make you tell me...you're pregnant and I sure as hell didn't get you that way. So how?" She sat back down on the bed and took her hand. She didn't want to be angry; she needed to understand. There was something going on here that didn't fit, and she needed to know why Nicole now looked as though she was terrified. She changed the tone of her voice. More softly now, she asked again, "Nicole, what are you not telling me?"

She watched Nicole as she closed her eyes and took several deep breaths to calm her sobs. The look of fear and shame on her face was almost too much for Lucy to bear.

He was ripping her underwear away. She could hear the sound so clearly, and when he forced himself inside her, the searing hot pain caused her to cry out. "That's right bitch, beg for it," he had snarled.

"Paul forced himself onto me." And there it was, the last part of her story out in the open. The part she had desperately tried to forget. The part she had refused to think about.

"He, he raped you?" Lucy said in disgust. The more she learned about this man, the more she wished him harm. Her eyes fixed on Nicole. She wanted to leave this room, this home and track him down, but she pushed the anger down, held herself steady and calm. She would be the person Nicole needed her to be. She would never be like him.

Nicole nodded slowly, all the while watching Lucy for any sign she was disgusted by her. Instead, she felt strong arms wrap around her and pull her in close, a soothing motion of hands down her back, and lips that kissed her hair. The silence settled between them.

"He never...before, he never did that before." She cried more quietly now. "I knew then that I had to get out. I couldn't let him...not again. A-a-and I...with Storm." She shook her head vehemently. "I couldn't stay anymore."

"You did the right thing." Lucy held her tighter. "We're going to get through this." She didn't say that it would be okay, because she didn't know, but she knew they would find a way through it. They stayed that way for a while, both contemplating what this news meant for each of them individually, as well as a couple. "You're pregnant?" Lucy whispered again. It really was unbelievable. She was already overwhelmed by all the change that had taken place so far: three kids running around the house, making noise and dragging her slowly back into the real world again; a woman who wanted to love her and be loved by her; and now, now another life would be joining them. It was all so surreal.

Nicole nodded slowly again. "Yes." A whisper. "And I understand that you will want to—" She didn't get to finish what she planned to say because Lucy cut her off.

"That I will want to raise this child with you?"

"What?"

"If you want to have it I mean, you have to decide what you want to do, but I will raise this child with you," Lucy said to her again. "Do you want to have it?"

"I...I don't know. I hadn't thought that far. I was too concerned with you leaving me."

"Why would I leave you? I..." She took Nicole's hand in her own and studied the way their fingers naturally interlinked. Her eyes raised back to Nicole's before she continued, saying words she once thought she would never say again. "I love you. And I will love this child like I love your other children."

Nicole gasped. Her eyes misted in an instant as Lucy's words imprinted themselves on her heart. She was a pregnant woman with three children, a violent husband making threats, and here was this woman just loving her, unconditionally.

Chapter Thirty-Five

"Do you know what I think?" Lucy said as they lay in bed together that night. Nicole was lying on her back and Lucy had her head resting on her chest, her fingers stroking lightly over her stomach. She was relaxed and calmed by the soothing rise and fall of Nicole's chest as she breathed in and then out.

"What honey?" she said gently as she pulled her fingers lazily through Lucy's hair.

"If two women could create a child, then we would have done so last night when we made love. So, let's just pretend we did, let's pretend this is my child, our child, a child we made from love," she said, not lifting her head. Her fingers stroked the area where somewhere beneath, life was growing.

"I think that I would like to do that," Nicole said, her throat constricting around the solid lump of emotion that grew whenever Lucy said anything lately. She moved her fingers through Lucy's hair again and felt her heartbeat quicken. She couldn't imagine her life without this gentlewoman in it any longer.

"And I think you need to get a doctor to confirm things...and that you should report him to the police, and file for divorce." Her fingers stilled as she waited for Nicole to answer. "If you want to, of course."

Nicole thought it through; the idea of going to the police terrified her. He terrified her. "He won't give me one."

"Then we will go to court and force him to."

"I can't afford to do that."

"I can... and I won't hear another word about money Nic, if we are raising a family and are going to be a couple, then you are going to have to deal with spending my money," Lucy said, as she repositioned herself so she could look at Nicole. Her hand stilled but remained protectively against Nicole's abdomen.

"He will drag it out and it will cost a fortune," Nicole implored. She wasn't sure she had the courage to face him just yet, to go to war with him.

"Nicole, I made more money than I need when I was in the band. It has sat in my bank account for all these years and I barely touched it. We can beat him," she said, pleading with her to trust her on this. "Otherwise my only option is to kill him," she said it with a smile, but she was only semi joking.

"Now, that's an idea I like!" Nicole said, laughing. "But only if you don't get caught, I don't want to lose you." It was difficult for her. She had spent the last ten years with a man who didn't allow her to have any access to money unless it was acceptable to him and necessary, and now she was involved with someone who willingly wanted her to spend money that wasn't her own.

"Oh, I have no plans to get caught." Lucy's lips were compelled to kiss her; there was no other option. Her body was responding to something within her that was innate. Her attraction to Nicole was something she had no control over. "Do you know how sexy you are?" Lucy whispered between kisses.

"I know how sexy I feel when you kiss me like that." Her breathy reply came naturally, her heart rate quickened, and her body reacted to the touch of her lover's fingers instantly.

"Yeah? I want you to always feel sexy."

"Then you had better keep kissing me then, hadn't you?" Nicole smiled into the kiss and enjoyed the sensations she was feeling throughout her entire body. Every cell was alive and every nerve ending tingled as she submitted to their carnal urges, allowing Lucy to make her feel sexy and confident and loved.

Chapter Thirty- Six

The school summer holidays began at the end of June. Nicole had made a lot of plans, and the three children were eager to enjoy it all for a change. So when Lucy came back from a trip into town one evening, the last thing she expected to find was Storm lying on her bed, inconsolable because Lucy's friends had died.

Learning from Lucy that she had been famous once had piqued Storm's interest. So, she had used her laptop and googled all about Lucy to find out everything about the band and the accident.

"But it's so unfair Mom," Storm cried.

"I know sweetie, but accidents happen and people we love are sometimes lost to us," Nicole tried to explain. She looked up and found Lucy standing in the doorway watching the scene in front of her. Nicole beckoned her in. At first, she hesitated, unsure if her presence was going to help or hinder, but Nicole just held her hand out to her, and so she trusted her judgement. Storm noticed the change in the room and looked around. She reached out her arms for Lucy, and when the older woman pulled her close, she wrapped herself limpet-like around her.

"Hey, what's going on?" Lucy soothed as the little girl clung to her. Nicole stood next to them, one hand rubbing gently back and forth against Lucy's back. With Storm tucked into the crook of her neck, Lucy kept talking. "Do you want to ask me more questions?" She felt a small nod and figured this was going to be more comfortable sitting down in the living room.

"So, what do you want to know?" Lucy asked, seating them both on the couch with Storm now sitting in her lap. Her big brown eyes, so much like her mother, were teary and wet as she blinked several times to clear them.

"I don't know, just...it makes you sad," she answered. Her fingers stroked down the scarred cheek in front of her. Lucy choked up a little. The idea that this little girl could be so clued up on the world around her and the people in it astounded her.

"Ya know, you're right. It does make me sad, but d'ya know what else?" Storm shook her head. "Every day that I get to spend with you and your sisters and your mum," she caught Nicole's eye and smiled, "makes me a little bit happier."

"Really?" Eyes wide as saucers, her face began to light up a little.

"Yeah," she nodded. "So, ya see sometimes things happen in our lives that make us sad, but it always gets better."

"Even for me?"

"Especially for you." She tapped Storm's nose playfully. "You're happier now, right?" The little one nodded. "See, things change. People come and go, but it's all okay. We end up where we're supposed to be."

"And I'm supposed to be here, with you?"

261

Lucy nodded. "Yep, right here with me and your Mum."

For the rest of the evening, Lucy had a shadow: Storm. Anywhere that Lucy went, Storm followed. If Lucy sat down to watch TV, Storm sat as close to her as she could possibly get and snuggled into her. Lucy didn't complain; she wrapped an arm around her and pulled her in closer.

When Lucy moved to the kitchen to cook dinner, it was Storm who helped peel potatoes and butter bread. Nicole tried to help, but they both insisted that she put her feet up.

"We got this, Mom," Storm said, smiling at Lucy. Lucy nodded her agreement.

Nicole wasn't going to argue with them. She loved watching her girls work together. She giggled to herself at the thought of Lucy as one of her girls, but she was. From her vantage point on the couch, she watched the two of them as they got all the vegetables ready, playfully pushing each other and joking around together as they worked. Storm was happy. There would be moments when Storm would find things difficult, question her place in the world, but time and love would one day win over, she was sure of it.

"Mommy!!!" screeched Rain from her bedroom. Nicole got up as fast as she could. Lucy and Storm both stopped what they were doing and stared towards the bedroom.

"Rain?" Nicole said urgently. "What is it?"

"Mommy!!" she screamed again, running from the room until she crashed against her mother's legs, wrapping her arms around them. "There's a spider!"

Nicole laughed hard. If this was the worst torment her young daughter had in the world, then she was happy too. "Okay, I'm coming...where is it?"

Chapter Thirty-Seven

Nicole had finally been to the doctor's and had her pregnancy confirmed a couple of weeks earlier. By mid-July, she was at the end of her first trimester, the safe zone. She and Lucy had discussed telling the girls and Rita, because they all needed to know. It was going to be several odd conversations, but conversations they needed to have; Nicole's belly was now beginning to show signs that she was expecting.

It was a quiet time of the day, and the girls traipsed along behind them. Holding Nicole's hand, Lucy led them into the store. The girls quickly rushed past them both and into the back room where Rita kept some games and a TV for moments like now when they needed to be entertained.

"Hey, guys," Rita said cheerily.

"Hi," replied Nicole and Lucy simultaneously.

"So, what's the big news you needed to talk to me about?" she asked, glancing from one to the other. They were sweet together in Rita's opinion, and she was so grateful for Nicole and the girls coming into Lucy's life.

Nicole looked at Lucy, who raised an eyebrow and grinned. "This is your show, Nicole," Lucy said gently.

"Yes." Nicole nodded and looked around, a little nervous now that the spotlight was on her. "I just don't really know where to start." She tried to smile, but it didn't quite reach her eyes. She had come a long way in these last few weeks and months, but her life before this was still difficult to talk about.

They waited patiently for her to find her words. Rita passed them both some lemonade and Nicole began to tell her story: how she met a man and fell in love, a man that was every girl's dream, only he turned out to be a nightmare. She told Rita of the beatings and the emotional abuse; she talked about the times he would hurt her and how eventually he began to hurt Storm. She explained his gambling and how he had used all of her money to pay his debts and continue to bet, that when it went wrong she would become his punch bag. How she finally made the terrifying decision to leave him after he forced himself on her and now, when she was constantly watching over her shoulder, he had found them and hurt her again.

Rita wiped away a tear. "Good God, Nicole! I...God, I don't know what to say." Rita's expression was one of sympathy and admiration. That someone could go through all that she had and still come out smiling at the other end amazed her.

"That's not all," Nicole said quietly, watching as Rita sat as still as she had ever seen her. "I've since discovered that I'm pregnant."

Rita's eyes went wide with surprise. "Pregnant?" She was about to ask how it was possible, but then she realised and understood. "Oh Jesus, are you-?"

"Happy? Yes." She grinned as she looked towards her partner. "Lucy and I are going to raise this baby." Lucy returned the grin as she considered once again the fact that she would be raising a family. She would be a parent; it was still so foreign to her. Sometimes she felt like it was someone else that Nicole was talking about, but then she would catch Nicole smiling at her and she would remember just how excited she was about the prospect of it.

"Then I am happy for you both," she said to the pair of them. Lucy's grinning face was seemingly stuck in place.

"I am going to go to a lawyer and start divorce proceedings, but first I need to explain things to the girls and put Sherriff Jenkins in the picture in case he returns," Nicole said worriedly. The thought of Paul returning really did fill her with dread; he was so unpredictable.

"This community won't allow him to come here and terrorise you, Nicole," Rita said seriously, taking her in her arms. "You're one of us now."

Chapter Thirty-Eight

They took the girls for pizza; not just any pizza, but Joey's pizza at Joey's Parlor, the best pizza this side of California and possibly the best pizza full stop if you had asked Storm.

With a lot of chattering and laughter, their table was certainly the place to be. When Andrea, their waitress, placed bowls of ice cream on the table, Nicole took the opportunity to get the girls' attention.

"So, Lucy and I wanted to talk to you all about something important," she said, looking around the table at her brood. Each pair of eyes set on her with smiling faces mostly covered in tomato sauce. They were all so beautiful and carefree, considering everything they had all been through.

"You love Lucy? We know, Mom," Storm said while rolling her eyes. Her spoon dug deep into the ice cream and came up loaded. She opened wide and shovelled it in.

Lucy blushed and giggled, which earned her a look from Nicole that said, 'please be serious.' She regained her composure and spoke up. "And you're all okay with that then?"

Three heads nodded in unison along with mutters of "yes," "yep," and "hmm mmm" as ice cream continued to be shovelled into three eagerly waiting mouths.

"Okay then. Over to you again." Relaxing back into her seat, she smiled at Nicole.

"Thanks, so as much as I am pleased that you are all happy with that issue, I actually have something else I need to tell you all." She took a breath and looked at each of them one by one, all three keenly awaiting their mother's announcement. "Alright so, here's the thing. I...well we...Lucy and I...well...." She struggled to find the right words and looked to Lucy for help.

"What your mum is trying to tell you is that we are having a baby," Lucy said clearly and easily to them.

"A baby?" Rain said loudly, causing Nicole to sweep her eyes around the restaurant hoping nobody heard that. Why she cared, she wasn't sure.

"A real baby that we can play with?" asked Summer, her eyes wide with excitement at the prospect of another plaything.

Storm was yet to speak and that worried Nicole a little, but she persevered with the conversation. "Yes, a real baby." She said smiling as Lucy took her hand in her own and squeezed.

"What do you think, Storm?" Lucy asked. She too had noticed the lack of comment from the eldest so far. Storm continued to push her spoon into her ice cream and then watch it fall off and splat into the dish before doing it again. "Storm? This baby is an addition to our family, not a replacement," Lucy said as she moved around the table to sit with her.

"You will still have time to play with me and do singing and stuff?" she asked, a little teary.

"Of course I will, sweetheart. This doesn't change anything, it just means we have more love to share around," Lucy explained. Storm took the opportunity to look her in the eye and check she was being true to her word.

"You promise?"

"I swear on my life that I will never, ever forget about you and we will always have our time to do the things we do together," Lucy said solemnly. "We are a family, Storm. I love you, your mum loves you, and everything we do is because of you and your sisters."

"Where is the baby going to sleep?" Storm asked.

"With me!" shouted Rain as she giggled. Nicole smiled at her daughter. Such a happy child in general, she lit up every room she entered with her smiles and giggles.

"Well, that was the other thing we wanted to talk to you about. I am going to move my things into Lucy's room and then Storm, you can have my room. And the baby will sleep in with Lucy and me for the first few months just like each of you did until he or she is big enough, and then we will have to reconsider things." Lack of space in the cabin was going to be an issue at some point. "But...."

"I get a room of my own?" Storm gasped, excitedly interjecting.

"Yep, how does that sound?" Nicole asked her, knowing full well she was about to go supernova on the excitement scale.

"My own room again! Can I paint it and have posters and friends over, can I have a TV? Can I?" She was cut off by a laughing Lucy.

"Okay, sunbeam, let's see how things go once we have moved it all around first, alright?"

"Ok!!! But I am officially planning my new painting scheme." She beamed her 100-watt smile, dazzling. She looked so much like her mother, it amazed Lucy. "I can't wait."

Chapter Thirty-Nine

When they returned home, Storm made a beeline straight for her new bedroom and threw herself onto the bed. She jumped up and down on it with the biggest smile on her face. Meanwhile, the twins ran around the cabin from room to room with their dolls, talking to each other about diaper changes and feeding times. It was a whirlwind of noise and movement. Lucy took a moment to just stand in the centre of the chaos and absorb it all and revel in it.

"Okay, your kids are officially nuts," Lucy said, smiling across the room at Nicole. The brunette returned the smile instantly. She still had to pinch herself at times that this was now her life, that her kids could just run around screaming and singing and being kids without any of them worrying that violence would be the final result or hiding in their beds with their hands over their ears to block out Mommy's scream. All of that was gone now. What they had now was beyond any dream she had ever had.

"It's taken this long for you to notice?" Nicole chuckled. Her hand automatically rubbed her tummy in soothing circles.

Lucy crossed the room and took her other hand, spinning her in a half circle before her arms reached around and lay over Nicole's own, her chin resting upon Nicole's left shoulder. "You look so beautiful like this," Lucy whispered in her ear, sending a light shiver down Nicole's neck and arms.

"You really mean that, don't you?" she responded quietly, allowing their fingers to link together. She was finally beginning to believe the words that Lucy offered up so often.

"Absolutely, I didn't think it was possible for you to be any more beautiful, but I was wrong, being pregnant and having our baby is the sexiest thing I have ever seen or imagined." She nuzzled into the crook of her neck.

"I've never felt so loved, Lucy," Nicole said, turning in her arms to catch Lucy smiling at her. Every time Lucy said *our baby,* it filled her with a warmth that she had barely felt before. "I love you, Lucy."

"I love you." Lucy kissed her lips in response and was rewarded by a double *ewww* from the twins as they came running up to Nicole with a question.

"When can we get the baby?" asked Summer. "We wanna play with the baby". Lucy giggled at the scene. Every day these two managed to say or do something that gave Lucy pause to think or laugh.

"Well, we have to wait a little while yet," Nicole explained, internally wincing at the idea of having to have the birds and the bees conversation with them soon.

"Can we go and pick one at the baby shop?" Rain inquired, which only increased Lucy's giggle. "I want one that looks like me."

"Okay, come sit with Mama," Nicole said, taking their tiny hands and leading them to the couch. She sat them either side of her as Lucy sat in the armchair opposite. There was no way she was missing this discussion. She pulled out her phone and put it on video.

"What? This is going to be gold!" She grinned at Nicole's reaction to the phone.

Nicole stifled a smirk. "All right, now there isn't a shop to go to, and we don't get to pick the baby we want," she explained gently to two very eager little girls.

"Well, how do we get it?" Summer asked. "I really want it now."

"The baby is already here, kind of," Nicole said and watched two pairs of eyes dart around the room looking. She smiled at them and their innocence. "The baby is in Mommy's tummy." Two pairs of eyes went wide with shock.

"You ate the baby?" Rain asked incredulously. Lucy laughed out loud at that remark, it seriously was one of the sweetest conversations she had ever witnessed.

Nicole smiled and tried desperately not to laugh, but she failed. "No sweetie, the baby was put in Mommy's tummy by love, and he or she has to stay there until they are big enough to be born."

"When will it be born then?" This was Rain again. Summer hadn't taken her eyes off of Nicole's tummy the entire time.

"Sometime in January."

"How long is Janwry?"

"Well, first you go back to school, then we will have your birthday, then it will be Thanksgiving and then Christmas. Once we have New Year, we are almost there."

"New Year?" Summer exclaimed, finally looking up into her mother's face. "We have to wait for a new year?"

"I am afraid so. The baby needs that time to grow. At the moment they are the size of a peanut. So, they are very small."

"That's tiny," Summer noted in awe.

Rain had gotten up from her seat and had walked around to stand in front of her mom. She tentatively reached out to touch her tummy and said, "Hello Baby." Tears brimmed in Nicole's eyes as she watched her daughter lean her head down to hear if the baby replied. "He isn't talking yet," Rain stated.

Chapter Forty

The following day Rita had the girls again, while Lucy took Nicole to see a lawyer. Agnes Danson was an expert when it came to divorce and arsehole ex-husbands. The short redhead took no prisoners when it came to dealing with abusive partners.

Nicole explained her situation in as much detail as she could manage, and Agnes agreed instantly to take on her case; it was that simple, and the initial paperwork would be done within the week. If Paul Nixon planned on dragging this out then he was going to find it a very expensive route to take, which went in Nicole's favour as it was unlikely he really would have the funds for such a battle, but that didn't mean Nicole wasn't worried. He had friends. Rich friends, friends in high places. If he needed to then he could get help to fight this. She was his, as far as he was concerned; she existed only because he said she did. Their kids were his. They were all nothing more than possessions, and Paul Nixon did not like having his things taken away from him.

Lucy made sure that Agnes added an injunction to keep him away too. They had not seen hide nor hair of him since Lucy had seen him off, but that didn't mean he wouldn't reappear anytime soon. They needed to make it clear to this bastard that he wasn't going to be hurting any of them again.

"I don't want him having any access to my kids," Nicole added. The redhead wrote that down and then looked up to address the matter.

"You may not get a choice. The courts could suggest he has access, no matter how limited."

"Then make sure it doesn't happen, whatever it takes," Lucy interjected. "Storm is just about getting back on track, and that bastard is not going to scare her again."

Agnes held her hands up. "I am just making sure you know the possibilities, but I will do whatever I can to make sure he doesn't get any access, or at the very least it is limited to supervised visitation. He will never be allowed to be alone with them." Lucy nodded; she wasn't happy with that idea, but they would deal with it if it happened.

With his mounting debts and gambling addiction, it shouldn't be too difficult to prove he didn't have the capacity to parent a child. Lucy agreed to pay for the services of a private investigator who would find out all there was to know about Paul Nixon's gambling and any other vices he might have.

"Would you be willing to allow Storm to speak with a psychiatrist?" Agnes asked Nicole. "It could help prove that he is an unfit parent who is a danger to the children."

Nicole shook her head. "No, not if we can do it another way. I don't want Storm to feel like it's her fault if the courts went in his favour."

"Which they won't," Lucy insisted. "I'll take you all to England before I let that happen!" Nicole smiled; it was sweet and Lucy had good intentions, but she knew it would never be that simple.

When they left the lawyer's office to go across town to Sherriff Jenkins, Nicole was feeling a little more at ease with the whole situation. She had spent so many years being frightened of this man that now she had Lucy and friends like Rita to support her fight back, she felt a little lighter in her step.

Sherriff Jenkins was a woman in her fifties. She had worked through the ranks and became Sherriff four years ago. She was a fair and honest woman who did things the right way and so, when Nicole and Lucy came to see her, she took down every detail and filed it all accordingly. There was no crime to answer to as far as the law was currently concerned, but if this Paul Nixon came calling on her patch and so much as blew too hard in Nicole's direction, then she was going to throw the book at him and use this statement as evidence if she could.

"I just wish I could go and hunt the bastard down and sling him in the cells for a few nights," the Sherriff said energetically. "You say your daughter was treated for a broken arm?"

Nicole nodded tearfully. "Yes, she tried to help when he attacked me one night and he grabbed her arm so hard it fractured. She needed an operation to put a plate in."

"I see, so there is a record of that somewhere?"

"Yes but, he made both of us say it was an accident, that she fell and he grabbed her to stop her from hurting herself."

"Bastards always got an answer for everything, ain't they?" she said, looking from one to the other. She sucked at her teeth.

"Well let me assure you, Ms. Granger, that nobody will be behaving that way on my watch, not in my town. You hear me? You get even the slightest whiff that he is around and you call it in. I'll have him locked down quicker than he can fart."

~E&F~

"I can't believe that everyone here just accepts my story," Nicole said to Lucy as they waited in line at the bakery. They were picking up some treats for the girls, well that was the excuse Nicole used, but mainly she was craving cream slices.

"Why wouldn't they? What reason do you have to lie about it, they can easily check you out."

"Yeah, but if they do that with the local police from back home, then they will probably get a whole different story from him."

"Nic, look at me," Lucy said gently. "He can say anything he wants to and it won't change a thing. You are safe here, and I am not going to let anything happen to you or our girls, okay?"

Nicole took a moment to take in what Lucy had said, to read her face and fall into the sincerity shining brightly from her eyes. And then she was there: she saw and felt the safety of Lucy. She felt the honesty, the love, the life free from cruelty, and she wanted nothing more than to grab it and hold onto it, so she did. She reached out and threw her arms around Lucy's neck and clung to her.

"I'm not going to let him anywhere near you," Lucy promised once more.

"Take me home," Nicole said quietly in her ear.

"What about the girls?"

"I think they will be fine with Rita for another hour." She smiled coyly and headed for the door.

"Okay, but I am still buying these cakes." Lucy laughed and handed over some cash to the assistant. Not even waiting for her change, she quickly followed Nicole out of the door and to the car.

They drove quite sensibly considering that neither of them could keep their hands off of one another. Thighs were stroked and cheeks were kissed. Whispers were spoken of desires and promises, all of which would be given the fullest attention once they finally got home.

Nicole pulled into the front of the cabin and they both leapt from the vehicle, crashing through the front door attached to each other. Lips parted and tongues battled as fingers and hands stormed the fortifications of clothing. Buttons popped and zippers pulled as they backed and pushed and twisted to the couch, half-naked and desperate for each other and for relief, an ache building in each of them that only the other could relieve. This was the first time that desire had eclipsed all thought, when urgency had overcome the need to take it slow. This was not going to be making love; this was something new.

Insatiable was how Nicole felt, totally and utterly insatiable, whether it was just the effect that Lucy had on her in general or a helping hand of hormones from the baby she wasn't sure, and she didn't care; she just needed Lucy, over and over and over. She felt the grip of Lucy's thumbs in the hollows of her hips as she arched. Her mouth warm against her as knowing lips devoured her.

"Oh God, what have you done to me?" she gasped as once more an orgasm pulsed through her.

Lucy laughed as she kissed her way back up Nicole's torso. "I'm not sure I know what you mean?"

"Oh, I think you know exactly what you do to me!" She laughed along with her as she rolled towards her and kissed her softly. "I love you, you make me so happy."

"Ditto, I never thought I could be this happy again. I love you too."

Chapter Forty-One

The summer holidays were over all too soon, and Storm was finally looking forward to the school pageant. She had practiced and practiced her song over and over, and Lucy was sure she was going to be the star of the show.

Celebrating 100 years of the school being formed, one pupil from each class had been selected to perform. Ms. Arnold was Storm's music teacher, and it was her decision to push Storm forward. Although she had only been at the school a matter of weeks before the holidays had come, Ms. Arnold wanted to involve Storm.

"I thought Storm needed a little help in asserting herself. She is a very intelligent young lady, but she lacks a little in self-esteem I fear." She spoke avidly about Storm to Nicole and Lucy. "I am hoping I haven't pushed too far. though."

"I think you will be pleasantly surprised, Ms. Arnold," Nicole gushed. "Storm has been practising all summer and well, she is very good."

"Oh, I have no doubts that girl will be brilliant at anything she sets her mind to," Ms. Arnold replied. "I wasn't aware she could play the piano though."

"She couldn't. She has learned this song over the summer, and we are continuing with her lessons," Lucy announced proudly to the intrigued teacher. She was so pleased with Storm and the twins. They had all enjoyed learning to play, but Storm had the talent for it, and she was good. Lucy was contemplating buying a real piano if she continued to impress and enjoy as much as she did right now.

"Well, here she is." They all turned to face the stage as Storm walked out, head high like Lucy had taught her. She sat on the piano stool and looked out. She couldn't see anyone in the audience because of the lights, just as Lucy had said it would be. She imagined herself sitting in the cabin, with Lucy and her mom and sisters. Taking a deep breath, she steadied herself before she brought her fingers to the keys and began to play, just the way Lucy had taught her. With each key she played correctly, her confidence grew, and by the time she opened her mouth to sing her first words, she had no fears left. She owned the stage; it was just her and the piano, and before she knew it, it was all over and people were clapping. Clapping for her. She heard whistles and calls for an encore, and not even the lights could outshine the smile on her face.

~E&F~

"Kelly and Maggie asked if I can come over this weekend, they're having a sleepover," Storm said excitedly once she had worked the crowd like Lucy told her to do. "Can I go?"

"If you want to, of course, you can, just have Kelly and Maggie's mom give me a call to confirm times, okay?" Nicole said. Storm was already rushing off to tell her new friends that she could come over.

"That went well then," Lucy said, grinning as she watched her go. "So, we have a happy eight-year-old. What are we going to do with these munchkins?" she said, squatting down to the twins and grabbing hold of them both, which earned her giggles and hugs from them both. She stood with one on either hip. "Shall we go home and watch one of those cartoon DVD things you love so much?" She looked between them as they nodded furiously in agreement.

"And ice cweem?" Summer asked hopefully.

"And ice cream?" Lucy questioned.

"Yesssssssssssssssssssss," They both said in unison.

"What do you think, Mum? Do these two munchkins deserve to have ice cream AND a cartoon?" Lucy asked, stifling a giggle.

"Well, I am going to have to think about it."

"Pweeeeese," said Rain, desperately trying to convince her mother that she needed ice cream!

Nicole gave a short gasp and clutched her tummy. She stood completely still, fully focused on something only she could feel. Lucy let the girls down on their feet again and watched Nicole's face for any kind of clue.

"What's wrong?" she asked as Nicole looked up and smiled at her.

"Nothing. I felt the baby move, that's all."

"Let me feel," Rain said, followed by Summer's, "And me!" She let them place their hands on her tummy.

"I don't think the baby is big enough yet for you all to feel it," Nicole explained, but it didn't stop Lucy from placing her hand there either. All of them grinned with excitement.

~E&F~

When they pulled up outside the cabin, the first thing they noticed was the car parked out front. A nice car, an expensive car; a Mercedes with a broken headlight.

"Oh no!" Storm cried. "Lucy, don't let him take us."

Paul Nixon sat in the driver's seat, a face full of rage and bitterness. He didn't like to lose.

"He isn't taking anyone anywhere," she said firmly to Storm before her eyes travelled around every set of terrified eyes staring back at her. "Take the girls and go inside, lock the door and call Sherriff Jenkins," Lucy said calmly. She didn't want to panic the children, and she needed Nicole to do just what she said, to keep the girls safe, as well as the baby and herself.

"What are you going to do?" Nicole asked her.

"Nothing, I'm just going to keep him distracted so that you and the children stay safe," she replied, reaching over and stroking her belly, making sure she was clear about the baby. "All of you stay safe."

284

Lucy climbed out of the car and put herself between him and the door. Nicole ushered the children out of the vehicle and straight into the cabin, already on her phone to the sheriff's office. She watched through the window as Paul Nixon climbed out of his vehicle, and she stayed on the line with the Sherriff's department just in case. Her heart was racing. Storm took the twins and switched the TV on. She down next to them, but her eyes darted across the room to where her mother stood watching the scene outside. The police were on their way, and Lucy said she would protect them, but even still, it terrified her that he was here, again. She kept watching her mother's reaction for any sign that they were in danger, that Lucy had failed in her promise.

Outside, Lucy had not moved. "You are not allowed to be here," she said to him firmly. Standing to her full height, she planted her feet solidly. She wasn't budging, and he wasn't going to be passing. Not today, or any other day.

"Says who? You? You think you can tell me what I can and can't do?" he sneered at her. He looked like a caricature of himself, his face contorted with anger, his clean-cut image long gone under an unshaved chin and dishevelled hairstyle that had grown and now looked messy and unkempt. Remnants of a black eye from his previous visit splashed red and purple across his nose.

"Actually, yes. This is my property, and I know full well you have been instructed to stay away."

"I don't give a fuck what you know full well, dyke. I want my kids and that slut of a wife, and I want them now." He smirked. The man was a moron if he really thought he could turn up like this and just make demands. Lucy felt the tug of a smile start to appear on her face as she realised just how stupid he really was.

"Do yourself a favour, get back in your car and leave," she said, turning to walk away.

"Don't turn your back on me, bitch!" he shouted. She stopped in her tracks and slowly twisted back to face him. Something about her made him pause; it was the look in her eyes. A look that told him she was done playing nice. She had something worth protecting now, and she would. She stepped towards him and he moved back a step. He could still feel the pain of the punch she threw last time.

"I won't tell you again." She spoke quietly, almost menacingly. "Get off my property."

"I want—" he began.

"You want what?" she smirked. "She doesn't want you, the kids don't want you. So, there is nothing for you to want."

"She owes me," he growled. His face contorted more. She couldn't see anything redeemable about this man.

"Owes you?" she snorted desirously at him. "What could she possibly owe you? You beat her black and blue, you fleeced her for every penny to gamble with." He looked suitably ashamed for all of a second and then it hit her, how to get rid of him. "I have an offer

286

for you. Tomorrow, be at our lawyer's office in town, and I'll pay you to sign those documents," she offered.

"Fuck you!" he screamed, taking a step towards her, but the sounds of sirens in the background spooked him. "We're not done!" he shouted as he climbed into the driver's seat of his car.

"10 a.m., I'll be there," she shouted to him. He drove off, dust billowing out behind as his wheels spun in the dirt.

When it was clear he had gone, Nicole ran from the cabin and straight into Lucy's arms. She held Nicole tight. This man would not hurt her again, not while Lucy was breathing. "Oh God I was so scared, are you alright?"

"I'm fine babe, he has no control here."

Nicole tried to smile. She wanted so much to believe Lucy when she said things like that, but she knew Paul, she knew him well, and one thing he wasn't was a quitter.

By the time the police cruiser arrived, Paul Nixon was well gone. Lucy gave the officer all the details anyway, further evidence logged against him.

"We will do a drive-by every hour for the rest of today, but any sign of him and you contact us instantly," the officer said, tucking his notepad back inside his breast pocket. "Any sign of this jerk and we will take him in."

"Thank you."

Chapter Forty -Two

The rest of the evening had been a quiet affair. It had taken a while to calm Storm down. She was worried that her father would appear in the middle of the night and snatch her from her bed. But, eventually, she had fallen asleep wrapped in Lucy's arms on the couch. Lucy carried her to her room and got her settled under the covers.

"I promise you, I will protect you," she whispered to the sleeping child. She closed the door quietly and returned to the living room to find Nicole yawning. She reached out her hand and led her lover to the bedroom. An early night for all of them would probably be a good idea.

"I told him to meet me tomorrow," Lucy said quietly as they undressed and got ready to climb under the covers.

"What?" Nicole said, instantly panicked by the idea of Lucy dealing with Paul again. "What do you mean?"

"I told him to meet me at the lawyer's office in the morning and that," she considered how to say this without upsetting Nicole, "I said I would pay him to sign the papers."

Nicole turned slowly to face Lucy and make sure she heard correctly. "Pardon?"

"I said..."

"I heard what you said. Just how much are you intending to pay him?" she said with a slight tilt of her head. "I mean, what am I worth, Lucy?" Lucy was confused at her remarks; that wasn't her intention. She just wanted to be rid of him, and the easiest way to do it was to pay him.

"I am not buying you," Lucy said, turning the cover back and climbing onto the bed. The sheets were cool against her skin as she slid between them.

"Aren't you?" She had already been owned once. People paid for possessions, didn't they? *Things* had price tags, not people. She didn't want to react like this, didn't want to accuse Lucy of such things and yet, she couldn't stop herself. She was angry. She was hurt. Didn't Lucy understand how this looked?

"No!" Lucy answered instantly.

"How much?" Nicole demanded as she too pulled the covers back, but she didn't climb into bed just yet. Instead she stood, glaring at Lucy for an answer.

"I don't know. Look, I'm not buying you or the girls. I'm buying you a divorce and your freedom," Lucy answered. Her eyes had misted over. She could feel the tears pricking and ready to roll wretchedly down her cheeks.

"I can't believe you would do this." Nicole finally climbed into bed, bashing her pillows hard as she set them upright, no longer feeling tired.

Lucy turned to her, her eyes boring into her. "I would do *whatever* it takes to keep you safe and happy and give you back your independence," Lucy said firmly as she held Nicole's gaze. "*Whatever* it takes! And money is easier and quicker than murdering him."

"Don't even joke about that."

"Who said I'm joking," she replied seriously. They sat in silence for a few moments before Lucy spoke once more. "I love you, I love our girls, and I want them to be free of this torment, and if it takes every penny I have to do it for them and for you then so be it." Lucy took Nicole's hands, kissing her knuckles. "You mean so much more to me than any amount of money ever could. I would rather be penniless than without you."

The tears that had threatened finally spilled over. Her heart felt like it would implode. All she wanted to do was to protect her family. Because that's what they were now, her family.

"You would do that for me?" Nicole finally said. It was still so difficult to really accept that anyone would love her so much that they would do anything for her. With Paul, everything had been about money. How much he earnt, how much she could or couldn't spend, how much he owed. But Lucy would give away her last penny so she could be free. It was such a contrast.

"Don't you know that by now?" Lucy smiled. "I am besotted with you, with us, with our family," she said as she reached out to touch Nicole's pregnant tummy, always including every member of this family they were creating. Nicole looked away, her own tears readying to fall. She felt a little ashamed at her reaction to Lucy's solution.

"Can I come?" she asked. Lucy must have looked confused, because she clarified, "To the lawyer's office...when you meet him, can I be there?"

"Of course, if that's what you want?"

"I do want." She paused. "I want him to see I am not frightened of him. That he has no control over me anymore."

Lucy smiled at that, oh god did she smile. "Yeah, you show that bastard."

~E&F~

They were woken an hour or so later by Storm crying out in her sleep. Lucy was up and on her feet in seconds, telling Nicole to stay put and go back to sleep.

Opening the door to Storm's room, she could see the little girl sitting up in bed with her knees drawn up to her chin. When she saw the door opening, she had scrambled up the bed, crying out in fear until she was sure that it was Lucy, and then she reached out her arms to her. Lucy moved as speedily as she could to the bed, tiny limbs wrapping around her neck in an instant. She lifted her and then carried her back to her own room, shushing her and soothing her until she quieted down and her cries became whimpers as she snuggled into Lucy's neck. Nicole pulled back the cover and Lucy lowered them both into the bed, placing her gently between them.

291

Storm rolled over and burrowed into her mother, her sobs now just stuttering breaths.

"It's okay baby. Lucy is going to fix everything tomorrow," Nicole soothed, her hand stroking down Storm's back as her eyes fixed with Lucy, an unspoken acknowledgement that she was now completely onboard with whatever Lucy needed to do to remove that man from their life, for good.

There were no more nightmares that night.

Lucy lay awake for a while, contemplating the day's events. How fabulous Storm was, how she had evolved over the summer from this shy bookworm to a confident performer. And now, after tonight and her father's visit, she was back to being a frightened little girl. She wouldn't allow it to happen again; they had worked so hard on this, every one of them had demons to face, and they were facing them together. Paul Nixon wasn't going to ruin it. She didn't care the financial cost.

"What are you thinking about over there?" Nicole said quietly in the dark. She had been lying awake herself, unable to drop the image of Paul outside their home, how Storm had instantly retreated back into her shell.

"How did you know I was awake?" Lucy said, smiling she turned to face her lover in the darkness.

"Your breathing is different when you are asleep. So, what were you thinking about?" She didn't mention that she was adept at listening to his breathing to judge when he was asleep and it was safer for her, that she could tell the difference between sleeping and passed out, or awake and lying in wait.

"You. The girls. Us. How great Storm was today." She paused before adding, "Him!"

"I've spent many nights doing that," Nicole said, reaching her hand across Storm's sleeping body to touch Lucy.

Lucy grasped Nicole's fingers between her own and squeezed as they lay in silence for a moment.

"Have you thought of any names yet?" Nicole asked Lucy.

"Names?"

"For the baby." She chuckled.

"No, I assumed you—" She didn't get to finish.

"Lucy, this is our baby, not mine. I want you to have input on everything."

"Oh, okay. Hmm well, it has to be something that matches the other three." Lucy's eyes began to close as she thought about naming their child.

"Night, darling," Nicole whispered, happy to have gotten Lucy's train of thought back on a good track.

Chapter Forty-Three

Sitting in the office of Agnes Danson at 10 a.m. precisely, they waited. Lucy had called Agnes the previous evening and informed her of the idea she had to offer Nixon a payoff. Agnes made sure to have all the paperwork in place. All that was missing was the figure they would agree on, if he turned up.

At 10 minutes past the hour, Nicole was ready to go. Her left leg bounced gently up and down to no particular rhythm.

"He isn't coming, we should just go," she said to Lucy and then to Agnes. Her anxiety levels were spiking and the longer they waited, the more she was losing her confidence.

"Five more minutes babe, okay?" Lucy said gently. She placed her palm gently on Nicole's thigh, calming the uncertain bounce. "He will come, I'm sure of it."

Nicole got up and paced around the room. She filled a polystyrene cup with water from the chilled fountain in the corner and had just sat down again when there was a gentle knock on the door. When it opened, one of Agnes' secretaries entered and introduced the arrival of Paul Nixon. Nicole felt her heart beat faster, and she realised she was holding her breath until she caught sight of him. And then all the fear dissipated in an instant.

He looked like he had slept in the car. Still unshaven and wearing the same clothes as the day before, he looked like someone sleeping rough. Like someone who didn't have the money to spare to get a hotel room. Lucy relaxed a little more. This plan was going to work, she knew it.

"Mr. Nixon, thank you for joining us this morning," Agnes Danson said, reaching across to shake his hand and offer him a seat.

He looked at Nicole and just glared, a deep penetrating stare that on any other day would have unnerved her, but today she could feel Lucy's hand back on her knee, anchoring her, reminding her she was safe, that Lucy would not allow anything to happen here. So, for the first time, she held his stare, her face neutral and composed. When he looked away first, she felt a small victory that boosted her confidence.

"Let's begin then, shall we?" Agnes said to the room.

"Yes, let's do that. I have an offer—" Lucy began, but Nixon had other ideas.

"I don't care what you have to say or what offer you have," he said loudly, his voice gruff and mean. "You want to buy my wife and kids, then it's going to cost you."

"I don't wish to buy Nicole or the girls. I'm buying Nicole her freedom from you," Lucy countered. "Now, I want to offer—" Again, she was cut off from speaking any further.

"No," his voice boomed as he banged his fist on the table. Nicole flinched. "You don't get to make any offers here. I will tell you what I want, and if you can't pay then I walk out of here without signing anything, and I will be going for full custody," he sneered, his gaze drifting back toward Nicole. This time it was her that looked away.

"Fine, go ahead. What do you want? What is it going to take?" Lucy spoke calmly. This man really was a prick. A look of victory crossed his face as he sat a little taller and adjusted his tie. When he spoke next, he spoke only to Nicole.

"I want 10 grand." He spoke slowly and enjoyed watching his wife squirm. Nicole sucked in a breath and waited because she knew he wasn't finished. "For each of them." He then turned his attention to Lucy. "And that includes the little bastard she is carrying." Switching back to Nicole he said, "You thought I wouldn't notice you've gotten fat again?"

"Shut the fuck up, Arsehole," Lucy said, standing quickly. Her leg ached with the sudden movement, but it wouldn't stop her from punching him square in the face again.

"Oh, big bad butch going to put me in my place, huh?" he said, laughing. "Sit down and give me my money." She stared at him for a full minute before finally she sat back down in her chair and regarded him once more. He really wasn't bright, but he clearly figured with witnesses around that he was safe. He was wrong, but she let him think it.

"Fifty thousand dollars? That's what you want?" she asked, her face neutral. She wanted him to think that she was thinking about it. But there was nothing to think about; she would give him the money.

He sat back in his chair and leered at her. "That's right, fifty big ones."

Lucy nodded to Agnes. "Fine, now sign the paperwork."

Agnes passed across the divorce papers, and he paused before picking up a pen and signing. He couldn't believe how easy it was; to be fair, he didn't think she would have the funds, and he kicked himself for not asking for more. But, his luck was riding today.

"And I'll double it if you sign away your parental rights to all children born or unborn between you and Nicole." Nicole gasped; she hadn't been expecting that. Paul Nixon's eyes lit up at the prospect of doubling his money. He didn't even have to think about it.

"Fine. Where do I sign?" he said to Agnes, who passed him another document that he signed and dated.

It was done. Nicole and the girls were finally free – well, almost.

"You'll also understand, Mr. Nixon, that the restraining order stays in place and that you are not to go within 500 feet of your ex-wife and her family, including Ms. Owen."

He nodded at Agnes. "Sure, sure, whatever." He grinned at the lawyer before turning his attention to Lucy. "Well, it was great doing business with you." He smirked as she stood.

"Oh, the pleasure was all mine." She smiled, unable to hide her glee any longer. "It's just a shame you didn't let me make my offer first."

"Yeah, I'm sure we saved a lot of time without me having to turn you down."

Nodding, she laughed and couldn't help herself. She held up the cheque with her offer on it.

"I was willing to give you one million," she said as she tore it up and looked at Nicole, whose mouth was now agape. "And I would have paid whatever it took to make her happy and keep those children safe from a monster like you. You don't deserve to breathe the same air as them, you worthless piece of shit."

He moved the pieces of paper, picking up the tiny piece that had the sum written on it, and looked again. Rage instantly reared its ugly head. His whole face reddened and his eyes bulged as he launched himself at her.

"You bitch!" he snarled.

She dodged him by moving to her left, and he fell to the floor. A crumpled heap of crap, in Lucy's opinion.

"Twice I tried to give you that offer and you told me to shut up, Mr. Big Balls. So, do not complain, you got exactly what you asked for." And with that, they walked out of the office with the sound of Agnes reminding him again about the restraining order and that he would be arrested if he remained in town for any longer than 10 minutes.

Chapter Forty-Four

The room was warm, the bed was inviting, and both women came together, naked and wanting. Nothing was going to spoil it.

Nicole writhed against the sheets, her fingers clutching at Lucy as she brought her to orgasm for the second time since they had arrived home.

She was euphoric, both physically and emotionally, all because of the woman currently between her thighs, loving her in the most intimate of ways. "Lucy." Her name tumbled from her lips in a whisper. Her back arched and her baby bump rose higher as she felt the delicious feeling of absolute love wash over her. "Don't stop," she begged. She could do that now: ask for what she needed. She could give and take with her lover and enjoy all the in-betweens.

For the first time, she was enjoying being pregnant. Her last two pregnancies had been awkward. He had gone from being violent and mean to leaving her alone, and that included sex. Her body had been primed and she was more aroused than ever, but she had nobody to enjoy that with. Not that she wanted him pawing at her and slobbering all over her for his own satisfaction. Until now – now she had Lucy, and Lucy made everything about being pregnant exciting.

Long gone was the body-shamed fear that she carried. She wasn't fat, she was pregnant, and she loved it. Loved her new shape as the baby grew and her stomach stretched. Loved the way that

Lucy would caress her and enjoy her. Even when Lucy was tired and Nicole had woken in the middle of the night with a sudden urge to make love, Lucy had never turned away.

Right now, her hormones were hypersensitive, and she was going to make the most of it.

Scrabbling up the bed for post-coital snuggles, Lucy found a home in Nicole's arms. She could curl herself around her and fall into a feeling of utter bliss, the outside world banished.

"We need to get up soon," Lucy said, her words a whisper as her lips pressed gently against the soft skin they rested upon.

"I know." Summer and Rain were with Rita. They would just about have time to go into town and pick up groceries before Storm would be finishing school too. "I still can't believe he has gone."

"Forever babe, it's just us now. Us and our girls." Lucy hummed as she thought about that. Her girls. She never really imagined she would have a family. She was far too young to even consider it when she was with Nicky, and all those years in between, it had all just seemed so pointless. But now...now was a different time, and she was a different person.

~E&F~

Storm was quiet on the ride home. The previous night's events when her father had arrived out of the blue had scared her. She had been clingy again that morning, not wanting to let go of Lucy's hand at the school gates.

301

Eventually, she had been persuaded that she would be safe at school. Lucy was angry on her behalf, however. Just 24 hours ago, she had been the happiest kid in town. Getting up on stage and confronting her fears the way she had had been a miracle, and now she was back to square one. All because Paul Nixon was a selfish pig of a man.

Now though, Nicole had had the last laugh, and they couldn't wait to share the good news with their eldest daughter.

Summer and Rain had lots to talk about on the way home. Their day had been eventful. Apparently, Summer had a boyfriend, and Rain wasn't impressed with him at all.

"He is very loud and he wants to be with Summer all the time," Rain complained. "Now I don't have anyone to play with."

"Yes, you do," Summer argued. "Anoki wants to play with you."

"Yeah but..." Lucy watched them both through the mirror as she drove. Rain had her hands out palm up as she tried to explain her point. "You're my sister."

Storm's head twisted back and forth between them.

"I know... doesn't mean we can't have other friends."

"Fine. Tomorrow I will play with Noki and see if I care."

"Why don't you all just play together?" Storm said, ever the grown-up. Rain and Summer considered this option before both agreeing that was a better way.

302

"Well, I am glad we sorted that out," Nicole said, as the car drove them all home with Lucy smiling at the helm.

~E&F~

The cabin was alive with noise as the twins ran back and forth playing some kind of chase game they had invented. Lucy chased after them while Nicole took Storm by the hand and led her outside.

"How are you feeling now?" she asked her eldest. Her palm stroked Storm's cheek gently.

"I'm ok, I guess." She shrugged.

"Really? You seem a little quiet still."

Storm didn't reply; instead, she just looked forwards, towards the lake.

"So, today Lucy and I...We met your father." Two watery eyes looked up at her in fear. "It's ok," Nicole reassured her quickly. "We met him because, well...we agreed that we're going to get divorced."

"For real?"

Nicole nodded and smiled. "Yes, for real, but that's not all," she continued. Pulling a piece of paper from her bag, she passed it across to Storm. "This piece of paper says that from now on, your father isn't allowed to come anywhere near you." She passed the second sheet across. "And this one...this means that he has no rights to you or your sisters...or this one." She rubbed her tummy. "Legally, he isn't your parent anymore."

"What does that mean?"

"It means that, unless you want to, you never have to see him again."

"Really?" Her chin began to tremble, eyes watery. "You promise?"

Nicole nodded, her own eyes filling with tears as she watched the years of hurt and horror finally lift from her daughter's shoulders. "Yes baby, I promise."

Chapter Forty-Five

It was nearing the end of November, the world around them had turned completely from green to orange as nature burnt its leaves readying for winter. It was Lucy's favourite time of year, autumn moving towards winter. She loved the vibrancy of all the changing colours. It smelt different too as rain moved in and dead leaves were turned to mulch. And with winter just around the corner, they were making the most of the last few days of the nicer weather.

Nicole blossomed and bloomed. In fact, she blossomed so much that Lucy often joked she was probably having another set of twins. Of course, she wasn't; they had confirmed that with all the scans she had had to make sure the baby was healthy and on track. They had decided not to find out what they were having, wanting it to be a happy surprise for them all.

Paul Nixon was nothing but a nasty memory.

Lucy had even suggested to Nicole that she stop working now. At first Nicole had become a little angry with Lucy that she wanted her to stay at home. It was only after some thought that she realised it was because that was what Paul had done: encouraged her to stay at home, distancing her from her friends and keeping her a virtual prisoner in her own home. In her heart, she knew that Lucy had different motives.

Nicole liked her job. She got to chat with all their neighbours and find out all the local gossip. Rita had become like a surrogate mother to her, and the girls loved her. It was nice knowing that she didn't have to work, but she chose to.

Time seemed to be moving at lightning speed as the days all seemed to roll into one. At seven months pregnant, Nicole hadn't seen her feet in a while. She also hadn't been allowed to do anything around the house. Lucy was very insistent that she rest up and relax when she got home.

She would arrive home to find dinner on the table and a bath run for her. She would get foot massages and shoulder rubs. In fact, she couldn't think of a time when she had ever been this pampered in her life. And if she was honest, she was enjoying it immensely.

~E&F~

In just three days, it would be the twins' 5th birthday, and to say that they were excited would be the understatement of the decade because Lucy had promised to take them to the shops to buy anything they wanted, within reason.

"Mommy!!" Rain shouted as she pulled on her coat, ready to do battle with the shops to find the best present.

"Yes Rain, I can hear you, I'm pregnant, not deaf." Nicole laughed as she pulled the zipper up to her chin.

"Sorry Mommy, I trying to tell you I want a bike." She grinned.

"A bike?"

"Yep, a pink one like Zoe has."

"Oh, I see, and can you ride it?"

"Don't be silly Mommy, I has to learn first," she said authoritatively. "Everyone knows that." She held her hands out palm up.

"Oh, well you are too clever for me!" Nicole smiled, she then turned to her left and picked up Summer's jacket. "What about you, Summer? What do you want for your birthday?"

"A skateboard!" she said simply without looking up from her bricks; she was building a castle.

Nicole raised her eyes at that one, Lucy smirked and looked away, too aware she was about to giggle, and that would cause a tantrum if Summer thought she was being laughed at.

"A skateboard? Are you sure?" Summer looked up, nodding. "They are quite dangerous for a little one like you," she questioned, holding up the jacket for her to push her arms into.

"I'm not that little, and José has one and he is smaller than me." Nicole helped her into her coat and zipped it up. "And girls can have skateboards too."

"Okay, is everybody ready?" Lucy asked. They all nodded including Nicole, who did so with the most adorable smile. Lucy had to take a moment to breathe; she was so overwhelmed at times by how she felt about her.

~E&F~

Lucy dropped Nicole off at her exercise class, Yoga During Pregnancy, and continued on to the mall with the girls. She was hoping the idea of bikes and skateboards would wane once they saw all the wonderful things they could buy. Alas, it wasn't to be, and soon Lucy was hauling a pink bike and a skateboard back to the car, as well as all the protective gear they would require. Storm was growing so fast she practically needed a new wardrobe every month, so she took the opportunity to kit them all out with new outfits and party clothes. Rain picked a pink dress to match her bike. Summer went for blue jeans and a white tee-shirt with a giant shark on the front, while Storm chose dungarees and a black polo neck jumper.

"Right, so we're all happy with our party outfits then?" She wondered if she should have gotten them all dresses, but then she considered that they were old enough to decide for themselves, and who was she to dictate what style they wanted to follow?

"Yep, thank you, Lucy," Storm answered.

"Thank you, Lucy," repeated the twins in unison.

"You're all welcome. So, who wants some lunch before we go and collect Mummy?"

~E&F~

They still had 30 minutes to kill before having to pick up Nicole from the yoga studio, so Lucy decided they may as well do the food shopping too. They ran down the aisles of Rita's store like a whirlwind, grabbing items and goodies, tossing them into the cart.

As they ran off again to procure more, Lucy would place some of it back on the shelves. They never noticed, as they were so engrossed in finding other treasures.

"I see you have trouble today then, Lucy." Rita laughed as she watched the twins try to decide if they needed hotdog sausages or not.

"For some reason, the twins are a little bit excited." Lucy smiled. "I can't imagine why?"

~E&F~

It took Lucy a further ten minutes to get them through the till and back into the car. They were going to be late picking up Nicole. She pulled her phone out and sent a quick text explaining that they were on their way.

As she slowed up looking for a space to pull into, she could see Nicole up ahead. She was sitting on a bench, her long dark hair swept up into a high ponytail, her face slightly flushed from the gentle exertion. She had her eyes closed and her face tilted to the afternoon sunshine just like Lucy always sat when she was in the sunshine. She looked beautiful, her big round tummy sitting cosily on her lap, her hands wrapped gently around it, cradling the baby, and she was talking. She was always talking to the baby, they all did. Lucy and the girls would often sit with her and talk to the baby. Summer would tell *him* all about her soccer games and Rain would explain to *her* that she was going to love pink and be her favourite thing to play with. Storm would read *it* stories and Lucy would explain how much she loved *them*, all of them, and how lucky they were to be joining this family.

She sat in the car just watching Nicole for a moment, enjoying getting to see her so unabashedly at ease with herself. She no longer had that haunted look she had arrived here with. Instead, she was tranquil and relaxed.

Nicole must have sensed she was being watched, because she turned slowly to the right and opened her eyes. She saw the car waiting for her, with Lucy just smiling at her like a proud momma bear. She couldn't help but smile back as she lifted herself gingerly to her feet and waddled over to them. Lucy jumped out and opened the passenger side door for her.

"Hello, Beautiful," she said quietly as she kissed her cheek.

"Hey." She climbed into the car and gave a quick wave to the girls before buckling up her seatbelt and relaxing back into the seat.

Lucy pulled the car out from the parking spot and into the traffic. "How was your class?"

Yawning, Nicole replied sleepily, "It was good, exhausting but good."

Before Lucy had a chance to reply, Nicole was already dozing quietly. She smiled as she looked around the car using the rear-view mirror to check on the girls. Everything was just perfect.

Chapter Forty-Six

The twins were having such a great birthday. The sun was out and it was warm enough for them and all of their friends to play in the sand by the lake. Many of the parents had stayed to enjoy the fun too.

It was an interesting time for Lucy. She had spent so many years around these people without ever really knowing any of them and yet, here they all were, in her home. She was a little unsure if all of them had stayed simply because of the children or if they just wanted to know more about the quiet woman who had lived amongst them so distantly all these years. She didn't care either way.

Lucy set up a karaoke machine. One by one the kids all took turns singing Disney songs. It was cute, but not half as entertaining as when the adults got up the courage to have a go. A little too much punch had helped them along.

As the evening progressed and they all moved inside where it was warmer, Storm began tugging urgently on Lucy's sleeve.

"Yes sweetheart, what is so urgent that you need to rearrange my clothing?" Lucy smiled at her, noting her wide-eyed excitable face.

"Sorry. Can you sing?" she asked brightly.

"You know I can sing."

"No, I mean can you sing, like now."

"Uh, why?" Lucy looked around the room at all the people she barely knew, her heart pounding a little harder at the thought of singing in front of them all.

"Well, I was telling Jodie and Robbie and Frankie and—"

"Telling them what?" Lucy squatted down to Storm's height so she could listen properly as she explained. It was something Storm loved about Lucy, that she always listened. She never looked down at her as just a child.

"That you could sing." She looked to the floor and fidgeted.

"And?" Lucy was studying her face. There was something more that she having difficulty saying. "It's okay, you can tell me."

She huffed and lifted her small palm to Lucy's face, touching her cheek and dragging her finger gently down the scar. "They said I was lying, cos you don't even speak to people so there was no way you could sing."

"Oh, they did, did they?" It wasn't that she was bothered about their opinion of her, or that she had a need to prove anyone wrong, but she wasn't having her...daughter? Yes, her child, called a liar for telling the truth.

"Will you?" Storm asked hopefully. Big brown eyes looked at her with such adoration that Lucy knew she would probably never say no.

"Sure, just let me finish my drink and I need to check on your mom first, okay?"

"Yes!" she said, clapping her hands with glee before throwing her arms around Lucy and kissing her cheek. "Thanks, Mama." She ran off, leaving Lucy to replay that over in her mind. *Mama?* She liked the sound of that. Smiling, she wandered around the room to find Nicole. She found her easily enough, holding court in the middle of a group of other ladies all discussing birthing issues. She was fine, and Lucy attempted to turn and escape, but she wasn't fast enough.

"Hey, you," Nicole said, smiling up at her.

"Oh hey, uh just checking if you needed anything, but I can see you have everything you need."

"Not everything," she replied with a wink, causing Lucy to blush.

"I, uh I said I would do my turn on the karaoke for Storm so, I'll be back later." With every pair of eyes on her, she was beginning to feel a little uncomfortable.

"Who knew Lucy was so adorable?" a redhead sitting next to Nicole said in amazement.

"I know, I am so lucky."

~E&F~

The room was bustling with the sound of chatter and laughter when Lucy sat down at the keyboard. Nobody even really noticed, and if they did, they didn't assume she would begin to play.

Slowly the room quietened down as one by one they turned towards the beautiful music.

Her practice over the summer with Storm had loosened her fingers, and she was able to play almost as well as she ever had done. When Lucy began to sing in that breathy whimsical way she had, she kept her eyes closed. This was the woman that for the last decade had barely said a word to them, and here she was playing the piano and singing. And she could sing.

Storm stood rapt in adoration for the woman that meant so much to her. She turned to her friends, who all stood wide-eyed. "I told you." She smirked before turning her attention back to Lucy, mouthing the words along with her.

When the song was finished and Lucy opened her eyes, there was silence and for a second, she wasn't sure about anything. All eyes were on her, mouths agape, but then one by one they began to clap. Faces smiled at her. She rose and took a comical bow, winking at Storm as she climbed off the stage and somebody flicked the music back on. The party was back in full swing, and Lucy disappeared into the crowd.

Nicole had watched in awe as everyone else finally got to witness the real Lucy, her Lucy. She had never been prouder to have everybody finally know what she was already aware of: that there was more to Lucy than just the silent hermit they thought she was.

The redhead, whose name was Carla, turned to her once more and added, "Adorable and talented."

"Yes, she is, will you excuse me for just a moment?" she said as she levered herself up from her position on the couch to upright, no mean feat when you can no longer see your feet and feel like you're carrying around a small elephant. She crossed the room and found Lucy by herself in the kitchen pouring herself a glass of orange juice.

Creeping up behind her wasn't possible any longer; the bump gave her away long before she got close enough to snake her arms around her waist. Immediately Lucy turned and grinned. "Hey, you're supposed to be resting."

"I am rested." She looked around the room to make sure they were not overheard. "And extremely horny," she whispered, giggling at Lucy's expression and the sudden blush that covered her cheeks.

"Oh, really?" Lucy replied quietly as she stared into lust-filled eyes and watched as Nicole nodded and pulled her closer.

"Yes, I heard you sing, and suddenly all I could think about was getting you naked and making love." The words hit Lucy's memory banks, and Nicole noticed a flicker of sadness dance across her face before the smile reappeared. "What? What's wrong?"

"Nothing, beautiful," she said, shaking her head. The smile she tried to force was not quite enough to convince Nicole.

"No, I said something and you got this look, just for a second. What did I say to upset you?"

"I'm..." She swallowed, her mouth suddenly dry. "I'm not upset, it's just..." How did she explain? "The last time I sang in front of people..." She paused. "I...I came off stage and—" Her eyes glistened, shiny and tearful. "Nicky was there and she said the same thing to me, only a little more graphically. It just brought back a memory, that's all." She wiped her eyes with the back of her hand, suddenly feeling vulnerable and a little nervous.

"Oh, sweet pea." Nicole kissed her face. "I'm so sorry."

"No, no you have nothing to be sorry about, I just...I never know what my reaction will be to things, and I didn't expect—" She stroked the back of her fingers down Nicole's cheek.

"Me to be horny over your talent and adorableness?" She grinned.

"Ridiculous I know, of course you should be horny about that." Lucy laughed. "I...I just don't want you to feel that you have to reign in your thoughts, that you can't say how you feel...I love it when you're horny." She chuckled.

"What's horny?" A small voice from below asked. Neither had been aware that Rain had wandered over.

"Toads!" Lucy said quickly. "I was telling Mommy all about horny toads, have you never seen one?"

Nicole chuckled and hid her smile behind her hand as Rain thought about it for a long moment, before announcing she didn't think she wanted to as toads were yucky, and promptly walked away in disgust.

"Toads?" Nicole laughed loudly.

"Yes, I happen to like horny toads." She laughed as she kissed her. "And later I'll show you just how much."

Chapter Forty-Seven

Christmas was fast approaching, and Nicole was finding everyday tasks just a little harder now that she was almost ready to pop. She was frustrated about always having to ask someone to help her. Lucy had reminded her that she had to have help with a few things because she was busy growing a baby, and that only made her cry. Her baby hormones this time around were so much different from the girls that she was almost convinced it would be a boy.

Her relationship with Lucy was moving smoothly along, to the point that sometimes Nicole had to remind herself that it had only been a few months. Barely any time at all and yet, life with Lucy, for herself and for the kids, was beyond anything she ever expected to have. It was unrecognisable to any relationship she had had in the past, with Paul or otherwise. They worked well together. Everything had a synchronicity as they moved around one another like dancers in a ballet.

Often, she would find herself drifting off into a daydream about her. She was doing just that right now when Lucy came through the door of Rita's store followed by three over-excited children all bundled up in winter coats and hats. The weather had turned cold. Lucy called it an arctic blast. All of them shouted excitedly at her, and none of them were making any sense. Nicole could do nothing more than laugh and wait them out until one by one they ran out of breath and the last one standing could explain.

"We're going to town to get a Christmas tree!" Storm shouted while jumping from one foot to the other.

"Oh, are you?"

They all nodded, including Lucy. Christmas had been a grand event in the Nixon household, but not for the reasons that would excite the children. The tree and decorations were not done for their enjoyment, but for the opulence of them in front of his friends. The tree would be the biggest he could find, and underneath would be boxes of all shapes and sizes. Only they knew that most of them were for show: empty wrapped cardboard.

Every Christmas Eve was spent with the house full of drunken ex-football players and other members of the community falling about in a stupor. The children would be allowed down for half an hour as he paraded them around. His need to be seen as the perfect father made Nicole feel sick, but she would plaster on the smile and go along with it anyway; anything for a peaceful night.

Christmas morning and the girls would have to stay in their rooms until he had fixed his hangover. If she had been lucky enough to avoid his mood swing, then she would get up and make his breakfast before finally ushering the girls into the living room to unwrap presents. They would have one each from their parents and a handful from Santa Claus, all the while he would strut around taking happy family snaps to show the world how wonderful his life was. Nicole hated every second of it as she watched their little eyes light up at the prospect of more presents, only to discover they were all fake. But not this year. She already knew that this year would be so very different.

"And then when we get back, these three terrors are going to decorate it while I give you a nice back rub," Lucy was saying, before she then leaned in close enough so that only Nicole could hear and whispered, "and when we go to bed I am going to spend a lot of time relaxing you further."

"That sounds, delightful!" Nicole spoke casually. "I can't wait."

~E&F~

Arriving back at the cabin, the first thing that hit Nicole was the smell. It smelt like Christmas. Lucy was baking cookies with cinnamon. The giant spruce stood grandly in the living room and gave off a piney aroma that inundated the senses. Three children set about decorating it with every piece of tinsel and bauble Lucy could find. It was lop-sided and messy, pieces of tinsel hung loosely. Nicole moved towards it and began to move baubles, tidying it up.

Lucy watched for a moment. At first, she had just assumed that Nicole wanted to be involved, but as she observed her, she could see a frustration developing, and something else: fear. She tried to think, what was causing her such emotional turmoil. Slowly, the girls came to a halt and stood back, all eyes on their mother.

"Nic?"

"It's not right." Nicole spoke but didn't stop her task of aligning each bauble symmetrically, shifting tinsel into place so that it was tidy.

"Babe, it's a tree...it doesn't have to be right." Lucy's eyes narrowed at her. She felt a tugging on her sleeve and looked down to find Storm looking up at her.

"Daddy gets mad if the tree doesn't look perfect."

"Oh..." Lucy looked towards Nicole once more and then turned back to Storm, bending down to her. "Can you do me a favour, take the girls into their room and play with them while I help Mummy?"

Storm nodded and took her sisters by the hand, leading them away from the frantic scene that was now taking place as Nicole began to cry and fluster. When the girls were safely ensconced within their room, Lucy moved across to Nicole. She reached out slowly and covered Nicole's hand with her own. She felt her flinch slightly, but then relax as Lucy began to speak.

"We can decorate this tree any way you want it done." She edged closer until she was just behind her, left hands together holding a silver bell bauble, her right hand resting gently on Nicole's waist. "If you want to have the perfect tree, if that's what makes you feel comfortable, then that's what we will do..." She kissed the side of her head. "But, we don't *have* to do that, you don't *have* to do that. We can give the girls any kind of Christmas that you want to...messy, noisy and fun." She waited.

"Oh God," Nicole cried, suddenly aware of what she was doing. Her hand dropped and she spun around to look at Lucy. She studied her face with her eyes, her fingers tracing the framework of her face. "I'm sorry, I don't know why..." She looked around for the girls.

"Storm took them all to their room while we talked," Lucy explained quickly. The last thing she wanted now was a freak-out because she didn't know where the girls were.

Nicole nodded her understanding. "It had to be so perfect, ya know, or else..."

"I know...we're making new memories now though, right?" Lucy smiled and led her to the couch. "So, why don't you put ya feet up, I'll get you a mug of hot chocolate and you can watch as the girls go crazy and make that the best, messiest Christmas tree the world has ever seen?"

"Yes, I like that idea."

Lucy leant forward and kissed her gently. "Right, hot chocolate coming up!"

~E&F~

Nicole sat quietly with her feet raised for the rest of the afternoon, watching on while Lucy helped lift the twins up one by one so they could add toys and baubles and other shiny Christmas decorations to the tree. With each one that found its home they would clap and cheer. Lucy's heart melted even more. This was their first Christmas as a family, and it was already the best she could have wished for. She glanced across at Nicole and found her equally as happy. A smile beamed across the room at them, the earlier moment of panic almost forgotten.

Nicole snapped pictures on her phone as they worked, constantly recording new memories to add to the album Lucy had brought her during the summer.

"Okay girls, let's take a break," Lucy said. "We can have hot chocolate and marshmallows, yeah?"

Four cries of "yes!" came back to her as she made her way into the kitchen to warm some milk.

Storm flopped down on the couch next to her mother. Her dark hair was tied up into a messy ponytail and her glasses had a small piece of pink tinsel stuck in the arm, but she made no attempt to move it, so Nicole left it in place. "Mommy?"

"Yes, darling?"

"I have a question." She gazed down at the floor until Nicole placed a soft fingertip beneath her chin and tilted her head so they were facing one another.

"What is it? You know you can ask me anything."

"Yes...I know." She took a deep breath before asking. "Is it ok if I call Lucy Mama?" She spoke quietly but her voice was confident.

"If you want to, is that what you want to call her?" Storm's question hadn't surprised her in the least; she could see how important Lucy was to her eldest daughter, how they had bonded and become like mother and daughter over the summer.

She nodded furiously, "Yes, I love her like I love you. I don't love Daddy and you said he couldn't be our parent anymore so, that means there's a vacancy." She grinned and pushed her glasses back up her nose.

"I think that Lucy would like that Storm, why don't you ask her?"

She jumped up instantly and hugged her mom before running off to find Lucy.

In the kitchen, Lucy was finishing off five mugs of hot chocolate. She sprayed cream on the top of three of them and then added mini marshmallows until they covered the drink and then, to top it all off, she sprinkled hundreds and thousands. There was a little tiny cough from her right and when she turned, she found Storm standing there patiently.

"Alright, kiddo?"

"Lucy, can I ask you a question?" she said, walking a little closer. Lucy noticed that Nicole had followed silently and was holding her phone up to capture something on the video or camera. She asked silently with her eyes, but Nicole just shook her head, smiling. This was Storm's moment.

"Of course, what's up sweetheart?" She glanced up at Nicole once more. Her lover was grinning like a Cheshire cat, but she held the phone steady.

"Can I call you Mama?" the small voice said. She was looking up at her with wide eyes as she waited for Lucy to answer her. Lucy thought back to the twins' party when Storm had inadvertently called her Mama before. She remembered how she liked hearing it, but actually being asked by an almost 9-year-old if they could think of you as their parent was something she would never forget. She felt herself choke up with emotion. Kneeling down next to Storm, she wrapped her arms around her, kissing her cheek.

"I would be honoured to have you call me Mama. You and your sisters, your mum and the baby are the most precious things on this Earth to me."

"I know." And she hugged Lucy again, harder this time. Looking up, Lucy noticed Nicole was crying too.

"Happy tears." She laughed.

"Right, hot chocolate then, daughter of mine?" Lucy said, laughing as she stood and watched Storm issue that smile that matched her mother's.

Chapter Forty-Eight

With just a week left until Christmas arrived, the cabin was a hive of activity as Lucy and Nicole ran around trying to make sure they had everything ready. To be fair, Nicole merely waddled around and spent most of her time organising what Lucy would need to do next, which Lucy was fine with. She enjoyed the whole experience that having children brought to Yuletide. It was exciting to see those three small faces light up every time Santa was mentioned or a new present arrived under the tree.

Cinnamon filled the air as Lucy pulled out a tray of rolls from the oven to be eaten later. She placed them down on the cooling rack and pinched a piece off to taste.

"So, we need to go into town and get some last-minute things I ordered," Nicole said quietly as she sidled up beside her and picked off a piece for herself. She didn't want the girls overhearing that there were more presents coming their way.

"Ok, let's drop the girls off with Rita and then we can go into town and pick those up."

Lucy rounded up the girls, pulling on coats and hats and scarves until they were all wrapped up and ready to go. She loaded them into the car and hit the play button on the CD player. The car was instantly filled with Christmas carols while the girls all sung along in the back seat.

Lucy drove at a leisurely speed along the road. They were in no hurry; it was the holidays, and the roads clear of traffic. It had been snowing quite heavily over the past few days, and the trees were drooping under the weight of it all. The lakes were frozen around the edges, but the roads were pretty clear of ice. Lucy glanced back at the girls via the rear-view mirror and smiled. It was such a wonderful time of year.

Following the road around bend after bend with little effort, Lucy was completely relaxed as they began a short descent down a reasonably straight part of the road. She applied the brakes and slowed gently as they approached a side road.

It was sudden. The impact of the truck slamming into the side of the car spun them around and around as the tyres lost traction with the road. It was disorienting; the kids were screaming. Nicole! The big red truck had hit Nicole's side of the car. The vehicle slid towards the bank and in slow motion began to slide down the hillside sideways. It was surreal. Lucy's mind flashed between now and all those years ago on the bus. Branches splintered and smashed into the car. The windscreen cracked and a tyre burst as it hit a rock but kept sliding on its downward decent until it finally came to rest against a giant tree trunk.

And then there was blackness.

~E&F~

Lucy could feel something hitting her face, gently tapping on her skin. She could hear her name being called over and over. Someone was crying. It was cold, and there was a feeling that scared her. It was like before.

She forced her eyes to flutter open, and it took a moment to clear her head and remember. The car, the truck, kids, Nicole, the baby.

"No, no, no." She sat upright and felt her chest tighten with pain and emotion. The tapping was coming from the tiny hands of Summer. She had managed to wriggle free from her car seat and climb over to sit on Lucy's lap. Her blonde hair was hanging loosely around her face because her hat had come off as she had scrabbled between the front seats.

"Lucy, wake up. Mommy is asleep." She was scared and crying. Lucy wiped away her tears gently.

"It's ok, I'm awake." She kissed her cheek and then looked around the car. The girls were all staring at her expectantly. They looked okay; frightened, but not injured.

"Are you all okay?" she asked them, and all three of them nodded back. "Good. Okay Summer, climb back over with your sisters so I can..." Before she finished speaking Summer was clambering over the back seat. Nicole was facing away from her and she didn't want to think about the possibilities, but they were there in her head. Memories of another time, another accident. She pushed them away; she had to. *They* needed her now. Three frightened little girls. "Okay, now huddle together and stay warm while I check on Mummy." They all nodded again. Lucy tried to push her door open, but it was stuck. The tree was blocking it from the other side. She tried the window, and thankfully it slid down and opened fully for her to climb out. It was difficult, as they were on a steep gradient and she couldn't bend her leg easily. If it hadn't been for the tree then they would have kept on going, gathering speed until they crashed to the road below, but it meant she could lean against it as she shuffled out.

The ground was slippery under her feet. Snow was deeper here, and underneath it was ice. She carefully inched her way around the front of the car, slipping a couple of times. As she reached Nicole's door she could see it was crushed; she had taken the impact. Grabbing the handle, Lucy tried to open it, but it was wedged. Nicole was unconscious, blood trickling down her face. Thinking on her feet, Lucy moved as fast as she could back around the car and opened the trunk. She searched around before her hand found what she was looking for: the tyre iron. The kids watched her every move. Ramming the metal rod into a small gap where the lock was, she wrenched hard and pried the door open.

"No. No. No," she whispered, "Not again, not again." She touched Nicole's face and heard her whimper. "Thank God." Lucy bent into the car and kissed Nicole's forehead. "Don't leave me." She closed her eyes. "I can't lose you too."

Rustling through her pockets for her phone, she checked for a signal. Nothing. "Shit, shit, shit," she muttered as she twisted around to look back up the bank. At the top, she could see the truck that had hit them. The front end of it was a wreck. Standing beside it was a man, a man she recognised.

"Should never have fucked with me," he shouted down at her. "What did you think? That I'd just let her walk away?" He sneered and wiped his nose with the back of his hand. "Next time, you won't be so lucky." He watched her for a moment more before calmly walking back to the truck and leaning against it. Paul Nixon.

She looked at the girls' faces, then back at Nicole. She needed to be where he was. She needed to call the emergency services. Lucy Owen wasn't an angry person. She didn't view the world through eyes of hate, but right now, she was ready to kill.

"Okay, I am going to climb up there and get a signal. I need you to stay here and keep talking to Mummy, alright? Can you do that?" She tried to smile and knew it was more a grimace than anything else, but it would have to do. "I'll be right back." She didn't wait for a reply from them. Turning, she started to climb. The pain in her leg barely registered as she took in the form of the man that nonchalantly leant against his truck. She had one thought and one thought only: get to the top and do whatever it took to make the call for help. He wasn't watching her now. He seemed more interested in his own phone. The shrill sound of it ringing had him scrambling to pull it out of his pocket. She could hear his voice, a little panicked. She kept climbing. She stumbled a couple of times and grabbed a hold of branches to heave herself up. He was out of view now; she heard the truck door slam shut.

"Please, just leave," she mumbled to herself as she took another step forward. Looking up, she could see she was just feet from the top. She pulled her phone out and checked. No signal. If Paul had one though, then she knew she needed to get up there. She pushed the phone safely back into her pocket and was relieved when she heard the sound of an engine starting up. She could hear the sound of wheels turning slowly on tarmac. There were just a few feet left, so with all the effort she could muster, she scrambled up there. As she pulled herself to her feet, she looked up along the road. Nothing to the right, but as she swivelled to look the other way, she heard it. The engine revving. She took a step forward and gripped her leg as pain shot through the joint. And then she saw it: the wrecked front end of the truck hurtling towards her.

"Shit." She barely had time to think, instinctively side-stepping, and then, in a last-ditch effort to safe herself, she threw herself sideways. The last thing she saw was his maniacal face screaming obscenities at her. Then there was fear, absolute fear as he realised: he had missed her, and now he couldn't stop. The brakes failed and a blur of red hurtled past her over the side verge.

Lucy sat up and scrambled to the edge. She watched in horror, and relief, as the vehicle gathered speed, passing by her own car, before it then hit a rock or a tree stump and flipped, tumbling twice before coming to a rest on the road below. There was no movement. If he survived that then he was hurt, but right now, she didn't care too much. She grabbed her phone and thanked the heavens that she finally had a signal.

With the emergency services on their way, Lucy scrabbled back down the bank. She was cold and her hands were numb as she grabbed hold of rocks and branches to help her. It took time. Her urge to move faster was only eclipsed by the thought of hurting herself. Then she would be no use to anyone, so she took the time it needed, but eventually, she made it back to them. Nicole was drowsy, but she seemed at least to be awake.

"Okay girls, I need you to be brave now and to do everything I tell you to," Lucy said. They nodded, wide-eyed and fearful. She yanked the back door open. "Alright, I want you all to climb out of the car on this side and start climbing back up the bank. When you get to the top you wait for me, okay? You don't walk into the road or do anything other than wait for me!"

"What about Mommy?" asked Rain, as tears fell down her cold, red cheeks.

"Baby, dry your eyes, it's too cold for tears. Mommy is going to be fine, I promise. Help is on its way." Rain rubbed at her face and sniffed. They all began to climb the bank, following Storm as she led the way. Lucy was thankful that the new boots they had just bought them had such a great grip. She watched them all the way, holding her breath with every step they took, until finally, they were there. Safe.

She turned her attention back to Nicole. Dark eyes were trying to focus on her. "Hey Beautiful."

"What happened?" Nicole asked.

"We got hit by a truck," she said honestly. "But the kids are okay, they are up on the roadside waiting for the ambulance. How do you feel?" There was no need to tell her about Paul Nixon right now.

"Okay, I guess," Nicole shrugged. She tried to lift her arm, but it was too heavy. Everything was just too tiring.

"Try not to move, you hit your head on the window, I don't know what other injuries you have, so you have to stay still. Are you warm enough?"

"Yeah. The baby is kicking like crazy though." She smiled. "You're cold."

"I'm okay." Her teeth might have been chattering by then, but she wasn't the one that was stuck inside the car.

There was shouting from above. Lucy looked up just as paramedics and firemen began descending the bank towards them. The girls were coming too.

"Please, can you get her out? She's 8 months pregnant," Lucy gushed as soon as the first responder arrived. She had been calm until now, but with help finally here, her fears were overwhelming her. She was having flashbacks to the roadside after the coach crash. Lights, blue and red, flashing over her. People were talking loudly around her, and yet it all sounded muffled.

"Ma'am, did she lose consciousness?" the paramedic asked Lucy, but she was rambling, almost incoherently lost in her past.

"This isn't happening, no! I can't do this again. Please, God, please not again."

The paramedic tried once more. "Ma'am, can you calm down? I need you to calm down."

"I can't, I just...you have to help her!" She was trembling, her breathing erratic, and when the paramedic went to touch her she freaked out. "Don't! Don't touch me until you have helped her!" she screamed, shrugging her off.

She felt a tiny hand take hers. Small fingers wrapped around her left hand and then another took her right hand. She felt the calm wash over as she realised she wasn't Lucy Owen, a pop star in a coach crash, anymore. No, right now she was Mama, and three little girls needed her. She looked down at them one by one, Rain to her left, Summer to her right, and Storm standing, facing her. Dropping to her knees to be on their level, she wrapped her arms around the twins, and Storm hugged her neck.

"I'm sorry, so sorry babies," she said to them all. When Storm finally let go and Lucy saw her, she almost screamed for the paramedic.

"Storm, where are you hurt?" She ran her hands all over her face and head, but didn't find a cause for the blood covering her cheek and coat.

"Mama, stop," she said quietly. "Mama. It's not me."

"What? You're bleeding."

"No, Mama. I'm not," she said gently as she raised her hand to Lucy's face. "You are!" Lucy stared at her, felt her fingers touch her, and watched as she produced them in front of her eyes as proof. She hadn't felt a thing, this entire time her face had been bleeding. "*You* are bleeding Mama, please let the lady look at it."

Lucy turned to find the paramedic waiting, smiling at the girls in thanks for helping to calm the situation. "Ma'am before I check you out, can you tell me if Nicole lost consciousness?" Lucy shook herself. She could do this, she had to do this. For them all.

"Yes, initially she was out, I think we both were. When I came around she was whimpering, but not awake for a while. Is she going to be alright?"

The paramedic gave the information to her partner before turning back to Lucy, "We're going to do all we can to make sure they both are, can you climb back up with your children so we can do what we need to do?"

Lucy nodded, looked once more at Nicole and saw her smile and nod. "Go be with our girls."

At the top of the embankment she found the girls huddled together in the back of an ambulance, laughing at something the medic was saying to them. Finally, Lucy allowed the paramedic to patch her up. She cleaned the wound and covered it with a bandage. "They'll wanna look at that when you get to the hospital."

"Okay, thank you."

Sheriff Jenkins arrived in her marked vehicle and pulled it over to park near to where Lucy was standing. Blue and red lights flashed a warning to others travelling the route. She waved over to Lucy and strode confidently across the road.

"You okay?" she asked, clearly concerned. Lucy shook her head, looking around to check that the girls were still out of earshot.

"No, I'm not okay, Sherriff. This wasn't an accident," she hissed. The police officer tilted her head, listening. "Paul Nixon, the truck hit fast and I didn't see much, but when I climbed out of the car and looked up the bank...he was there. Standing right here." She pointed to the floor.

"You're sure about that? You've had a nasty bang on the head."

"I am sure, yes...I'd recognise that arrogant prick anywhere. But you can check for yourself, he's down there." Lucy pointed back down the hill. They both moved closer to the edge and Jenkins looked down. "Over there, to the left. I climbed up the bank to call the paramedics and he drove at me."

"He drove at you?" Shock etched the face of the sheriff.

Lucy nodded. "He was mad, that much was obvious."

Jenkins threw out some instructions to other officers and sent them down to search the wreck of the red truck at the bottom.

"And he just drove over the edge?"

"I don't know if he intended to, but yeah." Her leg was starting to hurt, a deep throbbing within the joints. "I don't want Nicole hearing about it right now...or the girls, especially Storm." There was a lot of shouting from below. They were bringing Nicole up.

Chapter Forty-Nine

The girls arrived at the hospital with Lucy. Nicole was being brought in separately. For Lucy it was torturous. She wanted to be with the girls, to make sure they were okay. Not just physically; they had been frightened and were still worried. Lucy knew this was the moment she would step up and be the parent they all wanted her to be, but she was scared herself. Everybody assured her that the girls would be fine, that Nicole was fine, but she needed to see for herself.

She was sitting in a treatment room. Summer had climbed into her lap, and Rain was clinging to her arm. Storm was quietly sitting against the wall on a bench. The quiet was interrupted when a tall, dark-haired man in a white coat walked in.

"How are you doing?" he asked, kind eyes staring directly at Lucy before sweeping the room and acknowledging the girls. "Can I take a look?"

"Sure, but I am fine. Can you tell me about Nicole?" They all wanted to know where she was and when they could see her. Summer turned and burrowed into Lucy's chest.

"You have a gash on your forehead that probably needs stitching," he said, noting the amount of blood that was seeping through the makeshift bandage. "And, you're limping. I'd like to take a look at your leg."

"There isn't a need to do that, my limp isn't related to this accident," she explained, not really wanting to go into further details.

"Well, that's good. And, your arm?"

Lucy looked down at her left arm, wrapped around Summer. She could see a massive bruise appearing. Her head now felt sore. She had been running on adrenaline so far and had barely felt a thing until the doctor started pointing things out.

His name tag read Dr. L. Lau. Lucy allowed him to take a hold of her arm. He gently pressed around the area as he occasionally glanced up at Lucy. She kept her eyes on him the entire time.

"I think you might be lucky, it doesn't appear to be broken," he explained gently placing Lucy's arm back down. "So, can I take a look at your head?"

"Can it wait, please? I need to find—" He didn't take any notice and began to remove the bandage from Lucy's forehead.

"Nicole, yes..." He held up a mirror to Lucy's face. She had a half-inch long gash on her forehead that was bleeding quite profusely down her face. It was one of the reasons why the children had been so frightened.

"Okay." Lucy nodded. "Do it. But then I want to know about Nicole." Summer jumped down and sat with Storm.

"Of course, I will be as fast as I can, but I won't rush it as it will scar."

338

"Doc, I don't know if you've noticed, but it isn't really going to make a difference to my face."

The doctor blushed slightly. Of course, he had noticed the scar on the woman's face, but that didn't mean he had to make it worse. "I will do my job properly, thank you," he said, smiling at her.

"Can I make a quick call?" Lucy asked.

The doctor nodded. Rita answered after just a few rings.

~E&F~

"What's happening?" Rita asked worriedly as she rounded the curtain to find the doctor finishing off the last stitch on Lucy's face.

"I don't know, they haven't told me anything." She grimaced, the last stitch tugging a little as the Lidocaine wore off. When he was done stitching and had cleaned up Lucy's face, Dr. Lau left them alone to go and deal with another patient.

"Would you sit with the girls while I go and ask someone?" Lucy said, standing from the bed she had been lying on. She was a little unsteady on her feet. Her leg ached from all the activity of the last few hours. Painkillers would kick in soon, but in the meantime, she had to grin and bear it.

Rain had fallen asleep. Rita had brought some magazines with her and Storm had grabbed one. She was reading quietly to Summer about the actress that played Andi Stark, her favourite TV cop. Shelly Hamlin had just announced her relationship with another woman. Storm thought it was exciting that her Mom was just like Shelly.

"Of course, go, go." Rita waved her off.

Lucy kissed each child on the forehead. "I'll be right back, soon as I find out what's happening with Mummy. Stay here with Rita and be good girls, okay?"

As she stepped outside of the room, her phone rang. She admonished herself for not having turned it off. Pulling it from her pocket, she saw that it was Sheriff Jenkins calling, and so she answered.

~E&F~

The emergency room was hectic. Reception was busy and the staff there were already dealing with other people, taking phone calls and organising doctors. Lucy waited patiently in line and tried not to think about the reasons why it was taking so long to find Nicole. She was worried, even as she considered the facts and tried to keep herself calm. The accident was bad, but it could have been so much worse. Everyone seemed to be okay, Nicole was talking and alert. So, she should be fine. That's what she kept telling herself while she waited.

Finally, she reached the front of the queue. "Hi, I need to find Nicole Granger. She was uh, she uh was brought in earlier," Lucy stuttered as the woman on reception stared at her scarred face. "Car accident. She's pregnant." The woman looked down at her keyboard and typed in Nicole's name.

340

"Yes, we have her. I'll get someone to come over and speak to you." Before Lucy could even thank her, she was already addressing the next person in the queue. Lucy stepped aside and waited, again.

When a nurse came out and ushered her towards a small room, Lucy thought the worst. Her jaw clenched as she prepared herself mentally.

"What is happening? Why won't you let me see Nicole? Where is she? I want to see her now." The questions tumbled out. She had no control over it.

"Ma'am, I am going to take you through, but I need to explain a few things first, okay?" The nurse spoke gently, her hand guiding Lucy by the elbow as they moved inside the side room.

"Just tell me straight," Lucy said. She sat down slowly and waited, her breath held.

"Nicole is in labour."

"What? I need to..." The nurse placed a hand on Lucy's arm and gently pushed her back into a sitting position.

"She is in labour, but the baby is in distress. We need to help him or her out a little," she explained.

"What does that mean? Are they both alright?"

"Yes, they are both in very good hands. Obviously, the baby is a little earlier than planned. We think because of the shock of the crash, the little one has decided time's up." She smiled and sat down beside Lucy. "The baby is just under 34 weeks, so we're hopeful that everything has developed along as it should do, but the baby will be placed in the neonatal intensive care unit just to be on the safe side."

"And Nicole?"

"Will hopefully give birth naturally but, if the baby becomes even more distressed, then we are prepared to do a C-section. Either way, there is nothing to worry about, you're going to be a mama again anytime now," she said, standing and smiling. "So, come on then, let's go see Mom."

Lucy followed like a lost child, hands firmly in her pockets as they walked along a brightly lit corridor to a small room.

Entering, the first thing she heard was Nicole swearing.

"Honey, what's wrong?" Lucy said, rushing to her side. "You said she was okay." She reached for Nicole's hand as she spoke over her shoulder back at the nurse.

"Okay?!" Nicole shouted. "I am not okay. I am in agony; this baby is trying to kill me!" Nicole's face scrunched up in pain as another contraction hit.

"Oh."

"Yes, *OH!* Where the hell have you been?" she continued to shout. Every contraction had been getting longer and more painful. She hated being by herself, and even though she understood that Lucy and the girls needed to be checked over, rationality had gone out of the window. The baby kicking while she was in the car waiting to be helped out had been uncomfortable, but she hadn't been in labour until her waters broke as they were bringing her up the hill. Lucy was with the girls and so, she just assumed they would let Lucy know.

The grip on Lucy's hand was like a vice. "They wouldn't let me see you till..."

"Till what?" Nicole asked, only now finally opening her eyes from the pain of the last contraction to really look at Lucy. "Oh my God, you have stitches. Are you alright?"

"I'm fine. The kids are fine, they are with Rita."

"I want to see them," Nicole sobbed. Lucy looked to the nurse, who just nodded with a smile.

"Okay, I'll go and get them then."

"No, don't leave me again." She sobbed more.

"Okay, but..." Lucy was confused now, what the hell was she meant to do? "So, you don't want to see..."

"Of course I do, I want my babies."

"Right, I will be less than 2 minutes, alright? But I have to leave to go and get them. I promise you I will be back in 2 minutes," she said, kissing Nicole's cheek. Unclasping her watch, she handed it to Nicole. "See, you check on me. Two minutes." And she was off. She ran out of the labour room and into the corridor that led back to the ER. She forgot all about the pain she was in. Rounding the corner, she found the room where she had left them all. She opened the door and found four sets of eyes looking up at her expectantly.

"Come on, I found Mummy and she wants to see you all." She grabbed Rain and Summer under her arms, and with Storm and Rita both giving chase, she led them through the corridors, back the way she had just come until she came flying through the door of the labour room.

"You're 20 seconds late!" Nicole cried, and then gasped in pain as another contraction rocked through her. Placing the twins gently to the ground, Lucy moved quickly to take her hand and feel the vice like grip almost shatter her phalanges.

"Mommy!" Summer called out. She tried to run to Nicole, but Rita grabbed a hold of her.

"It's okay, baby." Nicole smiled, gritting her teeth as the contraction slowly eased. Rita loosened her grip, and both Summer and Rain edged closer to their mother, both of them frowning with concern. "It's just the baby coming."

"The baby is hurting you?" Summer asked. She pulled at the covers and tried to climb up.

"No...yes...It's not..." Nicole didn't quite know how to explain.

"So, are we ready for the rest of the birds and the bees discussion now then, Darling?" Lucy grinned, grabbing Summer and stopping her from her attempted ascent. She was aware of the glare she had just gotten. "Anyhow, so as you can see girls, Mommy is fine."

Rain tugged at Lucy's sleeve to be lifted. When she was high enough, she dipped her head down to Nicole's tummy and spoke to the baby. "Yay baby, come on out so we can play."

The baby gave a little kick.

~E&F~

Rita took the girls home with her, once Lucy promised to call as soon as there was any news. At first, they didn't want to leave, but Rita had promised they could stay up and wait for Lucy's call. She knew they would all be asleep long before that happened, but it had placated them, and she ushered them out of the room with a wave and a smile, leaving Lucy to deal with Nicole and the imminent arrival.

"I need to get up," Nicole suddenly said while already moving to stand.

"Woah! Hold up, let me help you?" Lucy said, quickly jumping to her feet to be by her side. Nicole's gown lifted slightly when she pulled back the cover and revealed an almighty bruise on her right thigh and hip.

"Jesus, why didn't you say you were hurt?" Lucy gasped.

"I'm fine, it's a bruise from the door. It isn't anything to worry about. I have been prodded and checked by several professionals. I am okay, Lucy." She spoke gently, knowing how tough this whole thing was on Lucy; not just the baby coming early, which was stressful for them both, but the crash. It had to have brought up issues for Lucy. "I'm more worried about you right now," she whispered as Lucy leant her forehead against Nicole's.

"Me?"

"Yes, you. I can't imagine how you are feeling about all this."

"I'm fine," she lied. She didn't intend to, she didn't want to, but with Nicole already under enough pressure and stress, and not forgetting the pain, she didn't need anything added. "I had a moment," she confessed, "But, ya know, I'm fine."

Nicole looked at her and took her face in her hands. "I have three children that try and lie to me all the time and I'm about to have a fourth, so tell me again how fine you are?"

Lucy had to smile at that. It was moments like this that really enforced in Lucy just how much she needed this: needed someone to see her, see through her and find the things she hid.

"I was having some issues with flashbacks, but since being here with you they have lessened, and physically I am fine." She smiled shyly and watched as Nicole nodded and then grimaced as a new contraction shot through her. She needed to walk, so she began to pace, back and forth across the room with Lucy by her side, supporting her elbow.

"Can I do anything?" Lucy asked. Never having been in this position before, she found it daunting.

"In a minute you can rub my back please, but…" She took in a deep breath and released it slowly. "Right now I just need to…" She moaned loudly and swore a few times. "Get through this." She sat back on the edge of the bed and took Lucy's hand. "I have done this twice already. Don't look so scared. I don't think it is going to be much longer."

"I love you," Lucy said to her as sincerely as she could, because she meant it. "I…I didn't think I could ever be this happy. Thank you." They held each other's gaze.

"Holy fuck," Nicole screamed. "Oh god, I need to push. Get the nurse," she shouted at Lucy. Eyes wide and ready for action, Lucy was on the move, grabbing the door and yanking it open before calling out for the nurse.

Chapter Fifty

Twenty-five minutes later and Nicole pushed into the world a beautiful, healthy baby boy.

Nicole was exhausted. Lucy was excited, and the baby was unaware of any of the fuss he had caused. He was taken to the NICU to be kept an eye on for 24 hours, just to make sure there were no complications, but only after he had been introduced to his two mamas. He had nestled contentedly upon Nicole's chest, doing skin to skin bonding, and he had gripped Lucy's finger tightly in his tiny hand.

While he was being settled into his tiny incubator, Lucy was calling Rita and speaking to the girls on speakerphone.

"Can we see the baby?" Rain shouted. Apparently if the phone wasn't against your ear, then you had to shout.

"Yes!" Lucy said excitedly, "You have a baby brother. And he is gorgeous and looks just like you all." She could hear a lot of excited chatter from them all as they shouted and squealed about a baby boy.

"How is Nicole?" asked Rita over the rumpus.

"She is good, they are just, uh, ya know, fixing her up," she said quietly, some things could and would remain private.

"That's great Lucy, I am so happy for you all, and I can't wait to meet the little man."

"Okay, I got to get back to Nic. I'll call you when we know what is happening next," she said, saying bye to them all by name before switching off the call and heading back into Nicole's room. She pushed at the door gently and slowly opened it. She could already see that Nicole was sleeping, so she crept in quietly and pulled the small armchair nearer to the bed and sat down. Finding her phone once more, she started flicking through the photographs that she had taken of Nicole with the baby.

She couldn't wipe the grin off of her face as she sent one to Rita to show the girls. Then she closed her eyes and let herself relax.

~E&F~

Lucy awoke to the feeling of fingers being pulled gently through her hair. She smiled to herself as she realised it was her lover. Sitting up, she found loving eyes staring softly at her.

"Hi there, sleeping beauty," Nicole said, smiling at her. She looked cute, all dishevelled and sleepy. She ran a finger across her forehead, gingerly skirting the new injury before cupping her cheek. Lucy raised her own hand and pressed it gently over Nicole's. She could feel the warmth and love in that one touch.

"How are you feeling?"

"Sore and tired, but other than that, I am all good," she said. "They said I can go home in a few hours."

"Why didn't you wake me?"

"Because you needed to sleep too."

"I haven't just pushed our child out into the world." She smiled at the mere mention of *our* child. She still had to pinch herself sometimes. It felt like her life had been one long dream, a nightmare really, and then, she had woken up and found she was a mother to four beautiful children. It was surreal.

"No, but you have just been in a car accident and had our other children to deal with, not to mention the stress of dealing with me. I had drugs to get me through." She laughed. Lucy's face fell at the mention of the accident. "Wanna talk about it?"

"Yes, but it's not what you think." She swallowed and tried to think of words to explain about the accident.

"It's okay, you can tell me anything, you know that."

Lucy nodded. "I know...it's just, it wasn't an accident."

"What do you mean?"

Lucy sighed. "It was Paul."

"What?"

"It was Paul, he drove his truck at us on purpose. He rammed us and pushed us off the road."

Nicole began to panic. "We need to get the girls...get out of here. Where is he?"

"Nicole." She placed a hand on her arm. "He can't hurt us. He's dead."

"Dead? How?"

350

"He was watching us, but I needed to get to the top of the hill to call for an ambulance. So, I started climbing, I thought I'd have to fight him, but his phone rang and then the engine started and so I figured he was leaving. When I got to the top and staggered to my feet, he...he drove at me."

Nicole gasped and began to weep.

"It's okay, he didn't hit me." Lucy didn't point out how obvious it was that she was fine. "I jumped out of the way, but he couldn't stop. The car went over the edge and well... Sheriff Jenkins said he was dead on impact."

"I can't believe it...Why? Why would he want to...to kill the...he must have known the girls were in the car!"

"He was a sick bastard, Nicole."

Nicole continued to cry, silent tears that slid slowly down her cheeks. Not tears for him; she was glad he was gone. But she was sad that she was happy about it, that he had turned her into the kind of woman who would be happy at someone else's demise. She was angry with him, angry for all the years of hurt and pain and now, for wanting her children harmed, or worse. "I want to see him."

"Paul?" Lucy was surprised but not shocked that she might want to. He was a like a demon that invaded your dreams. When you woke up, you were never quite sure if he was still there.

"No, God no. I never want to see him again," she insisted. "The baby, I want to see our baby." She smiled, feeling an overwhelming need to hold him and check all his fingers and toes were intact.

"Okay..." Lucy grinned. "So, do you want me to wheel you around to see him now?" she said, beaming at the idea.

"Yes, let me grab a quick shower first though and then we can go and see him."

"Are you allowed to do that?" Lucy questioned. She assumed Nicole would be bed-ridden for a few days while she recovered.

"Yep, a warm shower is allowed, but I do need someone to come in with me...just in case." She swung her legs over the side of the bed. "So, shall I get a nurse...or?"

"No need to bother them, they're pretty busy out there." Lucy grinned, jumping to her feet to help. "Here, take my hand." She led her slowly to the small room off to the side that housed a toilet and shower. Nicole shrugged off the hospital nightgown. Even after giving birth just an hour or so earlier, Lucy still thought she was the most beautiful person she had ever seen.

The shower was quick. Nicole had winced a few times and that had put Lucy into protective mode. She dried her off and helped her dress in her own clothes again.

Lucy wheeled her around the corridors slowly, turn after turn, up in the elevator one floor and round one last corner until they came to the big window where they could see him. He was in the 3rd incubator from the left.

"He is so tiny," Lucy said in awe. A tuft of dark hair in the centre of his head was dark as night, just like his mother's. He had a tiny button nose and he was smiling as he wriggled around in his swaddling.

"I know, the twins were as small too, but they were full term."

The nurse waved from inside the room and beckoned them in. Lucy felt like she hadn't stopped smiling for days. Her cheeks actually hurt and she loved it.

"He is due for his feeding soon and I am sure he would rather his momma fed him than a bottle," the nurse said sympathetically.

"Really?" Nicole almost cried. They followed the nurse through to a smaller, more private space, where she left them for a moment to go and bring the incubator with their baby in to them. Opening it up and lifting him gently, she placed him in Lucy's arms while Nicole undid her shirt and freed her breast, ready to take him.

After passing him over to her, Lucy bent and kissed her. "He is just like you, beautiful."

"He is," she agreed "He needs a name though."

"Have you thought of anything yet?" Lucy asked.

"Actually, I have," she said, smiling as he latched onto her nipple.

"That's the most beautiful thing I think I've ever seen," Lucy said, watching them both. "So, what name did you think of?"

"Wynter." She laughed. "Wynter Alexander."

"I like it, why those names though?"

"Well, Wynter because of the timing, it was really cold out there today and it matches with the girls." She chuckled. "And Alexander, after you." Lucy looked confused at that. "It means defender, that's what you are to him, to all of us. Our defender."

Tears sprung to her eyes. "Wow, I...I don't know what to say. I'm honoured." She truly was speechless.

Holding Wynter in one arm, Nicole reached for Lucy with her free hand. "Without you, this child would be like my others, living in fear. Without you, they would have no understanding of love from anyone else but me. Without you, I would have no life worth living."

"Welcome to the family, Wynter Alexander," Lucy said proudly. "I think you're going to be the happiest little boy in the world when you meet your sisters and Auntie Rita."

"He definitely is." Nicole smiled. "Just like his momma.

Epilogue

Christmas brought with it more snow, but there was nothing cold about Lucy Owen's life anymore. She had a house full of love, and the warmth of that alone would have kept her happy for a lifetime. There was laughter and music again. There had been a moment of upset when Nicole had explained to the girls what had happened to their father. There were tears from the twins, but Storm had kept her trembling chin under control. Though hours later, she too had finally succumbed to sobbing her little heart out.

Wynter had come home with them on Christmas Eve. He had spent almost a week in the NICU, but every day he grew stronger. He was breathing unaided and feeding without any concerns, and so the Granger/Owen family was complete in time for Santa visiting. For Lucy though, Wynter was the best present she could have ever asked for.

Christmas morning was a blur. Rain and Summer had had them all up and awake at just after sunrise, bouncing on the bed, shouting that Santa was here and pleading with everyone to wake up. It made Lucy smile to see them so excited.

Lucy had stayed up till after midnight the previous night. She placed all the presents from Santa under the tree, took a bite out of all three cookies and drank a glass of milk. She was reminded of her own childhood, leaving mince pies and a glass of sherry for Santa and carrots for Rudolph. Maybe next year she would see if she could make some mince pies. She put the carrots back in the fridge and then walked outside in her boots and trod in fresh snow all the way to the tree. Then she slipped the boots off and carried them back to the door, where she dropped them. In the morning Santa's footprints would just about be visible as melted snow left tiny puddles.

Wynter had them awake around three, hungry and in need of a change. Nicole and Lucy had agreed that breast was best, but for night time feeds, Nicole would express and Lucy would take her turn bonding with him. So, it was Lucy that woke to deal with him. She had never really understood what being tired meant before now, but she was determined to let Nicole sleep whenever possible.

Every toy unwrapped brought a new shrill of excitement and more jumping around. It was exciting for everyone. The place was a mess. Discarded wrapping paper and cardboard boxes littered the living room floor, but Lucy didn't care.

The TV was on, and *A Christmas Carol* was playing. Storm sat on the couch with half an eye on it. While Lucy herded the twins into helping her pick up all the rubbish, Nicole sat down beside her eldest, holding Wynter in her arms. Storm looked up and smiled, her attention now completely on her little brother.

"Hello Wyn," she said, ticking his chin. He wriggled and kicked out his chubby legs.

"Wanna hold him?" Storm nodded and Nicole gently placed him into Storm's waiting arms. He looked much bigger in her smaller arms. "He definitely likes you." Nicole said, and Storm grinned back. She had lost a tooth a couple of days ago and now had a gappy smile. Nicole snuggled up to her and they watched the film together for a while.

"Mom?"

"Yes, Storm?" Scrooge was currently being scared witless by the ghost of Christmas past.

"We're not going to leave here, are we?"

"No, baby. Why would you think that?" Nicole paused the TV and turned towards Storm. Her dark eyes filled with tears as they looked up at her mother.

"Cos daddy isn't here anymore. We can go home."

Nicole hadn't considered that option at all. It was true, they had a house there, but they had a home here. "We're not going back, Storm. I will make arrangements for our things to be brought here to us. But, our home is here now, with Lucy." She reached out and cupped her palm under Storm's chin, "That's what you want, right?"

Storm nodded, and Wynter began to mewl and wriggle in her arms. She looked down at him and smiled. "I think he wants Rain."

On hearing her name, Rain promptly dropped the trash bag she was holding and ran across the room to the couch, skidding to a halt by her sister's feet.

"Hey Wyn." Nicole chuckled; it was funny how they all seemed to have shortened his name. "Shall I tell you a story?" His eyes opened wide as he stared up at the voice he seemed to love the most. His little feet kicked harder, and Nicole moved to make room for her to join them on the couch. When she was settled, Storm passed Wynter along. Rain began her story about three little girls and how happy they were to finally have a little brother. Lucy and Summer wandered over. Lucy slid into the space left behind Nicole. The darker of the two turned and smiled over her shoulder at her lover. Summer climbed up onto her lap and they all listened as Rain explained that happy ever afters always happened.

You just had to wish hard enough for it.

If you have enjoyed this story, or any of Claire's other books, please consider leaving a review on Amazon, Goodreads or Facebook

Many thanks!

ABOUT THE AUTHOR

Claire Highton-Stevenson is the author of the Cam Thomas Series and The Promise.

To find out more about Claire, go to www.itsclastevofficial.co.uk

Or follow her on Twitter @clastevofficial

Facebook: Author Claire Highton-Stevenson

38517059R00203

Made in the USA
Lexington, KY
08 May 2019